USA *Today* Bestselling Author
ADRIANA LOCKE

Cover Design:
Kari March Designs

Photography:
Perrywinkle Photography

Editing:
Adept Edits

Interior Design & Formatting:
Christine Borgford, Perfectly Publishable

19/01

WRITTEN
IN THE
Scars

BOOKS BY

ADRIANA LOCKE

THE EXCEPTION SERIES
The Exception
The Connection, a novella
The Perception
The Exception Series Box Set

THE LANDRY FAMILY SERIES
Sway
Swing (coming 2016)
Switch (coming 2017)

STANDALONE NOVELS
Sacrifice
Wherever It Leads
Written in the Scars
More Than I Could (coming 2017)
Delivery Man (coming 2017)

DEDICATION

For everyone that has loved deep enough to have scars.
And for Jade.

ELIN

Seven years earlier

GLANCING OVER MY shoulder, the water below is reflected in Ty's bright green eyes. His chiseled face and sun-kissed skin smiles back at me.

I'm still no match for his grin. Without fail, a giddiness surges inside me when he flashes it my way. It's always been hard to believe *he* is *my* boyfriend; it's been even harder to wrap my head around being his fiancée. Being his wife tomorrow? Having his last name for the rest of my life? It's a level of elation I can't fathom.

"We really are getting married tomorrow, aren't we?"

"We are." He bends forward, kissing me sweetly on the forehead.

My body shifts with his as he draws a deep breath into his muscled chest. I let my back press on his front, the beating of his heart felt through the thin fabric of my sundress.

"Are you nervous?" I pick at the hem of my dress, waiting for any signs that my boyfriend of the last six years is reconsidering.

His deep laugh dances over the top of Moon Mountain, our favorite spot, as he wraps his arms around me and pulls me closer to him. "Absolutely not." He rests his chin on the top of my head. "We've talked about this day for years, Elin. Hell, even when I was fifteen, I knew I'd marry you one day."

"That day is in a few hours," I whisper.

"You aren't nervous, are ya?" He angles himself so he can see my face, his tone etched with worry that maybe I am.

"No," I laugh, a flutter of excitement creeping into my belly. "I feel like we're already married. Tomorrow just makes it official."

Our fingers lace together on my lap. My engagement ring, something that Ty put off buying until he could save his own money, glitters in the late afternoon sunlight. It's probably not worth a ton monetarily, but knowing he saved for it, went to the jewelry store and picked it out, called my father and asked for my hand in marriage—even though he knew he'd get it—makes it worth more to me than anything in the world.

"It'll be the two of us," I remark. "Mr. and Mrs. Whitt."

"It'll be the two of us . . . until I get you pregnant," he breathes against my ear. "I want to have a damn basketball team with you. Boys. All of 'em."

"Maybe one girl?"

The heat of his lips sears against my skin as he presses kisses behind my ear and down my neck. His free hand lies flat against my stomach before easing slowly toward the apex of my thighs. Bunching my dress and pulling it up into a ball at my navel, his palm rests at the base of my belly, his fingers hovering, taunting me with their proximity to my opening.

"We can start trying now," I offer, my breathing stuttered.

He stills, the only movement coming from the rise and fall of his chest. "I love ya, E." He squeezes my hand. "I know I've said it a million times, but I do love you. I've always loved you. You're everything to me."

"I love you too."

Scrambling to find the way to say all I'm feeling aloud, I realize: maybe there aren't words. Maybe that's what love is, something so beautiful and perfect that you can only feel it.

Snuggling as close to him as I can, I reiterate my words from before. "I love you, Ty. For better or worse."

"Til death do us part."

One

ELIN

"**I** DARE YOU."

Shooting Lindsay Watson a dirty look, I plop down in the chair beside her work station. Swiveling side to side in an extra hairdresser's chair, I watch her take the final snips of Becca Snowden's long, chestnut hair.

"But you'd look so good as a redhead, Elin," Lindsay gushes, ignoring my empty threat. "A crimson would make those green eyes of yours pop. Just let me."

"Ooh, you would look great with a little red," Becca chimes in.

"I'll keep basic variations of my dishwater blonde, thank you," I reply. "Pretty sure my Kindergarten class might freak out if I showed up with something new."

Lindsay laughs, her voice trickling across Blown, the salon she opened up a few years ago. Her blue eyes twinkle in the way they do when someone is living the life of their dreams, when everything is just the way it should be. It's an amazing feeling that I remember well, if distantly.

I let the chair come to a rest, my playful energy now falling with Becca's hair. Lindsay makes small talk with Becca as she removes the cape and leads her to the cash register in front, light shining in the windows from a beautiful fall afternoon. The city square in Jackson, Indiana, population six thousand, is bustling outside.

"I'm going to run to The Fountain and grab a drink," Becca says, digging through her purse. "Do you want me to bring you guys anything?"

"No, but I think I'll walk over there and grab a Bump when I leave here," I say. "Damn, I love those things."

"I haven't tried that."

"It's my favorite," I tell her. "A cinnamon citrus drink that's seriously the best thing in the world. We moved here my seventh grade year. After school that first day, Lindsay walked me to The Fountain and insisted I order one. I think we became best friends after that."

"Of course we did. How could you not want to be friends with someone with such great taste?" Lindsay jokes.

"Well, you did marry my brother, so I'd say your taste is impeccable."

"Wait," Becca says, turning to look at Lindsay. "You married Elin's brother?"

"I did. I befriended her so I could meet her twin." Lindsay sticks her tongue out at me. "Jiggs was the goal. Elin was a bonus."

Becca raises a brow. "Jiggs? That's his name?"

"It's James," I clarify. "I'm not sure why we call him Jiggs, but we do. Everyone does."

Looking at the floor so they don't see my eyes, I hide the fact that I'm lying. He's called Jiggs because our father was a woodworker in his free time. My brother was obsessed with the jigsaw when he was a little boy and Dad started calling him Jiggs. I don't share that because it'll just bring back the sadness I've managed to keep from completely swamping me today.

"Hey, we're having a bonfire this weekend," Lindsay tells Becca. "You should come."

"I don't know. This place still feels so awkward to me." Becca hands Lindsay her credit card. "I've been here a few months now, and I just feel so out of place. I've been considering going back to Texas."

"That's why you should go to the bonfire," I point out. "Meet people. Have fun."

Becca shrugs, not looking convinced. "Maybe."

The bell chimes as the front door is cracked open, a blast of cool autumnal air drifting through the salon. It brings with it scents of grilled hamburgers, crunchy leaves, and a certain spicy cologne that makes my breath catch in my throat. In unison, although for different reasons, our heads snap to the doorway.

Becca gasps.

Lindsay glances at me through the corner of her eye.

My heart topples to the floor.

Tyler Whitt's emerald gaze finds mine like there's nowhere to look but at me. It's heavy, pushing me into my seat from across the room.

I can't breathe. Even with my jaw hanging open much wider than I'd like, I can't draw in enough oxygen to make me not feel like I'm two seconds from passing out. He just stands there, not looking *at* me, but seeing right *through* me. Like he's studying every thought going through my mind. Once upon a time, that look, the feeling of being the focus of his attention, was the most comforting feeling in the world. Now it's downright violating.

Fuck him.

My chair rolls to a stop, the toe of my sneaker dragging across the floor. I rip my eyes from his, heat pinking my cheeks, and I'm not sure which emotion is causing it because every feeling in the world is roaring through me.

I've imagined this scenario a thousand times. The moment I saw him again has played over and over in my mind. The vision always looks different. Everything from us running in slow motion to each other, kissing like our lives depended on it, to me throwing every punch and kick I could manage straight into his gorgeous, frustrating face was possible.

Regardless of the version, I just hoped that maybe, just maybe, time would've weakened our connection. That I wouldn't feel the maddening tug that I've always felt around him. That somehow I'd be able to hold on to the anger that I've woken up with and gone to bed with for forty-three nights now. That I would see him and instantly forget all the reasons I loved him and would re-member all the reasons why I've convinced myself I don't. Looking at him across the salon, nothing has diminished. Not even a little bit. It's still there, all crackly and electrifying and enveloping and heartbreaking.

Fidgeting in my seat, I take a deep breath and try to get my bearings. The fear of uncertainty rocks through me. If we have to interact, it'll end in a fight. That's the only thing I'm certain of. It's the way we operate now.

Ty's Adam's apple bobs as he forces a swallow and hesitates, just a split second, before walking fully into the salon. After a look that tells me everything and nothing all at once, he clears his throat and pulls his gaze away from me.

The scent of his cologne, the same scent he's worn since I bought him the first bottle with my first real paycheck, drifts around the room.

"Hey, Linds," he says, his tone warm, yet distant. "Jiggs around?"

When he speaks, my throat clenches shut, trying to bury all the emotions that threaten to spill over. The emotions I don't have half the handle on I thought I did. Having him here feels like yet another punch to the gut.

"No. He's at home, I think. He was working on the truck in the barn."

Ty nods, running a hand through his thick black hair that's spiking up every which way. His angular jaw is dotted with stubble, more than a day's worth. I know what it would feel like if I ran my hand against it, how his head would cock to the side just before a playful smile kissed his lips. I can imagine the feeling of the scars marring his sculpted back from the mining accident that changed our lives in such horrible ways last year. I can envision his crooked smile, telling me everything would be okay. Clearly, that's a lie.

His six-foot-one body, clad in a pair of jeans and a clean white t-shirt, looks lean and healthy like the basketball hero he's lauded to be. He looks good. He looks like my Ty.

Again—*fuck him.*

Gripping the chair, I forbid myself from blurting the millions of questions rustling around my mind. I won't ask because I won't give him the power by speaking first. It's childish, I'm sure, but I don't care. I have to survive however I can. Knowing I held tight to something makes me a little less powerless in the most defeating situation of my life.

The limp in his gait is now fainter than I remember, and I want to ask him how he's feeling too. But I don't because he hasn't given a damn about how I'm feeling since he left.

My hands fold over my stomach, and I fight back the tears that wet the inside corners of my eyes. I won't cry. Not here. Not in front of him, the man that looks like the person I fell so madly in love with. But that's not him anymore. Hell, I'm not sure who I am these days. I just know that together we're too different, too volatile to work.

Lindsay looks at me out of the corner of her eye, her lips pursing together in sympathy for the brokenness I feel. She knows. She's the only person that knows the depths of my pain because she was there for it all, a front row seat to the misery.

I glance at Ty and he's looking at me.

The sides of his lips begin to tilt upward, to flash me that cocky smile that made me fall for him in the first place. As my breath catches in my throat, his start of a smile catches on his face and he looks at Lindsay.

"I'll head over there. If ya see him, tell him I'm lookin' for him," Ty says, a gruffness to his tone. He glances at me again. My optimism spirals entirely too high, waiting, hoping that he says something. Anything. *Hi. Screw you. How are you?* I'd take any of them. But I don't get a single word and that slices me to my already bleeding core.

I don't want to hurt. Not anymore.

He turns, jamming one hand in a pocket, and pulls the door open with the other and walks out of my life again as abruptly as he did the first time.

"Holy shit!" Becca exclaims, dropping her purse on the counter as the door swings shut. The keychain hanging off the side clatters against the top. I snap my head to her, my annoyance level brimming, and get a warning glance from Lindsay. "I changed my mind. If that man will be at the bonfire, count me in. *Who was that?*"

"Uh—" Lindsay starts, but I cut her off.

"That's my husband," I growl, sliding off the plastic chair and letting it twirl round and round as I barrel my way out the back door.

Two

TY

THE LEAVES MANAGED to turn colors and dry up to nothing while I was gone. They blow in the breeze and rattle as they bounce down the path that leads to the detached barn on Jiggs' property.

I wonder if Elin has brought out an old pair of jeans and sweatshirt and filled them with leaves. It's one of her favorite things to do this time of year, and I get roped into it without fail. I've wondered about it a handful of times, but I haven't driven past the house to see if the scarecrow is there. I've been in town long enough to see her car behind Blown and pull in.

That wasn't the plan. Sure, seeing her was the ultimate objective, but I was going to sort it out once I got here. Talk to Jiggs. See where things stand. But I saw her car at Blown—the truck pulled in on its own.

The sound of Jiggs banging on metal rings down the path. I have half a notion to get back into my pick-up and leave. Even though he's my best friend, he's Elin's twin brother, and their relationship is much more than your normal sibling banter. Their parents died in a boating accident six years ago, not long after our wedding, and that brought the two of them, although already close, even closer.

Seeing Jiggs should be interesting. We haven't talked since I left town either. I'm a jackass for just dropping by, springing this on him, but he's my best friend—the status of my marriage notwithstanding. At least, I hope so.

"What's up?" Jiggs asks, bringing me out of my reverie as I approach the barn door. "It's about time you show up. I need help getting this thing running."

"You're a shit mechanic." Relief washes over me at his easy, nonviolent, greeting.

He nods and leans against the doorframe of the rusty truck, the paint peeling off the antiquated structure. "Truth. But that's why we're friends. You're not."

"Asshole," I laugh, grasping his shoulder as I pass deeper into the barn.

"What made you decide to bless us with your presence?" The caution is there, the yellow flag warning me to proceed carefully. That he's Elin's brother before he's my friend.

I knew coming back to town would mean answering for things. Looking into the eyes of the people I care about and seeing fury or annoyance . . . or a broken heart. Imagining how to handle the judgement was easier in the farmhouse, fifty miles away.

"You gonna answer me, Whitt?" His work gloves come off and go hurling across the barn. "I'm glad to see that ugly mug of yours, but you have some explaining to do."

"I know." Cringing and gathering whatever pride I can find lying around, I suck in a deep breath. "I'm sorry."

"Not good enough."

"What do you want to know?" I ask, unsure where to even start. Everything is so scrambled, I don't know which way to go.

"Where the hell you been?"

"North of Terre Haute. Cecil Kruger's farm. He was a friend of my dad's back in the day."

"You didn't think to call? To answer any of our thousands of fucking calls?"

My head drops, my gaze landing on a discarded pop tab in the dirt floor. "I smashed my phone and didn't replace it. I was going to . . ." My chin lifts. "I'll be honest with ya, Jiggs. The quiet was nice. No fighting. No reminder of how fucked up I am or how fucked up everything is."

"So you just fucked it up worse?" he laughs angrily.

"I figured it might do Elin and I both some good to take a break. To, you know, have some time to think about things."

Dust covers my boot as I kick the ground, waiting on him to reply. I'm at his mercy. Whatever he doles out, I deserve.

"Why did you come back? Why now?" he asks finally.

"Because it's time."

Our eyes meet over the hood of the truck. He searches mine, looking for the meaning of my words. Together, our heads begin to nod in understanding.

"You can't expect things to go back to the way they were," he says, picking up a wrench.

"I don't."

"Then what do you expect?"

It's a simple question. One I can't answer. I don't even know what I have to come home to. My wife hates me. My best friend is skeptical of me. I even resigned from coaching the high school basketball team before I left, the one true passion of my life. What's left?

"Why didn't you come talk to me? Or to Cord, if you didn't want to talk to me about things with my sister? Why let it get like this, Ty?"

"I wish I knew," I mutter.

Jiggs sighs, resting his forearms on the truck's frame. "We worried about you. No one could get ahold of you. Elin was a fucking disaster, Ty, and I honestly thought she was going to have a breakdown. The only person to see you was Pettis—"

"Woah, wait. Pettis?"

"Yeah. Said he saw you in Rockville a couple weeks ago."

Racking my brain for where Pettis would've seen me, I come up blank. I didn't see him. I wasn't anywhere to see him to begin with. Before I can think it through, Jiggs speaks.

"Part of me wants to kill you and toss you in the lake back there," he says, jutting his thumb over his shoulder.

"Might be easier."

"Oh, it would. Which is exactly why I won't do it."

"Pussy," I tease.

Jiggs laughs, shoving away from the truck. "Why did you leave?" Before I can answer, his gaze narrows. "The real reason, Ty. Cut the shit. Give it to me straight."

"You know what it was?" I ask, a burn igniting in my chest. "It was like getting smashed by the timber at work destroyed my entire life."

The pain in my core smolders, taking the loneliness of not having Elin, the loss of my team, the fury of losing everything I've ever wanted and worked for, and stokes the flames until it's scalding.

"You can't go through all that, Ty, and not come out affected. Your leg was snapped in half a couple of hundred yards below the surface of the earth. We carried you out on a stretcher." His tone is somber. "We thought you were going to fucking die. That'll mess with you."

I nod. "Yeah, but I could've stayed sane. I could've managed everything better, but I didn't. I let my marriage go to shit. I walked away from the team."

They should've started practice this week. I looked at my watch at exactly five-o'clock on Monday and imagined them lined up at half-court, wondering why Reynolds was in front of them and not me.

I wonder what they thought, what they were told. How many voice messages were left in my inbox by them—Dustin, in particular. He'd have taken my leaving the hardest of them all and I should've reached out. But I didn't. I failed them all too.

"It was the right choice," I say aloud, maybe more for myself than for Jiggs.

"Maybe. But you aren't just their coach. You're their friend, their go-to. You can't just say fuck it."

"I already did."

He looks at me and waits.

"I don't know why I'm here," I admit. "Elin hates me."

"Yeah. Probably."

"I wish I could hate her."

Throwing me another cautionary glance, he strolls across the barn and gathers his gloves. "What are you gonna do? What's the plan, Sir Fuck Up? I know you went to Blown. Lindsay called, said Elin left right after you."

"I'll put it to you like this—my first move didn't go as expected."

"You couldn't have expected her to run to you. Cord calls her Pit Bull for a reason."

I can't fight the grin that spreads across my lips. Her fire and her fight are my favorite things about her. "I didn't," I admit. "But I didn't expect such a coldness from her. Like she despises me."

"Can you blame her?"

"No," I gulp. "But she told me to leave—"

"I don't give a fuck what Lindsay tells me," Jiggs barks, his eyes lighting up, "I'm not leaving her. I don't give a damn if she throws my shit in the yard and kicks my ass out the door, I'll sit on the stoop until she lets me back in. Get my drift?"

"I was at fucking rock bottom," I toss back, offended that he thinks I just took a vacation from my life. "Don't you get that? The accident, the pain, the bills adding up because there's no overtime. Watching E have to kill herself to keep us both going when that's my fucking job! Having to get into the savings fund we'd been putting aside for years to get in-vitro. I couldn't even fuck my wife without it being on some motherfucking calendar! Then, month after month, she takes the goddamn test and it's negative and I have to look at her face and realize it's me that failed her!" I shout, my face hot to the touch. "Damn it, Jiggs! I didn't leave her because it sounded easier! There was no other choice!"

"I had no idea," he whispers, his face paler than I've ever seen it.

Turning away from him, I drag lungful after lungful of air into my body and focus on calming down. When I turn back around minutes later, Jiggs is sitting on a cooler watching me.

"I just wanted to make things better," I say. "I couldn't stand fighting with her. There's nothing worse than looking in the face of the person you love and seeing . . . disgust. Indifference. Wondering if she thinks you're lazy or worthless or feels like you can't even do your job and give her the baby you've both talked about since before you were even married."

"Ty, man, I really didn't know."

"Do you know what that feels like? Do you know how emasculating it is to not be able to properly fuck your wife?" I pause, letting that sink in. "The one time she got pregnant, she miscarried. Do you remember that a few years ago? Yeah, well, she never got over that. Maybe it would've eased up if I could've made it happen again, but *I fucking can't!*" I scream. "I swear to God, it's just too much pressure. That's the problem."

"It all came to a head the day I left," I say, a hollowness to my voice that even I hear. "We lashed out. I think the hurt we both were feeling just hid behind so much anger. It's easier to be pissed off than to feel pissed on all the time."

Shaking my head, I lean against a work table. Saying this aloud to someone else feels good. Feels manageable. Jiggs offers nothing in response, so I keep going. "She told me to leave, and I left. I figured it couldn't get any worse if I left, and it sure as shit wasn't going to get any better if I stayed.

"I miss her," I sigh. "No matter what I try to think about, it's related to her. High school. The mine. The lake." My jaw clenches as I look at him. "Our lives are one and the same, you know? Everything we've been through in our lives we've done together. I held her hand at your parent's funeral, remember your mom's lemon pie every time I go through the produce section. I know she hates storms and love being there for her when she reaches out."

"So fix it." Jiggs raises his brows. "Go to her. Talk it out."

"I can't."

"You can," he laughs. "You're just a pussy."

"Maybe I am," I chuckle. "But I'm afraid I'll make it worse."

Jiggs rustles through a red cooler and pulls out a beer. "Want one?" he asks, extending a bottle.

"No. Thanks anyway."

The top flies off and hits the dirt floor. He takes a long swallow, wiping his face with the back of his hand. "You coming by the bonfire tomorrow night?"

"I'll pass."

"You can't pass, asshole. We do it every year."

Grabbing a wrench, I start to work on the truck's alternator. "Yeah, we always have. But some things have changed."

"Maybe in your life, but your issues aren't fucking up mine. You better show up or I might have to kick your ass." He waits for me to respond. "Elin's not coming, if that helps."

"Where's she going?" I ask too quickly.

"Some teaching thing or something," he says, his voice on the bridge of a laugh. "So be here."

"We'll see."

He leans under the hood with me, holding a wire out of my way. I glance at him out of the corner of my eye.

"By the way," I say, smirking. "You can't whip my ass. Let's not get it twisted."

He laughs, smacking my shoulder. Walking out of the barn, he leaves me with his broken truck and my thoughts of the woman I love too much to even love at all.

Three

ELIN

T HE BACK DOOR groans as I push it open into the kitchen. Letting it swing shut behind me, I sit my bag brimming with papers I need to grade on the kitchen counter. The thump resonates through the room, bouncing off the buttery-colored walls that Ty and I took forever choosing.

"I love this color!" I squeal, holding up a color swatch and flashing it in front of his face. "It would be perfect in the kitchen of our new house."

"It looks like piss." He grabs my wrist to stop the sample from waiving erratically.

"It does not," I pout. "It's beautiful."

Instead of pulling the sample out of my hand, he tugs me closer to him. Leaning down, his lips hover inches from mine. "The color is piss, Mrs. Whitt. But if you like it, then we'll take it, because my eyes won't be on it when I'm in there. They'll be on you."

I can feel the heat of his kiss lingering on my lips, even nearly seven years later, as my heart rapid-fires in my chest. He always let me have what I wanted, always made me feel like the only person in the world that mattered.

How did things go so terribly wrong?

The room feels empty, so barren, even with the knickknacks sitting on the counters and the dishes from last night's dinner in the sink. It's my home, but it doesn't feel comforting. There's no contentment to be found here.

It's been this way since he left. Even though I've purged the room of all of his physical belongings because I can't look at them without wanting to curl up in a ball and die, that or throw them into the fire pit out back and burn them to ashes, the little nuances of him still exist and still hit me at hard.

The oil stain on the floor beside the door is still there, a tarry looking spot made by his mine boots lying there after a shift. No amount of cleaner will remove it. I've tried them all.

The little basket that hangs under the cabinets is now filled with ink pens and highlighters, not for any reason other than to take the place of Ty's keys and gum packets. Even though it's technically not empty now, it feels that way. Because what's in it isn't what should be.

His face from only an hour ago pops in my mind, and I squeeze my eyes shut, like somehow that will make it go away. Like the action will barricade his rich, warm voice from echoing in my ears.

The door creaks again and I jump, my eyes jerking to the door, my breath automatically ceasing. I watch and wait for it to swing open, for a knock, for a certain voice to call through the air. Because only two people use that door. Me and Ty.

The wind rattles the glass against the wood and my hopes dash.

"Damn it, Elin," I mutter, my spirits sinking faster than I can gather them. I don't miss the defeat in my shoulders or the squiggle in my bottom lip as I glance into the living room. The little hairs on the back of my neck stand on end as I stare at the back of the empty sofa.

"Guess what happened to me today?" I saunter around the sofa and stand with my hands on my hips, trying not to melt down. He looks at me again. "I went to the bank to take some money out of the savings to pay the house insurance."

His face slips just a bit, the corners of his mouth dropping ever-so-slightly. Forcing a swallow, I suck in a breath and continue.

"There's over a grand missing from our account."

I watch him with bated breath, hoping to see him startle or confusion cross his features. He doesn't look at me. He just watches the television like it's the most interesting thing in the world.

"Ty?"

"Yeah?" His jaw is set, flexing under his grimace. "I took some cash. What's the problem?"

"What's the problem?" I exclaim, my head spinning. "It's a thousand dollars! It's the money to start our family! What did you do with it?"

He swings off the sofa, cringing as his weight settles on his leg. "It's my fuckin' money too, Elin. I don't have to explain shit to you."

"If it were twenty or fifty bucks—hell, if it was a hundred dollars—I'd agree."

Our heated gazes meet. Mine in disbelief, his in some state of defense that I don't understand.

I think back on the past few weeks and a chill slowly twists itself through my body.

The hours he goes missing. The sudden secretiveness of his phone. The hushed conversations, the distance he's put between us. The fights we have that start over nothing and the more than willingness on his part to sleep on the couch. My stomach hits the floor, my knees wobbling.

"Ty?" I ask, my voice shaking. "What did you do with that money?"

"It's none of your damn business." Although his eyes blaze, his tone is more uncertain now as the words drop, weighted with insinuations.

He stands, babying the leg that was hurt when a wall burst in the mine and snapped his fibula. He hasn't been the same since—physically or mentally. It's put a strain on our marriage as I've tried to keep up with him emotionally and financially.

"Ty?" I choke out.

He seems to understand my suggestion without me saying it, and I'm glad. I don't think I could ask him out loud if he was planning on leaving me, if he had another woman somewhere waiting on him. I couldn't handle that. I don't care how bad things have been. I can't stomach an affair. The thought alone sends bitter bile creeping up my throat.

"If that's true," I say, squeezing the words past the lump in my throat, "then get out."

"Oh, you're throwing me out now?" he asks, his voice rising. "Is that *how it works?"*

"Were you fucking around on me?" I cry.

"Was I fucking around on you?" he huffs. "Are you serious? What, you think maybe I wanted to have sex that wasn't dictated by a calendar and thermometer?"

The laugh in his tone, the mockery he's making of our attempt to have a baby incites me.

"Fuck you," I say.

"I'd love to, but we haven't checked the date yet," he says, amping himself up.

"How dare you! How dare you throw that in my face!" I shout, tears stinging my eyes.

"A spade's a spade, E."

My face heats, my cheeks scalding as the tears wash over them. "Are you cheating on me?"

"Elin . . ." he scoffs, like my name is dirty coming out of his mouth.

"Are you?"

"You want me to? Would that make this all so much easier for you? You can hate me and feel good about blaming everything on me."

"Yeah, I want you to. Of course I do." I roll my eyes. "I'm so sick of this, Ty."

"Not as sick of it as me."

"Then go."

He storms by, taking a wide circle so we don't accidentally touch, so I can't reach out and grab his arm. My jaw slams against the hardwood, words begging to be spoken, but I can't find them. I can only watch his back flex under his shirt as he walks out of my life, the door squeaking behind him.

A full-body shiver yanks me back to reality, to a kitchen that lacks the smell of his coffee or the sound of the television in the other room. With a lump in my throat, I head into the living room. Grabbing a pillow off the sofa and pressing it to my chest, I fight back the sorrow by setting my jaw and grasping for the anger lurking just beneath the surface.

"It's just because I saw him. That's it. Don't let this spiral, Elin,"

I say aloud. I miss him. My God, I miss him. Tears stream, an end-less testament to the emotion, the dreams, the rejection, the failure, that swirl inside my soul.

Maybe that's why he was eager to leave. Maybe that's why it just took a simple shot from me to go, and he hauled ass out the door. Maybe it's because after all these years, he realizes what a joke I am of a woman, one that can't conceive. With me, he can't play catch in the backyard with a little boy that looks like him or tuck a little girl into bed that looks like me. There's no hope for any of that with me, and that's the most humiliating thing anyone can ever experience.

Yet, here I sit, spewing hate his way, secretly wanting him to re-turn. My words say how horrible he was for not being there for me, and that's true, but my heart misses finding the rhythm of his in the middle of the night.

"I can't do this," I sputter, throwing the pillow across the room. It lands at the foot of the entertainment center, brushing against it just hard enough to rattle off a metal figurine in the shape of a coal bucket Ty's grandpa gave him right before he died—one miner to another. I watch it freefall to the floor, almost in slow motion. It falls end over end, twisting and turning in the air before it lands solidly on the carpet.

I know what I have to do. Or, rather, what I can't do anymore. The end of a journey of my own.

Racing to the garage, maneuvering the house by memory be-cause I can't see through the tears stinging my eyes, I grab a box. Coming in just as quickly, I start picking up what's left of Ty's be-longings and shoving them inside. I don't think about it. I focus on the fact that I can't live in this perpetual state of uncertainty any-more. I can't live loving a man that doesn't want me, in a situation in which I'm doomed to fail. It's time to accept reality.

Using the tail of my shirt, I sop up the wetness from my face.

The coal bucket figurine goes into the box. It's joined by a pic-ture of him from high school, holding the state title up in the air. My hands shake as I pick up his grandmother's quilt off the quilt rack and lay it on top of the other items. The pale pink linen is darkened by the fluid dripping off my chin.

Sniffing up the snot that dangles onto my lips, I start towards the bedroom where a few articles of his clothing still reside in the closet. I stomp by the room that would've been the nursery with the practiced "eyes straight ahead" so I don't break down. It's a dream that will never happen.

I grab his Tennessee Arrows hat off the hook on the closet door and dig out his favorite t-shirt from the dresser drawer. Before I can toss them into the box, I catch the scent of his cologne, and that's the straw that breaks the camel's back.

I fall to my knees, the box dropping to the floor in front of me. I hold his hat to my chest and sob.

Four

TY

RUSTLE THROUGH A trash bag against the wall and find a clean t-shirt. Pulling it over my head, I notice the smell of the laundry detergent. It's some brand I picked up at the laundromat yesterday. Waves of overly perfumed, cheap flowers drench my senses. It's not so much what it smells like that drives me nuts, but what it doesn't.

It doesn't smell like home.

Elin always uses the same brand, the same one her mother used. Every time I do a load at a random laundromat with a box of suds from the dispenser, I'm reminded how much I miss her and how every little part of my life goes back to her. Even my fucking laundry soap.

Collapsing on the futon in Cord McCurry's spare room, I rest my head against the rough material and close my eyes. Bracing for the onslaught of memories that floods me every time I don't intentionally focus on something else, I'm halfway relieved when the sound of footsteps thud through the room.

"You all right?" Cord's voice echoes from the hallway

"Yeah."

A few moments later, his head pokes around the corner. His sandy brown hair is cut short, his jaw set as he takes me in and decides how to approach.

"There's food and shit in the refrigerator. Washer and dryer are in the room off the kitchen." He leans against the doorframe and waits on me to answer.

"Thanks for letting me stay here."

"You've let me bunk with you a time or two. Glad to repay the favor. You can stay here for as long as you need to," he says, a slight slant to his grin.

It's one I return readily, an understanding between two men that met as a couple of rowdy boys in high school. Cord was a handful when he moved to Jackson, getting suspended for fighting on his very first day in school. I jumped in, not being able to stand watching the new kid from foster care—a fact I learned from my mother the night before—getting mauled by Shane Pettis, resident asshole, and got myself three free days to boot.

From that day on, Cord has had my back and I've had his. He's the most dependable human being I know, which is why I called him when it became apparent I wouldn't be going home tonight.

"Let's hope to fuck I won't be here long," I mumble.

His chin dips just a touch. "It was probably just a shock to her to see you out of nowhere. Just give her a minute to adjust."

"Do you know how bad I want to fucking go home and be with my wife? How I miss her? How I want to just forget all this bullshit and go back to the way things were before the fucking accident?"

He chuckles, his eyes sparkling. "I can imagine. She basically wipes your ass for you. I don't know how you're surviving."

A small laugh escapes me too. "That's true. But it's not even about that. I just . . . I don't even know what to do with myself, Cord."

"Follow your gut. Always trust your gut." He winks and shoves off the door. "I'm taking Yogi for a swim at the lake. Want anything while I'm gone?"

"You and that fucking dog," I mutter, falling back on the stiff pillow again.

"Laugh all you want. She doesn't put me through this shit," he teases before pulling the door closed behind him.

The futon springs rip into my back. They scrape against the scars etched there from the accident, the same ones Elin used to feather her fingers across at night while I slept.

Oh, how far we've fallen.

Loving her is so damn easy. It's as natural as breathing or the beating of a heart. Even when we were hurling insults at the very moment my rope was being frayed, a couple of seconds before she asked me to leave and I bolted—I loved her. That's never been a question. It's making life work around the love that's hard.

Life doesn't care about feelings. It couldn't give a shit about who you love and want to be with. It keeps tossing crap your way, trying to break you until all you know is the chaos of it all.

"What happened to your back?" Mrs. Kruger asks as I enter the farm-house, her silver hair like a halo in the early evening sun.

I place my sweaty shirt over my shoulders. Drops of sweat roll down my jaw and drip onto my chest from a long, hot day working for her hus-band in the fields. "It was from an accident in the mine."

She stops stirring a pot on the stove and turns to me. Her apron hangs over her round belly and she grabs the hem and dries her hands. "You know, it's better to have a scar than a bruise."

"Really? Why is that?"

"Bruises go away, Tyler. Scars stick around to prove you showed up for life. That you lived. That you fought. That you loved." She peers at me over the top of her glasses. "I knew it the night you came here, asking to talk to my husband, that your heart was broken. I've seen a lovesick man a time or two in my years. But can I give you some advice?"

I nod, my body breaking out in a cold sweat under her scrutiny.

"What would you say about your heart? Would you say your heart is bruised or scarred, Tyler?"

"Scarred in every direction possible," I whisper without hesitation.

She starts to smile, but catches herself. "When did you know you loved her?"

"From the moment I saw her."

"I see," she says, her voice barely a whisper. She thinks for a long moment before taking a deep breath. "You can't expect a relationship to

succeed based on the love you felt at the beginning. It succeeds because you continue to build on it until the end." She removes her glasses and smiles. "Your heart will be more scarred than your back by the end of your lifetime. That is, if you live the right way."

A warmth builds in my core, my feet shuffling beneath me.

"Go home, Tyler," she whispers. "Go build on the beginning."

Her words ring through my mind as I try to find a comfortable spot on this godforsaken futon. It sounds simple, to build on what we had at the beginning. So simple, in fact, that I'd raced back to town, sure as shit that I would find Elin, we'd see each other, she'd break into a tight smile, I'd smile back, and we'd figure this out.

Never did I expect the coldness in her posture, the disdain that filled her beautiful green irises. Anger? Yeah. Sadness? Sure. But hatred? It stopped me in my tracks.

Swinging my legs to the side, my footsteps create a circle in the room as I attempt to block out the idea that has me more worried than any other: she doesn't want to fix this.

The itch of frustration working its way up my spine has my skin on fire. This is my fault, this entire fuckup is my mistake in so many ways.

Taking a deep breath, I glance around the room. It feels empty, and I don't think it has anything to do with the lack of furniture.

Rising, I grab a pillow and a blanket out of another bag and toss them on the futon. It's going to kill my back to sleep here, but I have no inclination to get a bed. Buying furniture seems like planting roots somewhere, admitting that my marriage is over, and while I know it just might be, I can't see physical proof of that.

I might sleep on a futon for the rest of my life.

Getting as comfortable as possible, I try to block out Elin and focus on what I need to do. Yet her face slips across my mind as my eyes drift closed.

"Remember the good that used to be in me, Elin," I whisper, the words skirting past the lump in my throat.

Not the failure.

Not the weakness.

Not the man sitting on the couch popping pain pills with no job.

I swallow, forcing the lump down, and try to remember every line in her face. "I'm sorry, baby," I whisper again. "I'm so fucking sorry."

Five

ELIN

"WHEN DO YOU start at Ashby Farms?" I ask Jiggs, watching him take a marshmallow out of a bowl on the middle of his kitchen counter and pop it in his mouth.

"Monday. It's harvest time, so it'll be solid work for a while. Hopefully long enough for me to figure something else out."

"I wish someone else would start hiring permanently," I sigh. "I hate that the mine is basically your only hope for a consistent job."

"Even it's not consistent now." Jiggs shrugs, swiping another marshmallow. "It's good money though. I'll be glad to go back."

I watch him toss the candy in the air and try to catch it in his mouth. "Mom didn't want you working there."

"No, but she would've understood. It's Jackson, Elin. It's what we do here. Grandpa did it. Dad did it. It's our life. You know that." He tosses it up again. When it hits the floor, he looks at me and smiles. "May as well get used to it."

He leans over the island and presses his lips together, holding steady until Lindsay gives in and kisses him.

Laughing, he swipes another pillow of sugar. "I gotta figure something out, right?" He catches Lindsay's eye and they exchange a look that piques my interest.

"What am I missing?" I ask, furrowing my brow. Before I can

continue on and prod my brother and best friend, I hear a man's voice.

"Where y'all at?"

"In the kitchen," Lindsay shouts. She grabs bags of chips and tosses them into a picnic basket just as Cord comes into the kitchen with his trademark wide smile.

Cord McCurry has hung out with us since high school. We have a special friendship, one that's hard to explain. Maybe it's because he stayed with my family for a year or so after high school when my father got him a job at the mine. I don't know. All I do know is that Cord and I don't see each other daily, sometimes not weekly, even, but we always seem to be there for each other. It's almost a broth- er-sister relationship, although not quite. Cord would never allow someone that close to him.

"Hey," he says, patting me on the shoulder as he walks by. "Smells good in here, Lindsay. Whaddya got I can sample? I'm starving."

"You can wait like the rest of us," Jiggs says, reaching for anoth- er marshmallow.

"Oh, whatever, Jiggs," I laugh. "You've been into every dish we've made today. You probably still have brownies on your fingers."

He looks at his hands with a smirk before glancing up at his wife. "That's not all that's on these fingers."

"Jiggs!" Lindsay blushes and tosses a towel at him, making us laugh.

"Are you denying it?" Jiggs teases.

"Do you guys want to take everything out back?" Lindsay says in an attempt to change the subject. She glances out the window towards the fire that's starting to glow as the afternoon sun sets be- hind it. Upwards of thirty people are already here, lingering around the fire. "I think it's time to get this party started."

"Sure thing," Cord says, grabbing the cooler of snacks Lindsay and I put together earlier. Jiggs balances the picnic basket on anoth- er cooler and they head out the back door.

Once they're gone, Lindsay leans against the counter and

watches me. "You okay?"

"Yeah," I say, straightening out my red and grey flannel shirt, my fingers only slightly fidgety. "Why?"

"You've not quite been here mentally all day. Just wondering if everything is okay."

I snort, turning my back to her. I don't want to dampen the party by bringing up the fact that I feel like crawling in a hole and sleeping away my life. That I don't even want to be here. That seeing Ty has brought back, in vivid technicolor, the moment that forever changed the way I'll feel about him.

Dr. Walker sits down on the stool in front of the examining table and looks up at me through his black wire-rimmed glasses. He takes a deep breath as he sits my chart on the little table behind him. My hands find the edge of the white paper hanging off the sides and crumple it in my fists.

"What's wrong?" I ask, my voice trembling. I'm on the cusp of breaking down, my heart beating so fast in my chest that I can barely sneak in a breath. It's been this way since he left and I can't take it anymore. I feel like I'm going to die, like the world is starting to crush me with its weight. It's why I'm here. To fix it. To get something to help regain control of my emotions. But something's wrong. I can see it in his eyes, a benefit of seeing the same doctor since I was fourteen.

The glasses are removed and he clears his throat. "Where's Ty?"

"I don't know," I admit through the burn in my throat.

"Is anyone here with you today?"

"No. Why? What's wrong, Dr. Walker?"

"I'm sorry to tell you this, but your bloodwork showed you're in the process of a miscarriage, Elin."

My world stops yet starts a slow spin that wobbles me slightly as I take in his words. My gut churns, like I've drunk too many margaritas on a Thirsty Thursday with Lindsay, but something itches in the back of my psyche that tells me a margarita might be helpful right about now. I'm starting to sway in my seat, but no amount of grabbing the edges of the table helps.

"What?" I ask, trying to focus on the wrinkles in his face. "I'm not pregnant. It's impossible," I say, a sad laugh rolling past my lips.

Surely I misunderstood. The universe wouldn't do this to me, wouldn't take away the one thing Ty and I have wanted more than anything else. It wouldn't do this to me now, when everything else is falling apart. I won't be able to take it.

"I'm sorry," *he says finally.* "You were just a few weeks along . . ."

The rest is muffled by a screaming only I can hear. My heart thunders so hard I think it's going to explode as I touch my stomach and then pull back, like they're going to be burnt by contact.

I am pregnant. I was pregnant. I . . .

My head falls forward and I barely catch it with my fingers. All the times we tried. So many negative tests. Thousands of unanswered prayers. I can't . . .

My shoulders start to tip my body to the side, but I don't care enough to even try to catch myself. Let me slam against the cold linoleum. Maybe it'll wake me up out of this nightmare.

Dr. Walker's on his feet faster than a post-sixty-year old man should be able to muster, his arm going around my shoulders to keep me from falling off the table. Tears cascade down my face like an open sieve, my wail surely landing on the ears of everyone in the building.

He pulls me to him, and it breaks me that I'm being comforted by a medical professional and not my husband.

Ty. Where are you? I need you.

I hear the doctor whisper to someone to call Lindsay Watson at Blown and I feel like I should tell him not to interrupt her day, but I can't. All I can do is feel myself die a cell at a time.

"Elin?" Lindsay asks, shaking me out of my head.

I shrug. "What do you want me to say? Everything is peachy? My world is a bright and happy place?"

Lindsay rolls her eyes and drops her hands on the laminated countertop. "No, I don't want you to say that. You've just been lost in your own head more today than usual, so I thought maybe something happened. I'm sorry."

I look at her features and instantly regret my attitude.

"I just had a bad night," I sigh, thinking back to the night before and how I didn't sleep at all. Every minute that ticked off the clock,

I was there to watch it.

I've only wanted one thing in my life—a family with the man I'm sure, even now, is my soul mate. If I can't have that, what's left for me? How do you replace that dream when it's all that mattered?

"From seeing him?"

"Yeah," I mumble. "He's been gone for weeks and—boom! He's back. And then he doesn't even speak to me, Linds. Like I'm some stranger."

"Give it time."

"Time for what?" I look at my best friend, bewildered. She knows what I've been through. She picked me up that afternoon and sat with me in the middle of my bed and held me while I came to terms with losing a baby I never knew I was going to have. It was her that picked up the pieces that day. How can she tell me to give it time?

"Time to work out, Elin. He just came back. He was probably as overwhelmed as you were."

"He had the advantage of knowing what he was walking into." I sigh, exhaustion evident in the heaviness of my voice. "Late last night, I was sitting on my bed and a thought hit me: maybe it's over."

She blanches, reaching for my hand.

"No, really, Lindsay," I sputter, my voice cracking. "Maybe it is. Maybe I just accept that we aren't who we once were and we need to let it go."

Her eyes fill with tears, her bottom lip quivering.

"What are you doing crying?" I laugh. "You can't cry or I'll cry, and I've cried enough."

"I just hate this," she sniffles.

"I hate it, but I don't want to hate *him*. And it's getting so easy to."

She looks around the room before settling her eyes on me. "We always said we'd be pregnant together," she whispers.

I take off around the island before stopping dead in my tracks. A cold rush races across my skin. "Wait," I gulp. "Are you . . ."

I look up at my best friend and she nods slowly, her eyes filled with trepidation.

"Lindsay!" I exclaim, racing to her side. "Oh my God!"

Tears spill down her rosy cheeks. I grab her and pull her to me. I can't say anything, the lump in my throat too massive to get around.

I'm thrilled for her, my best friend carrying my niece or nephew that I already know I will love more than any human being on this planet. But at the same time, I'm heartbroken because she's right. We were going to do this together. Not only are we not doing it together, I'm starting from scratch. Without Tyler.

"I'm sorry, Elin," she sniffles.

"Don't you ever say that again," I laugh, pulling back and wiping the tears from her eyes and mine too. "I'm happy for you."

"I know. But I didn't even want to tell you. It just feels so unfair."

I paste a smile on my face for both of our benefits. "It's life, and you're bringing a new one, my niece or nephew, into the world. That isn't unfair in any way. That's exciting and exactly how it should be."

The front door closes, causing us to jump, and his voices rolls through the house. "Jiggs? You in here? Linds?"

I grab the counter behind me for stability. My cheeks are stained with tears, but I'm too frozen, too off-guard, to dry them before he sees.

Ty walks around the corner and his sight lands immediately on me. He stops in his tracks, the playful smirk on his face vanishing. "I, uh," he stutters, looking at Lindsay. "Linds?"

"Hey, Ty," she says carefully. "Jiggs is out back."

He doesn't move a muscle, only his eyes, and those just enough to find me again. The energy between us crackles, the air thickening by the second.

He pulls his hat off his head, smoothing down hair that's still damp from a shower. The movement is enough to rustle me out of my daze.

I look away, swiping a tissue off the counter and dabbing at my eyes. My hands tremble as they swipe at my face.

"You okay, E?" His words are so soft, so kind, I would think they weren't real if Lindsay didn't look at me, waiting on my response.

I nod my head, but of course I'm not all right. I haven't been in a long time, but why should he start caring now? Because he has an audience? Because Lindsay is standing there watching?

I focus on her, using her as a crutch to keep me level. "I'm going to go," I whisper, only meaning for Lindsay to hear.

"Don't," Ty says quickly from the other side of the room. "I'll go. Jiggs said—"

Laughter floats inside the room as Jiggs and Cord return. Jiggs stops in his tracks when he realizes what he's just walked into. He looks from me, to Ty, then to the ceiling.

I shoot him a dagger, knowing exactly what he's done.

"Jiggs said what?" Cord asks. He grabs a brownie and has it inches from his face when he looks up. Assessing the situation, knowing Ty and I wouldn't be in the same place at the same time on purpose, he puts the dessert back on the counter. "I can only imagine what Jiggs said to make this happen."

"Look," my brother starts, shoving his hands in his pockets, "you're both here now. Let's go outside and have a hot dog and a beer."

"I didn't know *she* was going to be here," Ty says, directly to Jiggs.

I look at Ty, baffled by the way he used a pronoun to refer to me. *"What did I ever do to you?"* I scream inside my mind. Instead of saying that or throwing the mug of coffee sitting in front of me at his face, I turn to my brother.

"I asked you if *he* was going to be here. You said no, otherwise, I wouldn't be."

Their heads whip to me, reacting to the fury in my voice. My cheeks are hot, half from pure anger at my brother and half from embarrassment. Even though they're my friends, my family, except for Cord and practically him too, it's still mortifying. They know he left me, and they must wonder, too, what is so wrong with me that my husband, the man I've loved my entire life, walked out and hasn't bothered to come home.

"Did you lie to me, Jiggs?" I ask, feeling Lindsay's hand rest on my forearm.

"Look, sis, I didn't lie to you. I didn't think he was coming."

"I can leave," Ty says, boring a hole into Jiggs' skull with his stare. "I probably should go, actually."

His shoulders slump, his navy blue Henley showing off the width of his shoulders and his trim waistline. He turns towards the foyer when Cord speaks up.

"Hey, man. Why don't you stay?"

Cord takes a step towards me, his sparkling green eyes soft. "That's an awful big yard out there, don't you think, Elin? I'm pretty sure we can all enjoy the night and give each other some space. I mean, fuck, remember the night Jiggs got drunk as fuck and puked all over himself? We all avoided him like the plague because he stunk so bad."

The memory eases the tension in the air just enough for us to chuckle under our breath. I can't look at my husband, though I know he's looking at me.

"You'd be all right with that, right, Elin?" Cord asks gently, coaxing words from my lips. "We're just five friends. Two of y'all are just fighting right now, which, by the way, has gotta stop. Ty is sleeping at my place and he's messy as fuck."

My gaze focused on Cord, I start to grin. "I know he is. Good luck with that."

There's no denying the relief in my posture at knowing Ty is at Cord's.

"I can leave, E, if it makes it easier for you," Ty says, causing me to shiver at the intimacy in his tone.

They all look at me again, the weight of their gazes too much to bear. I grab the plate of brownies off the counter and head to the back door. "I'm taking these outside. Ty can do whatever he wants.

He's been great at avoiding me for weeks now. I'm sure he can manage another couple of hours."

The door slams behind me.

Six

TY

THE FIRE CRACKLES, sending sparks shooting into the sky. Scents of burnt marshmallows and hot dogs linger in the chilly night air as most of the people I grew up with relax on hay bales and lawn chairs.

The party is a lot tamer than most of the bonfires out here. So many of the guys I grew up with, even some of our dads, worked at the mine and are now unemployed. It's not just a truck payment we have to cover now; we have families and mortgages and bills.

The lucky ones do, I guess.

Maybe that's why no one is doing anything that would need the fire department this time. Everyone has too much on their minds—real shit—for mischief. It's just as well. I don't even want to be here. I wasn't even going to stay, just stop by and say hi, until I saw her. Now I can't leave.

Twirling the bottle of beer between my fingers, I watch Elin across the fire. She's talking to Lindsay, her hand on her friend's stomach, and I realize they've told her about the baby. I take a swig of beer, more to squash the burning in my throat than because of thirst.

A baby—that's what we've always wanted. I felt guilty our senior year of high school when she thought she was pregnant and I was happy about it. There are worse things than a baby. I hated being an only child. I wanted the chaos the neighbors had with five boys.

Elin's mom used to say she and I had the same spirit. That's why we were so drawn together. I didn't correct her and say it was her daughter's ass that initially drew in, but it was her sweet, selfless spirit that kept me.

Her having my kids, my name, felt like such a victory. Such a coup. What more could a man want than to find a woman of Elin's caliber to have your family with?

Our life was built on that. The house we picked out has a large oak tree that Elin thought was the perfect view for a nursery. Her job teaching would keep her home on holidays and summers and my job at the mine would afford us plenty of money to raise a slew of children. It might even let her stay home, if she chose.

To think none of that might happen . . .

"Hey, man," Cord says, bumping my shoulder. He plops his tall frame into the chair beside me. "How are ya?"

I shrug.

"Yeah, I feel ya," he voices, following my line of sight. "She's pretty hot."

My head jerks to the side, my fist ready to pound his face. I don't give a fuck that he's one of my oldest friends. He just crossed a line.

"Oh, did you think I meant Elin?" he laughs. "I was actually talking about Becca, but Elin isn't bad either." He tosses me a wink.

"I just about ended you, McCurry," I chuckle, sitting back in my chair. "You were this close to dying tonight."

Cord laughs and stretches his legs. "Yeah, well, what are you going to do when you do see her with someone else? Have you thought about that?"

Yeah, I've thought about it, and it makes me want to end up in prison for a very, very long time. Instead of answering, I just watch my wife from the safety of the darkness.

The light of the fire highlights her delicate cheekbones and the fullness of her soft lips. Her hair brushes against her shoulders as it hangs straight, not curled or fixed up like she usually does. She's thinner than I remember, and I miss her curves and hate knowing that they're missing because of me.

"Have you talked to her at all?" Cord asks.

I start to respond but press my lips together instead. Whatever I say is going to make me sound like a pussy.

"Do you remember when my birth mother came looking for me a few years ago?" he presses. "Fuck, that was hard, Ty. I grew up hating even the idea of her. I was never the kid that wanted to know her. I was the boy in foster home after foster home, wondering why my own mother didn't love me enough to keep me. Wondering why I had to live with the alcoholic in a rage downstairs or the foster mom that had me only for the check, not to actually feed me or take care of me. I mean, if my birth mom couldn't love me, didn't want me, no one would."

He looks into the night, away from everyone, and I watch as a flurry of memories skirt across his face.

"You know, one night I remember lying in a bed with no blanket or pillow, and it was cold as hell," he says to himself more than to me. "It must've been December or so because I remember seeing Christmas lights out the window. My stomach ached," he cringes, "and I mean *ached*. I hadn't eaten more than a half a sandwich in a couple of days and a handful of iced animal cookies I snuck out of the cabinet in the middle of the night." His voice breaks and he pulls away from me, turns so I can't see his face anymore. "I remember lying there and praying that my mother and father, wherever they were, were hungry and cold and miserable. I prayed they died."

I watch his shoulders tense, his jaw clench, and I feel absolutely terrible for him. "Man, I'm sorry. I don't know what to say."

He faces me. "I hated my parents more than I ever thought one person could hate another. Their choices ruined my life. And then my mom showed up out of nowhere."

"I remember that. She came into Thoroughbreds, right?"

"Yeah. And she asked me who I was, and I told her, and she started crying," he says, the corner of his lips twitching. "I called her every name under the sun. I mean, I really ripped into her. But after I settled down some and the shock wore off, we went out to the lake and sat by the water and talked. It was . . . it was okay."

He quiets, stares across the night. "She made me all of these promises, swore she wanted to be a part of my life. Not that I believed her, but she said them anyway. Then she disappeared again."

"I'm sorry," I repeat. I wonder how often he thinks about that and how it feels to be all alone. Because he is. Without Jiggs and I and Elin and Lindsay, Cord is by himself.

He turns to me, his eyes boring into mine. His gaze tells me this isn't just a life story—he has a point. And if I thought hard enough about it, I'm fairly certain I could figure it out. But who wants to do that?

"You get what I'm saying, Ty?"

I take a drink and look for Elin.

"You need to attempt to fix this," he insists. "Your choices might have fucked shit up—her choices too—but you need to make good ones now to repair the damage."

Ignoring him, I take another swig.

"She may not forgive you for leaving her. She might not want any part of you."

Swinging around, I shoot him a glare. He shrugs.

"She might not," he repeats. "But I'm fairly certain her reaction right now is just an emotional overload. She's trying to figure this all out, and you're the one that caused the pain, so she's lashing out at you."

"Thanks," I grimace.

"Well, you're the one that left."

"Shut up, McCurry."

"Truth hurts, but I'm telling it to you anyway." He leans forward. "Don't you respect everything you've been through enough to at least go and talk to her?"

"And say what, Cord? That I'm a piece of shit that left when I should've fought, that took the easy road—"

"You didn't take the easy road," he says. "You did what you

WRITTEN IN THE $\mathcal{S}_{cars}$ 41

thought was best. You left so matters didn't get worse."

"I left because I was at the end of my goddamn rope." I stand, shoving off the chair so hard it almost falls over. "I left because I didn't know what to do to fix any of it. I left because I was a fucking pussy."

"Ty, wait—"

"I need to piss."

Heading for the house, I keep my eyes open for Elin but don't find her. I need to at least get a visual on her, make sure she's okay. The tears on her face when I walked in tonight stabbed me in the chest, and I think I've bled a little all night.

It's not that I think she hasn't cried. It's just I can't see it. I don't think I can shake the image. Two to four in the morning, the hours my mind goes through every mistake I've ever made, will be fun tonight.

Cord is right. Of course he is. There's a part of me that's desperate to talk to her, craving some form of interaction with Elin. But I know I have to tread lightly because something's different about her. Something's happened. I just don't know what or why it changed even more between us.

The kitchen is deserted when I walk in. I make my way down the narrow hallway to the little bathroom off the guest bedroom I've stayed in a number of times. My hand is reaching for the knob when it pulls open.

"Oh!" Elin yelps, her eyes going wide. She takes a big step back inside the bathroom.

Under the bright lights of the vanity, I can see the pink in her cheeks from the fire. I can smell her perfume mixed with the smoke from outside. It's a vanilla scent I haven't smelled since I went to the house the day after I left to get some of my clothes while she was at work.

My breath stills, my throat going dry. I'm unsteady on my feet and my hand reaches for the doorjamb for support.

She watches me like she's being cornered. Her chest rises and falls like she just got finished walking the five miles around town that she does every evening.

I should walk away. I should turn and walk down the fucking hallway and to my truck and leave. I should. Before I do more damage.

"How are ya, Elin?" I ask instead because it's her in front of me, and it's the most natural thing in the world. It's how my world should be, she and I, close enough to touch . . . yet she shouldn't have that look in her eye, and I shouldn't feel like a miserable puke.

"Ty," she breathes, her voice trembling as hard as her hands.

Instinctively, I start towards her, but her stumble back halts me. Shoving my hands in my pockets, I should get out of her way and let her pass. But after not having been this close to her in so long, I can't do that. I need every second she'll give me. I wouldn't have searched for her like *this*, but now that we're here, I can't break the moment. I won't.

"Are you okay?" I ask, searching her face for the truth because I'm not sure she'll give it to me. I'm not even completely sure I want to hear it.

"Sure."

She fidgets and that's enough to cause the air to escape my lungs, an invisible knife to slice the wall between us.

"Elin," I start to plead, "I just . . ."

Tears flood her eyes, but her lips form a thin, hard line. "You just *what*, Ty?" she spits. The words come out, a sob mixed with a ferocity that knocks me back a few steps. "You just want to stand there and act like we're friends from high school just running into each other randomly at a party?"

"No," I snort, watching her body stiffen. "I want to see how you are." Her posture softens just a bit, and I decide to push a little. "I was thinking maybe I could swing by the house. We could talk."

A million expressions grace her features before her gaze steels. "You know what?" she says, her hands hitting me in the shoulders, "Fuck you."

My back hits the doorframe as she presses through. Her touch, even as hateful as it is, still causes a zing through my body that I instantly crave to feel again.

I want to reach out and grab her, kiss her, make her talk to me. By the time I get my wits together, the door is slamming in the kitchen.

Seven

ELIN

THE BEER IS bitter and ice cold and tastes kind of like what I think urine would taste like. I've never been a beer drinker, but I've also never been a pool player. I've also never felt as nervous about being at Thoroughbreds as I do tonight.

"Wanna play again?" Jiggs asks, racking the balls. "I'll take it easier on you this time."

"No, you won't," I laugh. Setting the bottle on the table next to Lindsay, I look at my brother. "But, yeah, rack 'em. Let's play."

Lindsay picks the pepperoni off a slice of pizza. "I'm all for you getting out of the house, Elin, but you drinking beer and playing pool has me worried. I don't even know you right now."

"Yeah, well, me either." I pick up the beer and down it and motion for Becca to bring me another. "I figure this is better than sitting at home and drinking alone. That's what they say, right? Don't drink alone."

"So the point tonight is to drink?"

"No. The point of tonight is to get out of the house, but I can't do that without some liquid courage."

Lindsay sighs and exchanges a glance with her husband. "I don't think this is a good idea."

Jiggs laughs, his eyes heavy with trouble. "I think it's a brilliant idea. Elin wants to have some fun. There's nothing wrong with that."

"But Ty . . ." Lindsay starts and then looks at me. "Are you sure you don't want to go home and watch chick flicks? Jiggs can go get us junk food and we can just veg out."

"No," I insist, my hand flying to my hip. "Like I told you when I called you earlier tonight, I need to stop sitting at home and wallowing. I need to have fun. God knows Ty has been out gallivanting over the fucking country."

"That's not true," Jiggs says, but shuts up when I shoot him a look.

"Whose side you on, brother?"

"Yours," he sighs, shaking his head.

I spin around to take the new drink from Becca and sway a bit. Grinning, I realize my head is feeling foggy. I like it. It's quiet. Kind of numb. Why didn't I do this before?

"Thanks, Becca," I say brightly, yet even I know my enthusiasm is put on. Still, it sounds better. It sounds like what I want to sound like, so I roll with it. "How you liking your new job?"

"It's okay," she quips. "I've waited tables all my life, so I knew what I was getting into. The drunk jerks in the front are making my life a little hellish tonight, but nothing I can't handle."

"Who is it?" Jiggs asks.

She shrugs. "It's really not a big deal. His name is Shane or something, I think, but don't worry about it. I need to check on some tables in the back. Find me if you need anything."

Disappearing in the back, I envy the ease with which she drops into new situations. It's what I'm trying to do.

This is the first night of the new me. Or the first night on the journey to being the new me, I suppose. This is me getting out there, having fun, doing things on a Saturday night.

This is me trying to do it without having an anxiety attack. I take another swallow.

"You all right, Elin?" Jiggs asks, handing me a pool stick.

"Yup."

"How many are you going to let her drink, Jiggs?" Lindsay asks from behind us. "She's on number four."

"Oh, hush, Linds," I say, realizing there's more of a slur to my words than I imagined there would be. "It's beer. I'm well overage. And while you're gonna be a mother, you're not mine. Remember that."

Jiggs laughs and cracks the cue ball against the others, the sound ricocheting through the little pub. It's the local hangout, the place everyone lands on the weekends. Everyone from teenagers wanting to play arcade games in the back to fifty-something couples wanting a sandwich or a slice of pizza to the seventy-year-old men rehashing every sporting event of Jackson in the last century—they're here.

He takes another shot before looking at his wife. "She's a big girl, and I'm driving her home. Let her get wasted."

"She'll be sick tomorrow," Lindsay objects.

"First of all," I say, feeling myself sway a little as I try to line up a shot. "I'm right here." I drag the stick through my fingers and miss the cue ball altogether. "And you have no idea how good this feels."

"I've been drunk before," Lindsay says. "It's not going to feel so good in the morning."

I stand quickly, teetering a little. "Well, here's the thing. I wasn't going to be feeling so good tomorrow anyway."

Lindsay's face twists in pity and I hate it.

"Hey," Jiggs says, handing me his stick. His head turns towards a commotion in the front. "Becca mentioned Shane Pettis is up there. I'm going to go check on her. Be right back." He gives Lindsay a quick kiss on the cheek, his hand resting protectively on her stomach, and walks towards the noise.

"You," I say, focusing my eyes on Lindsay as warmth starts to build over my skin, "are having a baby."

She giggles, her eyes lighting up. "I am. I can't wait to see if it's a boy or a girl."

"When are you telling everyone?"

"I want to get out of the first trimester first. We've just told you . . . and Ty," she gulps. "And Cord found out," she continues in a rush. "But that's it. We haven't even told my parents yet."

"Your mom will be so happy," I grin. "She won't be able to stand not having you close to her once you have a baby. I bet she moves back up here from Florida."

My mind starts to flirt with the idea of what my parents would've thought, but I push it out. Not tonight. I'm not doing the what-if's and what-could-have-been's.

"I've been thinking about that," Lindsay says, her finger drawing a line around the rim of her glass. "If Jiggs can't get a job here, you know, maybe we'd be better off down there with my mom."

"What?" I yelp, my hand slamming on the table in front of me way too loud. We both flinch. "You can't leave me here. Jiggs is the only family I have. Well, and you. And the baby."

"Shh," she says, her finger going to her lip.

"You aren't serious, are you?"

A hand touches my shoulder and I jump, nearly falling over. I'm steadied on my feet by Shane Pettis.

"Who's not serious?" he asks.

Pulling away from his touch, my lip curls in disgust. "What do you want, Shane?"

He grins in his smarmy way. "How are you, Mrs. Whitt? Or have you taken back the name Watson yet?"

"Go to hell, Shane," Lindsay fires at him.

He tosses his head back and laughs, his floppy blond hair falling over his forehead. "Easy there, spitfire," he says to Lindsay. "I was just asking a question. Everyone knows they're on the outs."

"Well, that's none of your business," I slur.

He studies me closely, but his gaze is too much, too strange, and I close my eyes. Ty's face tries to squeeze into my mind, but the alcohol helps block it out.

"You're right. It's not." He places a hand on his chest and looks at me sadly. "I wish I knew nothing about your split. It's just hard to look at you and know what a good girl you are and know, too, that your husband is a drug addict."

The words, the accusation, is the only thing I hear clear as a bell. My fist clenches around the pool stick until my knuckles turn white.

"He's not a drug addict, you dick."

His hands fly in the air in a defensive move. "Hey, I only know what I heard."

"You heard wrong," I spit, staring him down as best as I can with my head wobbling back and forth.

"Why are you defending him? You can do so much better, Elin, than a guy that's all gimpy and buying pills off my cousin. I heard he was staying across the river with some needle junkie."

"Shut the hell up, Shane," I say. The room starts to spin a heavy, slow turn and I reach for the table to steady myself, but can't find it. I can barely make out Lindsay's muffled voice to my right.

Shane takes my hand. I'd normally fight against it, but I need the stability. He leads me the few steps to the pool table and I go along, knowing Lindsay and Jiggs are here. His hand finds the curve of my hip, and I push it away in an awkward attempt at keeping him back.

"Leave her alone, Shane," Lindsay objects from somewhere behind me. "Jiggs will be out here in a minute and will kill you."

I trip and fall against the table, my hands finding the side and catching me.

"Careful," he whispers against my ear.

"I got this," I say. And I'm pretty sure I do. That is, until I look up to the doorway of the patio and see Ty standing there, watching me.

TY

"WELL, SHIT," CORD mutters beside me.

My blood boils as soon as I see Shane's face. I can't stand him. Never could. But seeing him with his hand on her hip—hell, seeing him within breathing distance of Elin is enough to make my head explode.

My eyes lock with my wife's and I know something's wrong. She barely reacts to seeing me, just looks at me like she thinks I'm going to disappear if she looks at me long enough.

"She's drunk," I say, shaking my head. The movement makes her look away.

"What the hell is she doing?" Cord asks, his hand on my shoulder. I'm sure it's so he can yank me back if I leap to rearrange Pettis' face.

"I have no fucking clue."

Shane Pettis is the asshole that exhibits your typical fuckboy behavior. He's the guy that will tell your girl you just got your cock sucked by some random chick so your girl might sleep with him in her moment of agony . . . even though your dick has been under lockdown the entire time. It's rumored that he slips shit into girls' drinks when they aren't looking and once had a minor accuse him of trying to fuck her. He, naturally, denied it and there was no proof, so he got off the hook. He's a pussy, a one hundred percent pathetic excuse for a human being.

Pettis doesn't see me and I want to keep it that way. Lindsay is sitting behind them, a look of mortification on her face because she knows, as much as I do, that if Elin were clear-minded, she'd never give Pettis the time of day. He came on to her once at the Coal Festival and she gave him such a dressing down right smack dab in the middle of the Cake Walk that he fled the scene.

No, if Elin was sober, this wouldn't be happening. Not even close.

I nod at Lindsay, letting her know I'm apprised of the situation, and then spot a table in the corner behind a potted tree.

"So, we're just gonna sit here and drink a beer and watch this bullshit?" Cord asks. "You fucking serious right now, Whitt?"

"Yup."

Looking around the room, I see Jiggs walking their way. He spies his sister with Pettis and cracks his hands in front of him.

"Seriously, Ty?" Cord asks. "You're gonna just let this go down?"

Pettis stands a few feet from Elin as she tries to take a shot. She misses terribly, her giggle floating through the pub and to my ears.

"Yeah. I am."

"Why?"

"Because."

"That's a fourth grade answer."

He's right, but I don't explain. I just want to see what happens. She deserves some space to have a good time, and right now, besides being with Shane Fucking Pettis, there's nothing I can say.

Elin downs what appears to be an entire bottle of beer. Jiggs says something to her and she tries to poke him in the chest but misses. He grabs her arm and steadies her.

My throat is burning, my hands itching to take the bottle away and shake some sense into her. This isn't Elin. She's not a beer drinker or a girl to make a fool out of herself. She's never been this way.

Pettis slides up to her again, his arm going around her waist as he takes her stick away. He leans them both up against the table and whispers in her ear. She leans her head on his shoulder, her lashes fluttering closed.

"You were right, Cord," I scoff. My chair screeches as it goes sailing behind me.

"What about?"

"I can't handle seeing her with another guy."

I start across the room. Out of my peripheral vision, I see Jiggs stand.

They're facing away, almost at the door, when I finally reach them. Pettis' hand is resting on the small of Elin's back.

Reaching out and wrapping my hand around his forearm, I squeeze as hard as I can and jerk it away from her, my fingers searing into his flesh.

"What the fuck?" he yelps, swinging around to see me. Instead of being smart and correctly reading the situation, he smirks.

He's always been a dumb motherfucker.

"Hey, Ty. What's happening, man?"

"Do yourself a favor and head on out of here." My tone lacks any warmth whatsoever, yet it carries the red-hot fury coursing through my veins.

Elin flinches. "What are you doing, Ty?"

"Saving you a bunch of embarrassment."

"I know what I'm doing," she fires back, teetering a little. "He's taking me home."

"When you can say that without slurring the words, sweetheart, I'll believe you."

Shane laughs and starts to reach for her again. I cut the distance between us in half. Looking down and as far into his eyes as possible, I try to drive home the severity of this situation.

"Touch her again, motherfucker. I dare you," I growl. "I have no problem with going to jail tonight."

"Ty!" Elin nearly yells, trying to shove me back. Instead, she falls head first into my chest. The feel of her body against mine, even if it's on accident, is enough to make me lose my breath for a quick second.

Pettis reaches for her, but stops when he sees my face.

"Get the hell out of here, Pettis," I snap, lacing my fingers through Elin's. She tries to pull away, but my grip is too strong.

"Why are you doing this?" she asks, her eyes filling with tears as she stops to remove her hand from mine. Her shoulders slump, her lips tremble. "What do I look like to you? Some piece of property you own?"

"No," I say, pulling her to my side. "You look like my wife."

"I'm not your wife," she whispers, her eyes struggling to stay open. "Not anymore . . ."

Pettis laughs and turns away. "Have fun with that." He's out the door, Cord on his heels, before I can say another word.

"How many beers did she have?" I ask Lindsay.

"Four."

"And how did you think you were going to handle that?" I ask Elin, shaking my head at her stupidity. The realization of what would be happening to her this very second if I hadn't walked in makes me want to come undone at the seams. "Do you have any idea what he would've done to you? What in the world has gotten into you?"

"Why do you care *who* or *what* is getting in me?" she asks, yawning.

I grit my teeth, trying to contain my temper. "Careful, E."

"Just leave me alone."

"I'm not leaving you like this?"

"Why? That's what you're best at."

"We can discuss this when we get you home, if you'd like," I growl.

Her eyes pop open. "I'm not going anywhere with you."

"Try again." I pick her up and toss her over my shoulder, kicking the door open with my boot. "Hey, Becca!" I call over Elin's objections. She looks up from the table she's serving and takes in the situation and laughs. "Put whatever she had on my tab, okay?"

She flashes me a thumbs up and I pause to look at Jiggs. The lines on his face are severe as he braces in anticipation of me going berserk.

"We *will* discuss this later, Watson," I promise him through gritted teeth.

Elin pounds on my back as I carry her out the door.

Eight

TY

THE TRUCK RUMBLES as I steer it off the highway and onto the gravel road. The cab is completely still, the only light coming from the glow of the dash as we get further into the country.

There are no other cars on the road. That's a good thing because I can't keep my eyes off the passenger seat. Elin sits with her head resting on the window, her eyes closed.

Her breathing is even, peaceful, and I try to match mine to hers. If I closed my eyes, I could convince myself we are home in bed. But we aren't, and my brain knows that, and it's a complete internal fight not to pull the truck to the shoulder of the road and pull her into my arms.

The part of me that has been agitated for months is now soothed. Just being in the car with her is a balm to the wound that's been seeping since before I walked out on her. She centers me, stills me, and I wonder how in the hell I let things get so out of control.

Elin mumbles something I can't understand. Her face twists sourly as whatever she's dreaming plays out in her mind and I wonder if she is realizing she's with me.

As much as I hate that I'm with her because of *this*, I can't think of another place I'd rather be. I push away the uncertainty of how to handle this situation once I get her home and instead revel in the feeling of being next to her . . . even if she was seconds away from being with Pettis tonight.

I can't imagine another man touching her, feeling her, knowing her in a way that only I do. My skin crawls, my blood reaching a boiling point. My palm smacks off the steering wheel, making Elin jump.

"Ty?" she asks, trying to sit up. Her hand goes to her forehead, wincing. She looks at me with utter confusion, leaning away against the door.

"Just taking you home," I say, trying to not alarm her. "Look."

The house is dark as we pull in. The security light along the walkway to the back door is out, and I wonder how long that has needed fixed and how many nights she's come home late and had to venture through the darkness.

She's drifted back to sleep by the time I stop the truck. I climb out and make my way around it. The air is crisp, the glow of the fireflies blinking in the darkness making me think back to nights on the porch with her.

Pulling the door open, I catch her as she starts to slide out. A grin tugs at my lips as I feel her body soft against mine.

She doesn't stir at the contact, so I gather her in my arms and lift her out. My heart nearly stops beating and goes wild at the same time.

I bury my face in her hair and breathe her in, fighting back the constriction in my chest. I glance at the house and know I have to take her in when I really just want to put her back in my truck and drive somewhere, anywhere, as long as we're together.

I need her.

Damn it, I need her.

"Mmm . . ." she moans, wrapping her arms around my neck. Her head nestles into my shoulder like it's done a thousand times.

I pick up my feet and walk towards the house. My head is already trying to convince my heart that I have to put her to bed and leave. Again.

I don't know if I can do it.

I have to do it.

Sticking my key in the back door, I'm pleasantly surprised that it still works. The door squeaks as I push it open with my hip. At least some things are the same.

A motion light on the stove flickers on and illuminates the room. The kitchen looks like it did when I left, but there's no note on the table like she used to leave for me when I got in late from work. No promises of what she would do to me when I climbed in bed, no directions on where to find the dinner she made, no lipstick kisses on a blank sheet of paper.

"Ty?" Elin whispers, her breath hot against my neck.

"Yeah, baby?"

"I think I'm gonna be sick."

I squeeze her closer to me. I'd rather be covered in her vomit than have to put her down. "You're gonna be okay. I'm here."

"Ty?" she whispers again, this time more sleepily.

"Yeah?"

"I'm glad you're here."

Unable to respond, I just keep walking towards the room she and I used to share.

The floor moans with our weight as I go through the living room and down the hall. The door to the bedroom is open and our bed is lit up by the moonlight streaming in the window. I walk to the side of the bed, but I can't lay her down. I just can't make myself do it.

The picture from our honeymoon in Tennessee is still framed on the nightstand. My reflective vest from the mine is still hanging on the hook on the back of the closet door and I want to make her wake up and ask her why. I want to jostle her until she tells me she misses me and doesn't hate me and still, somehow, loves me.

"Can you lay me down?" she asks roughly. "Please."

I look at her beautiful face, her eyes still closed, and consider saying no. Instead, I yank back the comforter with the little yellow daisies we bought on a Saturday morning in Terre Haute and place her softly on my side of the bed. She never opens her eyes.

Fighting a myriad of emotions, ones that threaten to spill out in an ugly mess, I remove her shoes and pull the blankets up around her. I tuck them beneath her body, sealing her in both to hopefully comfort her and to put a physical reminder to me that I can't climb in with her. I'm *this close* to doing just that. But I won't take advantage of this situation. We need to work through things, not add reasons to fight.

"Will you lie with me?"

I furrow my brows, absolutely sure I misheard her until she asks again.

"Will you lie with me, please?"

I shake my head, trying to walk a fine line between what I should do and what I want to do.

"You don't mean that. Just go to sleep. I'll be right here."

My soul rips apart to say those words, but the only thing that could make this situation any worse is for her to feel like I took advantage of her. And I won't mess it up, not more than I already have. Even if that means denying myself the very air I've been craving for so long, I will.

"You've promised me that before." Her voice is clearer than it has been, enough for me to know she's keeping her eyes closed on purpose. She just doesn't want to look at me. And that makes me want to die.

"Elin . . .

"You left."

"Elin . . ."

"You didn't come back."

Her words are strangled, both a fact and a myth because whether she knows it or not, my mind was always here. I never left. Not really.

"You wouldn't answer my calls," she mumbles. "Lie with me. Show me you don't hate me."

Tears cloud my vision and I struggle to blink them back. What she's asking is exactly what I want to do, what I *need*, but not like this. Not with her so drunk.

She takes my hand, the offer of her small fingers in mine

crushing me. She tries to pull me towards her, but she's too cursed by the alcohol. Instead, I hold her hand, stroking her knuckles with my thumb like I would do while we watched a movie or drove down country roads. Her hand was always in mine . . . just like this.

Her features smooth and her breathing evens out. I bring her hand to my lips and press a long kiss to the middle of her palm.

"The baby . . ." I can't make out the rest of the sentence, but it's salt in an already gaping wound that she's thinking of Jiggs and Lindsay's baby when we should be in that situation too. Our lives shouldn't have taken this turn.

"I love you," I whisper, choking the words out. She doesn't react, too asleep and out of it to hear. "I'm sorry. I'm sorry for everything."

The urge strikes hard, much harder than before, to slip into bed beside her and pull her into me. Before I can do that, I turn away and head back down the hallway leaving my heart beside her.

Forcing air into my lungs, around the pain that's nearly unbearable, I enter the kitchen and flip on the light. I need to get a grip. And I need to rip Jiggs' ass for, yet again, putting me in a situation with Elin before either of us are ready.

I whip out my new prepaid phone and find his name and press call.

"Hey," he answers. "You okay?"

"Fuck you, Jiggs," I spit.

"Settle down."

"Don't fucking tell me to settle down," I warn, feeling my body shake. "What the fuck were you thinking letting her get bombed like that? And what? You just sat there and watched Pettis try to fuck her right in the middle of Thoroughbreds?"

"Ty—"

"Fuck. You." I lean against the wall and try not to see double. "I don't know if you thought it was funny or—"

"How about," Jiggs interrupts, "you shut the hell up and think about this for a minute?" His chuckle rings through the phone. "She's my sister, Ty. Do you think I didn't have that under control?"

"Well, considering I was two seconds from ripping Pettis apart and am now standing in the middle of my house while Elin sleeps—yeah. It looks like you didn't have jack shit under control."

"That's where you'd be wrong."

The relaxed tone of his voice tells me he's right. I sink further against the wall.

"I knew you were on the patio, you fucking idiot. Cord sent me a text. So I let her do her thing, let her feel like she was being some kind of rebel . . . and let you see what can happen if you don't get your shit straight. Maybe it'll do you both some good."

Huffing, I pace a circle around the table. "It's not your place to do this, Jiggs."

"The hell it isn't. What am I supposed to do? Sit here and watch the two of you both be hard-headed and let your lives go down the drain?"

"They're our lives, so yeah. That's exactly what you should do."

He laughs. "It hurts to feel that, doesn't it? It hurts to face what you've done to her instead of running. Welcome to reality, Whitt."

"What do you want me to do?"

"Be the man I know you are. As much as you want to pretend you can't fix things and she's somehow not your responsibility anymore, you just proved tonight that's a lie. Hell, you proved that at the bonfire."

"Another time you shouldn't have interfered! You're just making it worse. You're forcing us together when we don't want to be."

"I'm calling bullshit on that."

A heavy sigh leaves my lips. Everything is so fucked up; I don't even know what I feel right now. And I sure as shit don't know what Elin thinks.

"Where's she at?" Jiggs asks.

"Sleeping. I think she's out for the count."

"What are you doing tonight?" His voice is careful and it makes me hang my head.

"Staying here. I can't leave her alone." I look around the kitchen. It still feels like home. It's enough to take a part of the weight off my chest that has been sitting there for a long time. "I've probably pushed my luck tonight. Why don't you plan on coming by in the morning and checking on her? Let her replay all this with you, not me. Then, maybe, I can build on this."

"Sounds good."

I don't miss the smile in his voice.

"I'm still pissed at you, Watson."

"You'll deal."

"Talk to you tomorrow," I say and end the call. My anger is diminishing and I don't want him to know it.

Turning the light off, I make my way back to the living room. Slipping off my shoes and sweatshirt, I open the trunk against the wall. A pillow and blanket we use for movie night are tucked away like they should be.

Arranging a little nest on the sofa, I lay down and stretch out. The house is quiet, so quiet, that if I listen closely enough, I can hear Elin's breathing in the other room.

The couch folds around me, welcoming me with its soft leather like it remembers me. Closing my eyes, I listen to Elin's rise and fall and pretend I'm next to her.

On a couch in a house I'm not quite welcome in—it's the happiest place I've been in a very long time.

ELIN

I'M GOING TO *be sick.*

Squeezing my eyes shut from the onslaught of sun pouring through the open blinds, I lie completely still in hopes that the putrid bile that's threatening to blast up my throat goes away.

My head pounds, my stomach gurgling away.

I place my hands on my belly and realize I'm in the same clothes I wore yesterday. As I run them down my stomach to my legs, I'm even in my jeans. I never wear jeans to bed. My mom used to tell me when I was a little girl that my skin would get stuck in the zipper while I slept. It terrified me from trying it. Still does.

Everything is foggy as I try to pick apart what I remember from last night. Jiggs and Lindsay picked me up and we went to Thoroughbreds for pizza.

Beer.

Gagging, I try not to upchuck the telltale bitterness of a bottle of brew.

I take a hefty breath, only to have it halt in my throat. A flurry of shadowy images whips through my memory, a muddy slideshow . . . except for Ty's face.

He was with me.

Oh my God.

I try to remember something, anything, that tells me what

happened. There's a blur of memories, of voices, of familiarity, yet nothing concrete.

A nervous energy courses through my body, my skin tingling with the possibility that Ty might still be here.

Dear God, please don't let him be here. Please don't let me have done something stupid.

I don't even know how I will process it if I walk into the kitchen and see him. *Did I sleep with him? Did I tell him about the baby? Oh, God . . .*

I open my eyes, hesitating before they flutter awake. Glancing around the room, everything looks completely normal. Nothing moved, nothing out of place. No sign of an argument. No sign of him.

Giving myself a second to adjust to the light, I ignore the throbbing in my head and pull back the covers. My feet on the floor, I stand, wobbling for a second as the alcohol settles in my stomach.

With a sense of anticipation mixed with a heavy dose of dread, I start down the hallway. I listen for the television, for his voice. It's quiet.

The couch comes into view and I grip the wall for support with one hand, the other covering my mouth. The pillow and blanket from the trunk are in a messy bundle. It's Ty's handiwork, the pillow lying length-wise and not horizontally like normal people use it. He always lies with his pillow under his head, neck, and top of his back long-ways.

He stayed with me.

My eyes sting as they fill with hot tears, my headache now blocked by a surge of emotion. With more urgency than I care to acknowledge, I make my way into the kitchen. I'm across the room in half the normal time.

Dashing to the window, only my car is in the driveway. A million questions fight for attention, a thousand possibilities and scenarios race through my mind. I struggle to piece together the events of last night.

I have no idea what happened. Fear hits me hard when I realize that regardless of what occurred—he's not here. Yet, through it all, a little bubble of happiness sits squarely on my shoulders because *he was here.*

It infuriates me that him being here makes me happy. I don't want to want him. I don't want to be happy that he gave me a piece of his time, like he can walk back in my life and decide he'll bestow some attention on me.

God knows what he was doing all day yesterday, or last week, or the month before.

My purse sits on the table. I go to it and rummage around until I find my phone. My finger hovers over Lindsay's name when I hear tires hitting gravel.

With a lump in my throat, I look out the window. Jiggs waves as he makes his way to the front door. Dropping my phone back in my purse, I head to the front and let my brother in.

"You look like shit," he laughs, ruffling my hair as he walks inside. "Feel like it too?"

"Pretty much," I mumble, following him into the living room. He picks up the pillow and blanket, and I automatically open my mouth to object, but shut it quickly. I don't know what he knows, and I don't want to muddy the waters.

Jiggs gets comfortable, kicking his feet up on the coffee table and watches me smugly.

"What?" I ask. I plop down in the recliner, my stomach roiling.

He shrugs. "Anything you wanna tell me?"

"No, but I know you know what happened last night, and I'd love to know too."

"You don't know?"

He seems surprised, uncrossing him arms. He peers at me through his thick lashes, a gift from our grandma.

"Jiggs," I ask, my voice unnaturally even, "Did he stay?"

"Yeah. He brought you home from Thoroughbreds."

My world spins in a mad dose of uncertainty. "Why? Why did he do that?"

Jiggs laughs. "Well, it was him bring you home or let you go home with Pettis."

"Pettis? I'd never go home with that son of a bitch."

"You almost did last night," he cracks.

"Oh my God." I cover my eyes with my hands, unable to look at him. Unable to look at myself. That's not like me. If I would've been willing to go home with Pettis . . . what else was I capable of doing? Or saying?

My cheeks flush, my stomach rolling again, sloshing with the alcohol that caused this big mess.

No, I caused this big mess. This one is on me. I chose to go to Thoroughbreds with the explicit purpose of getting wasted.

"It worked out well," my brother says. "Ty walked in and saw it and flipped his lid."

My chest swells, and I can't help the smile that tugs at my lips. "He did?"

There's no denying that this little tidbit of information feels good. That I was able to get under his skin, even if I didn't mean to. Score one for the alcohol because I never would've attempted such a thing sober.

"He actually carried you out of the pub. I was going to bring you home, but he didn't really leave it open for debate."

My gaze falls on the pillow at the other end of the sofa.

"He left around five this morning. He called me when you went to sleep, and I talked to him again this morning. I know you're thinking a million things, but nothing happened last night. He just put you to bed and slept on the couch."

Giving that a second to soak in, I imagine what last night must've looked like from his perspective—me, drunk, stumbling, and altogether foolish. And he comes in like some kind of savior and brings me home, watches me in my inebriated state.

So not the image I want him to have of me, and Jiggs knows that.

"Damn it, Jiggs."

"Listen to me. He—"

"No," I cut him off. "I can't think about this right now." I rise off the chair, my stomach all acidy again. "He can't just waltz back in here and bring me home and see me like that. It's not okay. And to hell with you for letting him! I'm your sister, James!"

"And he's your husband."

I whip around to face him. "Is he? Or did he just see something last night that contested his manhood? Did him seeing me get hit on by Pettis make him go all alpha? Like I was some kind of fire hydrant in a pissing match?"

"Don't do this."

"Why? Because he should be allowed to just come and go in my life when he feels like it? Because that's not happening."

He sinks back into the sofa and sighs.

My eyes narrow. "You have no idea what he's put me through." I'm sure it's the alcohol that's still pumping through my body that makes those words sound choppier than I'd like. He doesn't know I was pregnant. Only Lindsay does, and I swore her to secrecy. The coupling of losing my husband and our baby in the matter of a few short days was just too much humiliation to admit to. I wanted no pity, no casseroles, no cards. I just wanted to be sad. Then bitter. All of it alone if it wasn't with Ty. I deserved that reprieve and it's the only secret I've kept from my brother.

"I know he's broken your heart. I get it."

"No, you don't," I laugh angrily. "You don't have any clue how deep my scars go."

Jiggs scans my face, trying to see what I mean. He quirks a brow. "I'll listen if you want to tell me."

"I don't."

Rolling his eyes, his jaw pulls tight. "The two of you are going to be the death of me."

My heart breaks, but I say the words anyway. "I'm not sure there is a 'two of us' anymore."

We watch each other, a sadness in the room that's almost as thick as it was the day our parents passed away.

"Jiggs, I'm just . . . I'm really, really tired of this," I say through the strangle in my throat. "I'm tired of being sad and I'm tired of hoping he'll come back. Him bringing me home wasn't him coming back. That was him being jealous and while it's entertaining and I might even enjoy that a little bit, it's not us being together," I sniffle.

Jiggs rises from the couch but doesn't come towards me. He just stands, shoulders slumped, almost as saddened by this as I am. "When did it get this bad between you two?"

Walking to the mantle, I pick up the picture of us. I trace his jawline with my finger. "I can't even remember. He was fine after the accident. At first, anyway. Then everything folded on top of itself. I think he got depressed. I know I felt pressure to take care of it all. He received unemployment, but no insurance payout and no overtime. Things got so tight. So I had the infertility money we'd been putting back . . ."

"Ah, Sis."

"It just started feeling like this black hole, Jiggs. Like everything was shit and we both felt that. There was nothing to look forward to anymore."

My brother lets out a sigh, his hands clasping in front of him. "I knew he'd withdrawn some. When he put in his resignation from the team, I came over. Asked what was up and he just said he couldn't do it anymore. I knew that was bullshit because those kids were his everything. But the harder I pushed, the more he refused to talk."

"Dustin would come by," I say, my throat tight. "It didn't help. I didn't know what to do. I just kept thinking if we could have a baby, that would shine some light on this. Give us something to come together about. Instead, it caused even more stress, and then I had to use the money to live and then I found out he was taking some of it too . . ."

"The perfect storm."

"Yeah." Shaking my head, the fatigue of the situation drops hard. I sit the picture on the mantle. "Maybe we grew apart. That happens."

My voice breaks and as my eyes fill, my entire body begins to shake. Jiggs crosses the room and brings me into a hug just as my heart starts to splinter.

"I feel like I've just waited on a day when I would wake up and this would all be some joke, some nightmare. But it's not, Jiggs. This is real. And it's time I accept that. It's time I accept that so much has happened between us that can't be repaired."

I shake as I admit out loud, for the first time, what I know is the truth. My marriage is over.

Ten

TY

"I HAVEN'T SEEN you around here in a while," Melissa, the girl that works at Sullivan's most afternoons drawls, giving me a flirty smile as she takes my money. "Where've you been, handsome?"

"Around."

"I've missed that smile of yours."

I place a candy bar on the counter.

"No chew today?" she asks, obviously proud of herself for remembering what I usually get every afternoon.

"Nah, I quit." I don't go into the explanation that I really don't chew it anyway, that it's some kind of habit that I've had since I was a teenager—buying the can, sticking it in my pocket, then giving it to some poor bastard that asks if he can borrow some.

"You coaching again?" she asks, not missing a beat. "We need you. The newspapers from Indianapolis say we have a chance at a state title this year."

I shrug, ignoring the little bud of pride that unfolds in my stomach. "They're a good group of boys," I concede. "They can do big things this year. Reynolds will have them ready."

"I guess. We'll miss you on the court." She hands me my receipt. "Don't be a stranger, Ty."

I take my change and ignore her invitation that didn't have

to be spoken. Swiping my candy off the counter, I walk out. The sun is bright, despite the ominous clouds rolling in from the west. Squinting, I take a sip of my drink and make my way to my truck. I look up when I hear the distinct roar of Cord's diesel.

He bursts through the parking lot of Sullivan's and slides his truck in beside mine, the tires squealing as they lock in place. Flicking off the ignition, he grins. "Hey."

"Hey." I stop at the bed to give Yogi a scratch behind his ears. "What are you doin'?"

"Not much. Was taking Yogi out to Busseron Creek before this storm hits, maybe do a little fishing. I thought I'd swing in and see if you wanna go?"

I shrug. "Nah, thanks for the offer though."

"You got something better to do?"

"Not really." I look at my friend and laugh. "Wanna tell me what you said to Pettis last night?"

He smirks, trying to stifle a laugh. "I just properly advised him of his rights."

"His rights?"

"Yeah, his rights." He pulls off his hat and roughs his hand through his hair. "His rights to life, liberty, and the pursuit of happiness. I explained those were his Constitutional rights. However, those don't apply to dead men and if he is seen anywhere near Elin Whitt again, I'm afraid his rights would be terminated."

My laugh triggers glances from the patrons pumping gas a few feet away. "That's gold."

"That's fact," he grins. "Now, what are you up to? I haven't seen you at home all day. Was kind of hoping you were with Elin."

I kick a rock and watch it roll across the pavement. I don't know what I expected to feel like today; I guess I didn't give it much thought. I just reacted last night when I saw Elin with Pettis, and now I'm paying the price.

She's all I think about every day, but it's been worse since I slipped out of our house this morning. This time, when I left, I looked back. This morning, I hesitated, nearly walked back inside a handful of times before I forced myself in the truck and down the driveway. Even then, my eyes were on the rearview mirror.

Cord tilts his head, a smirk dragging across his lips. "Wanna tell me what happened when you took your wifey home?"

"Nope."

"I figured as much. Even if you had managed to try to say something to her, she would've been too out of it to remember."

"Come to think of it, that was the perfect time to talk to her about everything. Shit."

"Missed opportunity," he grins. "Things will work out. I feel it in my bones."

"Nobody wants to hear about your bones, McCurry."

He hops out of his truck and stands next to me. Pulling his Arrows hat down as the wind gust rips through the parking lot, he winces. "Damn, that's cold."

"They were talking about it in there," I say, flinching as the cold goes right through me. "Said it's gonna be a helluva storm coming through here in a bit."

"Guess that means no fishin'. Better grab what I need and get home."

"Got someone waiting on you?" I ask, even though I know the answer. Cord doesn't get close to people. He's friendly with Jiggs and I and our wives, but that's the closest he's ever gotten with any-one. He's dated here and there, but never anything meaningful. The few girls he's brought around us over the past few years he inten-tionally keeps some barrier between them. You can almost see it.

He's cool about it. All the girls he dates, if you call it that, re-main his friends afterwards. Everyone loves Cord McCurry. Cord just doesn't necessarily love them back by design.

"Nah," he grins as Yogi licks his face. "This is my girl. My one and only."

"That's sad, Cord," I laugh.

"Sad but true," he says, locking his truck. "I'm not built like you. I don't have some part of me that women can relate to."

"Bullshit."

He shrugs, a faint frown tickling across his lips. "Maybe, maybe not. Either way, we're gonna get blown away if we stand here much longer." He claps me on the shoulder and heads inside. "I'll pick up some frozen pizzas and cold beer. How's that sound for dinner?"

"Good as anything." I climb in my truck and back out of the parking lot. The wind shoves me all over the road, the sun now hidden behind a steely set of clouds that move so quickly across the sky it's like they're on fast forward. "Shit," I say, dodging a tree limb that flies in front of me as rain begins to pelt my windshield.

My phone buzzes in my pocket, and I pull it out to see a severe weather warning encouraging everyone to take shelter. As my truck is pushed into the other lane by a crazy gust of wind, I make a quick right and head towards Cord's.

ELIN

ALCOHOL HELPS YOU make bad decisions.

Nearly twenty-four hours after my little drinking party, I'm still making them hand-over-fist.

Curled up on my bed, e-reader to my right, phone to my left, I have blankets tucked around me. A candle flickers on my nightstand just in case the power, which is blinking like a disco ball because of the storm, goes out. And on my body, all soft and wrinkled, is Ty's old Tennessee Arrows t-shirt.

Not once since he left have I done this. There hasn't been a single instance where I've become *that girl*, the one that wraps herself in his clothes and tries to find the scent of his cologne buried somewhere in the fibers of the fabric. I've managed to maintain my dignity, never stooping to that level. Until tonight.

I blame it on the alcohol.

I'm hungover, both on the beer and on the emotions of the day. Time had granted me the small luxury of choice and I chose anger. It was the easiest to handle. But after seeing him three times in as many days and having to deal with him seeing me and touching me and God knows what else, things I still can't remember, it's like a hurricane came in and whipped all my feelings together, spilling them into one giant, confusing heap.

His shirt helps. I don't know why, but it does, and even more disturbing is that I don't feel weak because of it. Maybe it's because I made the choice to put it on. I wasn't crying when I did it. I wasn't grieving or praying for some kind of direction from the man upstairs. It was a very calm moment after my shower and I saw it hanging in the back of the closet.

My biggest fear is letting my feelings get so mixed up by remembering who we used to be together and not who we are now. The thought of living with him and fighting like we did is unbearable. It's not us and not the way either of us should want to live, and I'm afraid if I don't stop this, once and for all, we'll find ourselves in that very same place. And I can't handle going through this again.

Thunder cracks outside my bedroom window, making me jump. I snuggle deeper into the pillows and clutch my phone for good measure, wondering why the worst storms happen after midnight.

Storms have always made me feel like a child. I hate the darkness, the unpredictability of the danger associated with them this time of year. I used to stay awake until Ty would come home from work if a storm was particularly bad. We would joke about what would happen when we had a baby and I had to be the grown up.

My heart sinks in my stomach.

Another clap of thunder rings through the air and I shudder. It lasts for a long few seconds and ends with the sound of the back door being rattled.

"Don't even," I mutter, swiping a tissue off the nightstand and dabbing it against my eyes. "Don't mess with me tonight, Mother Nature."

The rapping sound rolls through the house again in the midst of the tree limbs scratching at the window. Hearing it again, it sounds intentional. Deliberate.

I pull Jiggs' number up on my phone and uncurl my legs from

the blankets. Drawing in a quick breath, I drop my feet to the floor.

The windowsill shakes as the wind assaults it, rocking the old farmhouse to its roots.

The floor is cold against my bare feet as I slip through the room, my thumb hovering over the call button. My breathing echoes off the walls of the hallway, my senses on high alert. Listening closely, I try to hear the knocking sound again but all I can make out is the howling wind.

I round the corner and scream, dropping my phone.

"Elin! It's me!"

My hand searches frantically for the light switch, and when I finally find it and flip it on, I can't believe what I'm seeing.

Ty is standing in front of me. His grey t-shirt is soaked all the way through, his jeans pressed against his body from the rain. His hair is smashed to his head and water droplets trickle down his cheeks.

"What in the hell are you doing?" I gasp, my heart speeding out of control.

"I didn't mean to scare you."

"Oh really?" I eke out in between gasps, trying to regulate my breathing. "You think you can just walk in here in the middle of the night and I'm going to be expecting you?"

"I hope you're not expecting another man to be walking in here in the middle of the night," he says, a gravel to his voice that just incenses me.

Laughing in disbelief, I throw back my shoulders. "I don't think you have a right to an opinion on who's coming in here in the middle of the night."

"My name is still on the mortgage."

"We can have that fixed."

We glare at each other, a standoff neither of us wants to lose. This is us, our new roles as combatants.

I bend down to pick up my phone. Standing as tall as my five foot four will allow, I stare at him. "You don't live here anymore,"

I spit, a break to my voice that is just enough that I know it is unmistakable.

He forces a swallow, unfazed by my attack. "Settle down, Elin."

"Don't you dare tell me to settle down!"

"I just wanted to make sure you're okay. I know you hate storms."

"Really, Ty?" I ask in pure disbelief, my jaw hanging wide. "You wanted to make sure the storms didn't scare me? *How considerate of you.*"

"Come on, E," he sighs.

"No, you *come on*, Ty. It's a little ridiculous that after everything, you come waltzing in here acting like a fucking saint over a storm."

"I was just *checking on you.*"

"Here I am," I say, holding my arms out, almost touching either side of the hallway. My chest shakes right along with the quick breaths, but I hope he doesn't notice. "See me? I'm still here. Doing just fine without you. Not that you probably give a fuck—"

"Are you serious?" he booms. "You think I don't give a fuck?"

"Do I look serious?" I shout back.

"Of course I give a fuck! Damn it!" He tugs at his hair in frustration. "You have no idea just how much I *do* give a fuck, Elin. *You have no idea.*"

"No, I don't know. And you know something else? I don't care," I seethe, lying through my teeth. Because I do care. So much. But I can't care anymore.

He takes a deep breath and allows the air to settle in his lungs. He starts to speak a few times before catching himself and starting again. "I just wanted to make sure you're all right. I'm sorry."

"I'm fine, as you can see. Now you need to go."

"You look good," he says softly, ignoring my request.

I should have some sort of compassion for him because he's obviously trying to play nice. But I don't allow that soft spot for him because that weakens my strength. And what do I know–maybe he's just still worried I *am* with someone else? Maybe he's been with another woman and wants to come home?

Squaring my shoulders, I lace my arms across my chest. "I *am* good. No thanks to you."

His shoulders slump and his eyes hit the floor. "E . . ."

"Don't. You have no fucking idea what you've done to me." I see the door to what would've been the nursery out of the corner of my eye, and I choke back the lump in my throat. "But let me tell you this," I say, walking close enough to him to poke him in the chest, letting my pain drive me, "I. Am. Still. Here. And all you've done is proven that I can live without you."

His eyes draw slowly to mine. "I've proven I can't live without you."

"Don't even say that to me," I gruff, tears tickling the corners of my eyes. His words, coupled with the look on his face, would break me if I let them. "You don't have the right to say those things to me! This was a marriage—" I yell, as he cuts me off.

"It *is* a marriage—"

My hand shakes as I glare at him, pointing my finger at his face. "No, it *was* a marriage, Ty, and you walked out."

"You told me to!"

"Yes, I did," I say, biting back the memories flooding my mind. "But I didn't mean it. I just said it in the heat of the moment and you took full advantage."

His eyes narrow, his jaw ticking, but he doesn't respond. He just stands there looking at me like he doesn't know where to start.

"A marriage isn't something you can just come and go from as you please. You ruined this. Not me." My voice is steadier than I anticipated and it gives me some courage.

"You're right," he says carefully, his Adam's apple bobbing in his throat. "I ruined it and I will fix it."

"That would mean I want it fixed."

The hallway closes in on us, the air between us hot and thick. We just stare at each other, feeling each other out.

"You have no idea—"

"No!" I yell, my hand going back into the center of his chest. It's wet and hard and feels so familiar. "You have no idea what you've done to me. To *us!*"

His hand wraps around my wrist and my breath escapes in a smooth gasp. The contact, skin-to-skin, is not something I'm prepared for.

It's not fair.

Bending down so his face is inches from mine, he says, "To *us*. Because it's still *us*, E."

I snort, trying to ignore the feeling of his touch. The corner of his lip curls, his gaze darkening. The look is ferocious and as he takes a step towards me, I take one back.

"Don't act like I don't know what *us* means, Elin," he snaps, taking yet another step forward. "Everything I do in my life is for you."

"So walking out on me was for my own good? You did that for me?" The cockiness in my tone is to hide the anticipation of reaching the boiling point. We are almost there. I feel it, the temperature rising and ready to topple over. I just don't know which way it's going to fall. "Gee, thanks, Ty. That makes this so much easier."

Thunder cracks outside just as my back hits the wall. My chest rises and falls, touching his with every intake of breath. He peers down at me, his eyes boring into mine.

"There hasn't been a damn thing easy about this," he says, his breath hot against my skin.

"That was your choice."

I try desperately to hold on to the anger that's being replaced quickly with my need, my desire, my craving for this man. The only man I've ever loved. The man that is my other half—whether it's fucked up or not. Being this close to him puts me at a disadvantage, but there's no denying the little balm of peace that's washed over some of my wounds by his presence. By his touch. By the way he's looking at me.

"It sure as hell didn't feel like my choice," he gruffs.

"Maybe that's the problem," I say, the words full of hesitation. "Maybe we aren't the same people anymore. Maybe we've changed. I know you're not the Ty I once knew."

"No, you're right," he says with an arrogant shrug of his muscled shoulders. "I love you more than I ever have."

"Fuck you," I say, a slip to my voice that he hears.

His eyes glimmer, distracting me, and I don't see the kiss coming. But the feeling of his lips against mine sends a zip of energy screaming through my veins.

"Ty!" I object half-heartedly, pressing him away with only a portion of the gumption I could put behind it if I wanted to. He doesn't care. He just kisses me harder, his lips soft and smooth like I remember.

My knees go weak, like it's some kind of first kiss, my breathing ragged like the first time he kissed me under the steps at the high school.

He drops his grip on my wrist and clenches my hips with both hands. His lips are unrelenting, working mine with such precision, such skill, that it's all I can do to follow along.

And really, it's all I want to do.

Our kisses grow quicker, our breathing more labored. My head is spinning, shouting at me to stop the madness. My body, my heart, lobbying in tandem to stay put because this is where I'm supposed to be.

I can't process the arguments. All I can do is fall into an easy rhythm, be played like an instrument in the hands of the man that knows it like the back of his hand. A man that's played it a million times, that's crafted how it plays by his touch.

My fingers find the back of his hair and I lace them through his wet locks. He growls against my lips, the heat of his breath tingling my mouth and eliciting a fire between my thighs.

His fingers dig into my hips, his body pressing mine into the wall. The intensity of the contact at every level makes me desperate for more.

Ignoring the tick of my subconscious that tries to remind me why I shouldn't be here, my hands hurriedly find the hem of his shirt. It's wet and heavy, and when my skin touches the defined lines of his abdomen, we both flinch.

My fingertips skirt his chiseled torso, his body rolling against my skin, itching for connection the same as me. In a swift movement, I find the waistband of his jeans and frantically undo the button. The zipper slips down over his hardened cock.

"Ah," I moan as his lips finally leave mine and work their way to the skin just below my ear.

Before I can register it, my shirt is up and over my head.

"Fuck, E," he breathes as he takes in my nude body. "Damn, baby."

"Ty," I whisper, my voice barely heard over the storm raging outside. It's no match for the explosion happening inside me.

His eyes never leave mine as he slips off his shoes and jeans. I watch, pinned to the spot by the words he's telling me without saying anything at all.

"Come here, sweetheart," he whispers as the light in the bedroom flickers and the power goes off.

My hands shake as I reach for him in the darkness. He takes my hand mid-air, like he knew where I'd be, and guides me to him. Our bodies press together, skin to skin, our hearts thumping at the same frenzied pace.

"God," he mutters, holding me tight against him.

"Ty?"

"Yeah?" he asks as his fingers stroke my back.

The war raging inside me tears me in half. For once in my life, I go not with what makes sense, but what makes me feel better.

This time, just this once, I'm going to give in. After this, I know what I'll have to do and it's been a long time coming.

I take a deep, shaky breath and go for it. "Fuck me before I change my mind."

Eleven

TY

THE SECURITY LIGHT kicks on at the end of the hall, a soft glow that illuminates the woman in front of me. She watches me, her chest rising and falling quickly, her eyes wild even in the dimness. She looks so fucking beautiful.

Her hair is in a wild knot at the top of her head, her cheeks pink. Although I loved seeing her in my t-shirt and hope that means she was thinking of me, I love her more like this: bared, just for me.

It takes a split second for her words to sink in, and once they do, the fire in my gut is stoked into a raging inferno. Stalking the minimal distance between us that feels like a canyon, I pin her to the wall. My hands are on either side of her head, my cock pressed against her belly.

A small, quick intake of breath escapes her lips as she feels how hard I am.

"Feel that?" I ask, my lips brushing across her cheek.

She hums, tilting her neck so my lips find the crook of her neck. I drag the pad of my tongue against her skin, tasting the sweetness beaded from the anticipation of what's to come.

She takes my left hand off the wall, dropping the back of it onto her shoulder, and with her hand wrapped around my wrist, trails it slowly down her chest, over her breasts. Her nipples are stiff, wanting to be sucked, and my cock throbs at the thought.

My rough hand draws down her smooth torso, gliding over her belly button. Her back arches off the wall, her eyes floating closed as a soft moan escapes her lips. I let her stay in control.

My hand is twisted so the palm is centered over the apex of her thighs. She takes one of my fingers and presses it against the opening of her pussy.

"Feel that?" she moans.

"Fuck." She's soaking wet for me, her body begging for my attention. I flatten my palm against her body, cupping her pussy. Two fingers press firmly against her opening, and I watch her head fall back against the wall. "Feel good?"

She doesn't respond, but she doesn't have to. I know how to work this woman better than I can work myself.

Kneeling in front of her, I part her with one hand, putting pressure on her clit with my thumb. She gasps, knowing what's coming and I smile up at her when she looks at me.

I lick her slowly, my flattened tongue soaking up every bit of sweetness I can find. Her hips roll against me, needing the friction that I'm deliberately withholding.

I dip my tongue into her, strumming small circles against her clit. Her moans fill the air, a straight shot to my dick.

Sliding my tongue up her slit again, I can feel her start to go off. I know from hundreds of times of doing this very same thing, she will explode if I touch her for much longer.

So I stop.

"Tyler," she moans, grabbing my hair and attempting to force my face against her.

Smirking, I stand and wipe the wetness off my face with the back of my hand. "What, Elin?" I tease.

"You know what," she groans, pulling me towards her.

I wrap my arms around her, each hand cupping her ass. Her mouth forms a perfect "o" at the contact, her body turning into putty. I knead her backside in my hands as I look into her eyes.

I lift her, letting her thighs rest on my forearms. I pin her back to the wall and her legs wrap around my waist like it's an automatic response. I feel the heat rolling off her. The muscles in her legs clench as our bodies make real contact. She reaches down and palms my rock-solid length and guides it into her.

"Ah," she moans, as the tip parts her. She bites her bottom lip, tugging it between her teeth. Her wetness coats me as I slide into her tightness. Her body squeezes my cock, her nails digging into my shoulder.

Beads of sweat pop on my forehead and I fight the urge just to slam into her. It feels too damn good. So fucking right.

Her skin glows in the low light, her cheeks a beautiful shade of pink. Her hair now falling wildly over her shoulders and she presses her lips together and smirks.

"That all you got?" she asks.

"Oh," I say, dragging my cock out and then pushing it roughly back in, making her yelp. "You want more?"

"Yes," she breathes.

Readjusting her weight on my arms, feeling her nails tug at my skin and her legs cinch around me, I slam into her once more.

And again.

And again.

The pictures on the walls rattle, one next to the light switch falling to the floor. The sound of the glass breaking echoes down the hall, adding to the sound of our damp skin slapping against each other.

"Ty!" Her breasts bounce against my chest, her legs starting to shake. It's sensory overload.

A full-body tremble rolls through me and I have a strong need to close my eyes and enjoy the sensation of her getting off on my cock, but I'm not about to miss a moment of this. Watching her come is the most spectacular event of my life.

Her lashes lie on her cheeks, her delicate lips falling open. Her chin tilts to the sky as she intakes a quick breath and moans the sexiest sound I've ever heard.

She tightens around me in every way, and I push into her as far as I can go and let myself fall over the edge with her. It's an execution we've perfected.

"E," I growl, feeling myself explode into her body.

"Ah," she moans, letting her head fall forward on my shoulder.

Moving slowly inside of her, I milk her orgasm, drawing out the most pleasure for my girl. Her heartbeat thumps against me, eventually slowing and evening out right alongside mine.

I want to hold her in my arms forever, feel our naked bodies touch in every way. Damn, I've missed this. More than I even realized.

"I hate to do this," I say, my voice shaking, "but I have to put you down."

My arms feel like they're full of lactic acid as I ease Elin to the floor. She doesn't say anything, and when she's on her feet, she doesn't look at me.

Instead, she scurries to the end of the hallway and finds her t-shirt, *my t-shirt*, and slips it over her head.

"I thought you hated that shirt," I joke, attempting to put some levity into the air that's suddenly full of awkwardness. Pulling my jeans up and searching for my shirt, I can't pry my eyes away from her.

"I do."

"So why are you sleeping in it?"

She runs a hand through her tangled hair and looks at me. "I'm not sure. It was just the first one in the dresser."

I know that's a lie. She hides that shirt from me all the time because it's so ratty. But I let her go with it.

Nodding, I get myself back together and feel the strange build between us. I hate it and scramble to find a way to fill the hallway with something else.

"What have you been up to?"

As soon as the question is out of my mouth, her brows shoot to the ceiling. "Really?"

"Yeah, really," I say, confused. "Why do you act like it's an odd question?"

She huffs and leans against the wall. "I was thinking you'd go now."

"Elin, I—"

"Please. Go."

"We need to talk," I say.

"Not really."

"Yes, we do. Let me explain . . ." My heart kicks up in my chest because I don't know what I'm going to say, but I have to. And I will. I'm ready. I'm ready to get my life back. Our life back.

She pulls at the hem of her shirt. "Not tonight."

"Will you be okay?" I ask, not wanting to leave. My hands itch to pick her up and carry her down the hallway to our bedroom. I want to pull her on top of me and show her how sorry I am, how much I love her, over and over again until she understands.

"I'm always okay."

The bite to her words hits me full-on, and I must flinch because she reacts to it, seconds from offering her apology.

"If you need anything, you'll call me, right?"

"I'll call Jiggs," she whispers.

Pressing a kiss against the top of her head, I let it linger for a few seconds longer than necessary. Hoping it tells her all the things I can't say, I pull back. "Call me," I insist and leave, making sure to lock the squeaky door behind me.

Twelve

ELIN

"YOUR REGULAR?"

My eyes adjust to the light in The Fountain as the door closes behind me. I search for Ruby, the owner for the last fifty years, and find her at the sink.

"Please," I smile, standing at the counter next to Lindsay. Fishing out two dollars from the bottom of my purse, I lay them beside the napkin dispenser for a large Bump.

"What are you doing here?" Lindsay asks, sipping on a strawberry milkshake.

"It's sixty-degrees outside," I say, pointing at her glass. "Why are you drinking a milkshake?"

"I told her I won't tell a soul," Ruby says, sitting my Styrofoam cup in front of me. She leans on the counter with a knowing look.

"Tell who what?" I ask.

She leans closer, her eyes sparkling. "That's she's pregnant."

"Hush," Lindsay giggles, looking around the deserted building. "I don't want anyone to know. Not until I'm out of the first trimester." She looks at me and then away just as quickly.

I hate this. Lindsay should be asking me to throw a baby shower, having me help pick out names. Instead, she's not discussing it with me and I'm not bringing it up and it's just wrong on every level.

It has to stop.

I gulp.

It's going to stop.

Ruby picks up on the awkwardness and clears her throat, backing away. "I understand. And like I told you earlier, no matter how much you try, I won't serve you caffeine. It'll be milkshakes for a while. Or juice. But the acid won't do you any favors." She goes back to the sink and Lindsay looks at me out of the corner of her eye.

"How are you feeling?" I ask her.

"Good."

"When are we going shopping and buying all the things?"

A wide, genuine smile splits her cheeks. "I want to. Now," she giggles. "I just don't want to make you feel awkward in any way."

"Stop worrying about me! You are having a baby," I grin. "I am so ridiculously happy for you, and I want in on everything. And I mean everything. The only weirdness is you avoiding me."

She blinks back tears and laughs at herself. "I'm so hormonal. Jiggs is afraid to say anything because I just start crying. Poor guy," she says, wiping her eyes with a napkin.

"I think it's going to get worse," I tease.

"I don't know how," she says, laughing at herself. "I'm worried about everything from the health of the baby to the best kind of crib to if I can nurse to if we should move to Florida."

I toss her a pointed glare. "We're still talking about Florida? Why?"

"I'm scared, Elin. What if we can't support a baby here? It's not just about us now."

"No, it's not. But . . . have you talked to Jiggs about it?"

She rolls her eyes. "Yes and it goes nowhere."

I find a little satisfaction in that, that my brother wouldn't just up and leave me.

She digs around in her purse and places her money next to mine. "So, what are you doing in here at two-thirty in the afternoon?"

"I took a half day today," I say, fiddling with my keys. "I had some errands I needed to run."

"Things you can't take care of after school?" she asks, picking holes in my obvious excuse.

"Yup."

"Okay," she says, drawing out the last syllable. She drinks the rest of her milkshake, slurping the last few inches from the glass like a little kid. "There. I've given you a few seconds. Now you can start all over."

Glancing at the clock, I settle my purse on my shoulder. "What are you talking about?"

"You don't take half days, Elin. What's wrong?"

The somberness in her voice is enough to break me, but I don't want to do that in front of Ruby. I don't even want to do it at all in public because the first breakdown—because I'm sure there will be more than one—should be somewhere private so I can just ugly snot down my face. That can get disgusting. I know because it looked exactly like that last night when I looked in the mirror.

I watched myself cry. It's not the first time I've done that. But it is the first time I felt calm instead of being frantic. Quite possibly, it was closure settling over me.

For a brief moment in the hallway of the home we once shared, we were us. The old us. The people that promised so many things to one another. But once we pulled back, that moment was over.

I didn't want to see the secrets in his eyes. The questions on my tongue were so dirty, so insane to consider that it felt like a slap in the face. The sting of abandonment was so piercing that I just couldn't imagine it ever completely going away.

The foundation of a marriage is love. The walls of a shared life are built with trust, loyalty, and respect. Once those are torn down, there's nothing left standing.

I love him, but that's clearly not enough.

It took everything I had to make the call this morning, including vomiting my breakfast in the toilet first. But it had to be done. I need to see what options there are and what I can afford.

Lindsay watches my hand tremble as I pick up my drink and refuse to look her in the eye.

"Elin?"

"I have an appointment."

"With?"

"Eric Parker."

Her hand flies to her mouth and she pulls me to her with the other. I push away because hugging my best friend before I do the deed will inevitably have me walking in the attorney's office with wet cheeks.

"Why, Elin? Did something happen?"

"I'm just going in to see what my options are. I probably can't afford to file anything anyway."

"Jiggs said—"

"I don't care what my brother said," I say, turning towards the door. She follows behind me, her hand on my shoulder. "Do you know how mentally fucked up this is making me?"

"I can't imagine," she whispers.

"It's like a special form of torture and the longer I let it go, the murkier it's going to get."

"I get that, but . . ."

A sob roots itself at the base of my throat. When I look at her, the tears blur her face. "He's going to break my heart. I know it," I sniffle, trying desperately to compose myself. I shake my head, warning her not to try to hug me. "We can have sex, but we can't talk. He tried to talk, but I don't want to hear what he has to say."

"Why not?"

"Because I'm too weak, Linds. What if I just break and then things go bad and I'm back to square one?"

"You don't know that is what will happen," she implores.

"You're right. But I need to know my options. I need to feel like there's a plan, some way out if I choose to listen to him and it doesn't work out. Right now, I'm just in this never-ending swirl of confusion and I can't do it anymore. I need something to ground me that isn't related to him."

"Well, I disagree with this. For the record."

"Noted."

Pulling the door open, the light makes me squint. Lindsay's lip quivers, and I have to look away before my walls collapse and I'm a heaping mess on the sidewalk.

"I need to go or I'm going to be late," I tell her.

Sighing, Lindsay walks the two doors down the sidewalk to Blown and disappears inside. I remember hanging out in there with her, planning dinners and nights out with our guys, like my world was untouchable. How foolish.

I'd give anything to close my eyes and be transported six months back. To walking in the house and having Ty there, the kitchen a mess from his attempt at fixing lunch, the television on entirely too loud.

"Stop," I mutter to myself, turning abruptly to head to my car. I jump when I almost collide with a hard body.

"Mrs. Whitt, I'm sorry!" Dustin Montgomery is standing in front of me, a wide grin on his face. His brown hair is cut short, his blue eyes shining.

"It's fine, Dustin. I think I ran into you," I laugh.

"How are you?" he asks, his eyes narrowing. "How's Coach?"

Pasting on a smile to hide my uncertainty, I deflect. "I'm good, thank you. Why are you not in school?"

"I skipped a day," he winces.

"Dustin . . ."

"I know, I know. I'm sorry."

I can't help the smile on my face. Dustin is one of Ty's favorite kids, a boy reminiscent of a younger Cord. He is a child of foster care, a kid that does the best he can. Ty picks him up a lot and gets him to practices, and I fix a bag of food for him a lot of nights so he has something to eat after school before practice.

Dustin's a good kid, and I know he loves Ty as much as Ty loves him, and it breaks my heart that he feels as abandoned by my husband as I do.

He furrows his brow, his face sobering. "We all miss Coach,

Mrs. Whitt. Is he okay? Is he coming back? Jason said he saw his truck at the gas station yesterday. I said it couldn't be him because if he was back, he'd have been at practice." He forces a swallow. "He would've called me. Right?"

My chest aches for him. "He just got back. I'm sure he'll be by to see you soon." I feel like a jerk for leading him on when I don't know what Ty's plans really are. "But you have to remember, he's not your coach anymo—"

"He'll always be our coach," he says with so much certainty it makes me feel like I'm being reprimanded. "You tell him," he swears, bending forward so his eyes bore into mine, "that we want him back. At least to see him, know he's okay. Tell him to come by practice. Okay? Tell him to call me, Mrs. Whitt."

"Okay. I will," I whisper, my heart tugging in my chest.

He flashes me a concerned smile before turning towards the Fountain.

"Hey, Dustin!" I call out.

He turns to face me. "Yeah?"

"Here." I fish through my purse and pull out a twenty-dollar bill. "Get a sandwich before practice."

Hesitating before reaching for the money, I can tell he doesn't want to accept it. He never does.

"Take it," I say, smiling. "Have Ruby make you a double cheeseburger. She's bored in there today anyway. You'll thrill her to death."

"Thanks, Mrs. Whitt." He reaches for the money, his eyes softening. "I'll do that. But the burger won't be as good as yours."

Shaking my head, I adjust my purse on my shoulder. "If you need anything this week, you know how to get ahold of me. I mean that."

"And if you need anything at all, call me. You've always . . ." His cheeks flush and he looks down the street for a long second before turning back to me. "You've always been good to me. Anything you need, Mrs. Whitt, I'm happy to help out however."

"Thank you, Dustin," I say, biting my bottom lip so the physical pain weighs heavier than my emotions.

He watches me carefully, trying to decide if I'm okay. Once he seems satisfied, he heads inside The Fountain and I head into Attorney Parker's office a few doors down.

Thirteen

TY

PULLING OFF MY blue hooded sweatshirt, I toss it into the truck before slamming the door behind me.

"Ball!" I yell out, and a few moments later, the basketball is in my hands. I step onto the court and launch the ball from half-court. It drains through the net. Grinning at Jiggs and Cord, I laugh, "Still got it."

Jiggs rebounds the ball and passes it to me again. "Didn't expect to see you here."

"And why is that?" I pull up and drop another through the hoop.

"I was hoping you'd be at the high school."

I let out a long breath. "I'm actually going to head over there in a bit."

"You are full of surprises today, Whitt," Jiggs says, whistling through his teeth.

"Yeah, I called Reynolds this morning and asked if he'd care if I came by tonight."

"He isn't gonna care," Cord laughs, stealing the ball from Jiggs. "That's your team."

It is my team, to me anyway. It always will be. I've watched most of these kids come up from elementary school, participating in the kiddie clinics and summer camps. They've grown from tooth-less faces to men ready to strike out on their own and I feel a vested interest in making sure that happens.

Besides my life with Elin, there's nowhere else I love to be more than with the team. Resigning felt like the right thing to do. I couldn't walk without a fucking limp, couldn't show them how to do the skills I needed to teach them. Not being able to give them one-hundred percent wasn't acceptable and admitting that in front of them, letting them see me broken, wasn't tolerable either. So, I tucked tail and ran.

"Don't get me wrong," Jiggs says, "I'm glad you're going. But what changed? The last time I talked to you the question of you going back to coaching was up in the air."

Elin's face darts through my mind, the taste of her lips against mine. The feeling of her body wrapped up against me.

Everything was launched into perspective. Even though I don't have answers on how to work everything out, I know there's no other option, no matter how long it takes or how hard it is.

"I saw Elin last night," I say simply.

"So you got some pussy?" Cord grins.

"We aren't going to talk about fucking my sister," Jiggs interjects, throwing up a shot. "I have limits, assholes."

Laughing, I rebound the ball and press it against my hip. "I had relations with my wife." Glancing over my shoulder, I catch Jiggs' eye. "Sound better?"

"Can we just say you talked to her? I can read between the lines."

Chuckling, I pass the ball to Cord. "But I didn't talk to her. Not yet."

"Ah, so you just got down to the point—"

"Shut. Up. Cord," Jiggs grimaces.

"I'm gonna deal with the boys first. Apologize for bailing like I did, maybe see if Reynolds needs a hand this season. Then I'll go see my wife."

"Sounds like a plan," Cord says. "I like it."

Jiggs turns to look at me. "I like it too."

"I expect her to be pissed and for this to take some time, but

she's ready to work this out. I mean, she made me leave last night after *we talked*," I smirk. "And that's fine. I can handle that. I feel good
about it today. Clear."

Cord's face lights up. "It's about fucking time."

"I—"

The sound of gravel crunching behind me cuts me off. We all
look to the entrance of the park to see Pettis' car pulling in.

"What the fuck does he want?" I spit.

"His rights terminated, maybe," Cord laughs, an anger palpable
in his tone. "Hopefully."

Pettis gets out of the car.

I've hated this fucker since high school. He's a year older than
me. When I took the starting point guard position on the basketball
team away from him my freshman year, things got heated. When
Elin chose me over him, things got worse. They never recovered.

The chip on his shoulder has my name on it. We've gone head-
to-head on just about everything, even our jobs in the mine. Seeing
him pull up with *that* look on his face sends me into high alert. This
look is one I've seen a million times over the years and it never—*never*—ends well.

"Hey, guys. Need another player?" he asks cheerfully.

"You can't be fucking serious," Jiggs laughs.

Pettis makes a face like Jiggs is crazy. "You're an odd number.
We can go two-on-two."

"The only two-on-two that will happen around here if you
don't leave is two fists hitting you in the face," Cord promises.

Pettis laughs and steps up to the court. "How are ya, Whitt?"

I eye him carefully. There's nothing pleasant or coincidental
about this run-in. While I'd really like to just dribble his face down
the asphalt after the incident at Thoroughbreds, for some strange
reason, I want to hear what he has to say.

"Yeah, that's what I thought," Pettis says, sighing dramatically.
"I'm sorry. You know, not everything is meant to be. Just keep your
chin up and you'll find—"

"What the fuck are you talking about?" Jiggs asks, walking so that his shoulders are lined with mine and Cord's.

Pettis flinches like he's caught off guard. "What do you mean?" His eyes grow unnaturally wide, putting on a show for me and my friends. His hands come up in front of him in some form of defense.

His sight is set straight on me. He makes sure I'm paying attention, a smirk hidden beneath his false surprise.

My alert mode flips straight into kill mode. Although the source of this little meet-and-greet is still unknown, what I do know is that it's going to end with me wanting to end him. Period.

Cord knows it too because I feel his hand on my shoulder, squeezing it. Reminding me he's there and if I need help ending Pettis, he's more than willing.

"Shut the fuck up, Pettis, and get to the part where you say whatever it is you showed up here to say or fucking beat it," Cord says.

"Easy there, McCurry," Pettis says, realizing just how precarious his situation might be. "I didn't realize y'all didn't know."

"Didn't know what?" Jiggs asks. He flashes me a look, apologizing for asking because it is, in a way, feeding the troll. But he wants to know. We all do.

Pettis looks right at me, the smirk playing on his lips.

My blood runs cold, my breath hanging in the air, as I wait to see what bomb he's going to drop on me. Because he is. He's too geared up for it not to be.

"That Elin filed for divorce today."

Pettis says the words so carefully, so clearly, then watches for the wound to open where his words cut me. He's smart enough to take a step back as I process his declaration.

Although I don't think it's true, not after last night, I can't help but feel the rug slip just a little beneath me. My world spins, my voice escaping me as the thought—*what if it's true?*—hits me.

"She did not," Jiggs says, laughing in disbelief. "Get the fuck out of here before I kick your ass and don't you ever, *ever*, go near my sister, you piece of fucking shit. You hear me?"

Pettis shrugs, still watching me. "I'll leave. Just wanted to give you my condolences. I offered her mine as she came out of Parker's office today. I might go by there tonight and see if she needs a friend."

Cord shoves me backward as he charges forward. Pettis scrambles to his car and locks the door, Cord and Jiggs on his heels. He starts the engine, his eyes now wide for a completely different reason.

"I will personally see that you feel pain for every cocksucking thing you've ever done!" Cord steps back as Pettis slams the car into drive and slides down the driveway and up the access road.

I feel nothing—no rage, no anger, no fear.

My friends are talking around me. I hear a basketball being tossed into the back of a truck. I sense movement, feel someone bump me, but I don't move. I'm afraid to snap out of this haze because I'll have to process everything, consider that there might be some truth to his accusations.

But it can't be true.

She wouldn't. Not after last night.

My shoulder is hit again and I look up and into Jiggs' face.

"Did she?" I ask point blank.

"Ty, if she did, I didn't know." He scrubs his hands down his face. "Fuck, man. I'm sorry either way. If she didn't, then Pettis just signed his death warrant. But if she did . . ."

My wedding ring catches the late afternoon sunlight. It shines in the light, reminding me of the day Elin placed it on my finger.

"I'll love you, for better or worse, 'til death do us part."

The chill that arrived with Pettis leaves me with his departure. Instead, a red-hot flame starts in my gut and burns every fiber of my body as it rolls through me. There's no way this is happening.

"What are you gonna do?" Jiggs asks.

Considering his question for a half a second, I turn my back to him as I storm to my truck.

"Ty?" Cord asks, leaning against the side of his truck.

"Hey, Cord," I shout, swinging my door open. "If I get hemmed up tonight, you'll bail me out, right? Because if I see Elin and this isn't true, I'm gonna fucking kill him."

"I got you."

Fourteen

ELIN

HOLD IT together through the appointment, to my car, and on the drive home.

Radio off, ignoring the envelope next to me that lays as heavily on my mind as it does the leather passenger seat, I keep my vision trained on the road ahead. The bright white envelope is full of papers that, if I fill them out, would officially end my marriage.

There should be relief in that, in knowing my options. But there's no relief in this. Really, how could there be? It's not a choice I want to make, but one that feels like the only possibility available.

I don't trust him. My respect level is barely hanging on. There's no loyalty between us, not anymore. How can he even understand loyalty if he would leave me and the boys like he did?

If I were dating him, I'd end things. Granted, I wouldn't've loved him like I do if that were the case. But when you're in a hole this deep, is love a big enough ladder to climb out? It certainly doesn't seem so.

Piloting the car onto my street, I focus on staying between the lines through the blur. Pressing harder on the accelerator, I rush to make the last few miles before the tears start. The harder I try to focus and block them out, the stronger the dampness gets in the corner of my eyes. The bridge of my nose is swollen with that tickle you get right before you start to topple over the edge.

Everything is spinning. I'm starting to lose control. Emotions take over, writhing inside me, and that panics me even more.

My breaths turn into quick hiccups as I glance into the rearview mirror and see a familiar truck. It's passing a car a few hundred feet back and I watch it fly into my lane and hover a few car lengths behind me.

Hands trembling around the steering wheel, a small gasp escapes my lips. I flick my eyes forward as he approaches close enough for me to see his face. Whatever composure I have now will be obsolete if I somehow meet Ty's eyes in the rearview.

Maybe I'm too tired to think clearly, maybe I just want to get this conversation over with as quickly as possible, maybe I just feel too scattered and afraid either way, but against my better judgement, I pull into the driveway.

The recklessness of his driving, the aggression I can feel ripple off of him—even being in different vehicles—is telling.

He knows.

He knows where I've been.

It's terrifying and a relief all in one swift, blazing swoop. It's enough of a shock to press the tears away, my body going into some kind of fight or flight mode because I can't predict his behavior. That's a part of why we're in this damn situation anyway. I don't know him anymore.

Breathe, Elin.

Just as I suspect, Ty's truck inches in behind me, its bumper almost kissing mine. He's out of the truck before I even turn off my car. I see the ferocity in his eyes in my side mirror, his jaw ticking as he gets closer.

I grab my coat and toss it over the envelope, like somehow that piece of fabric is going to protect my decision, make it easier to get through these next few minutes.

My door is jilted open and he stands in front of me, scowling. His eyes are narrowed, his body rippling in his jeans and long-sleeved, charcoal-colored thermal shirt that clings to his body.

I step gingerly out of the car, my gaze trained on the gravel beneath his grey and blue sneakers, and he slams it behind me before taking a step back. I'm not sure if it's for his benefit or mine.

I keep walking. Head down, shoulders pressed forward, heart thumping away, I stride as quickly as I can up the walkway and to the back door. I listen for his steps but hear none.

My mouth is dry, my nerves dancing with overstimulation as I realize I've forgotten my purse in the car. My stomach stinks as I try to figure out if I can get in through a window or if I can just sit on the back porch until he leaves because there is no way I'm walking back there.

The glass in the door gives me a warning that Ty is coming up behind me. I stand, facing the door, my breath fogging up the glass as he nears. Far too quickly than I'm prepared for, his chest is inches from mine, his arm around the front of me as he sticks his key in the lock.

His chest is not quite touching my back, but I can feel the energy pouring off of him. Knees weak, I fight myself not to fall back into him because he's not my safe place anymore.

Just as I start to disintegrate and lose all composure, the door groans, opening wide. I don't hesitate to step inside . . . and neither does he. The groan sounds again before I hear the lock latch shut.

"Guess who I ran into today?" he asks, his voice far too calm. The disparity of the tone against the look I saw in his eyes a few minutes ago sends a chill down my spine.

I have no idea why he's doing this, why he just doesn't come out and say whatever it is he has to say about my visit with Parker. But I'm in no hurry to get to that part of the conversation, so I play along. Hoping, praying, that I'm wrong about the purpose of this visit.

"Jiggs?" I offer, my back to him.

"Did ya happen to run into Pettis today?"

My hands tremble as they cover my face. The coolness of the metal of my wedding band caressing my cheek. It suddenly feels so heavy on my finger. "Yeah."

His hand smacks the table and I jump, the jolt dissolving the wall holding back the tears.

The wetness courses down my cheeks, my lashes heavy with the weight of the fluid. It's a silent cry—no sobs, no gasps for breath.

"What the fuck, E?"

The huskiness of his voice quickens my tears, the sadness so thick that I can't bear to endure it for the both of us.

"What are you talking about?" I ask, my own voice muddied.

"Pettis told me you filed for divorce."

Like a mortar hitting its target, even though it's a shell I shot, my heart bursts into flames. I swallow a sob, nearly choking as I do.

"Tell me he's lying, E," he says, a hitch in his voice that breaks me. "Tell me I need to go find him and bust his ass. Tell me I'm going to spend a couple of days in the county jail. *Please*," he adds, the pain so palpable that I can't take it anymore.

Thoughts, fears, questions, consequences, failures hurl through my mind, consuming me. I can't think, I can't make sense of anything other than the overwhelming desire to shut my eyes and succumb to the pain.

Reaching for the doorframe, I start to steady myself, but not before a set of strong hands finds my waist and does it for me.

A sob slips by my lips instantly, the sound filling the quiet of the kitchen. Another one rips from somewhere in my soul, and another, and another, and before I know it, I'm twirled around and my face is buried in Ty's chest. His arms pull me against him, his chin rests naturally on the top of my head like it's done a thousand times before.

My hands wind around his waist and I cry for everything we've had together, every moment of our life we've spent as one unit.

For every late night we sat in bed eating a pint of ice cream.

For every drive through the country with no destination in mind.

For every decision we made, inside joke only we understand, every minute we've spent loving each other.

For the two babies we lost, one he doesn't even know about, I cry.

This is this most peace I've had since he walked out the door. A bottomless pit of sadness, sure, but there's a stillness in this moment that allows me the opportunity to just mourn everything I've been up until this moment. Because when I pull back, I will never be this person again.

Even though I haven't done it, even though I'm not sure I could've done it if I had the money, it's inevitable. My heart knows it. My fears feed it. My soul loathes it.

Never again will I know the feel of his arms around me, the warmth of his breath on my cheek. Never again will I hear his heartbeat in his chest or feel the roughness of the palms of his hands on the small of my back.

I love him. Damn it, I love this man so fucking much.

His shirt stains with my tears, my body shaking like a leaf in his arms. I don't bother trying to control it because this isn't something that can be reined in for any reason.

Ty holds me, occasionally shushing me like he would when I heard a story about a disadvantaged child at school and would come home in tears or like he does when I cry at the end of *Steel Magnolias*. He strokes my back with such tenderness that even though he's the enemy, he still feels like my best friend. And that little fact is going to be the hardest to get over, if I ever can.

My phone rings in my pocket, breaking the tranquility of possibly the last good moment of my life. I press one final kiss into the center of Ty's chest and don't look him in the eye as I pull back and answer the call.

"Hey, Linds," I try to say. It comes out as a fuzzled blurb. "Ty's here."

"Oh, shit," she murmurs. "Do you want me to come over? Do you want me to send Jiggs by?"

Taking a deep breath, I look up. He's watching me, a need in his eye that I can't deny. I know we are going to have to have this conversation. We owe it to the life we've shared.

"No, I'm good," I lie.

She sighs into the line. "If you're sure . . ."

"I'm not sure about anything," I laugh, sniffling back tears. "But I'm okay. I'll be fine. I'll call you later."

"Make sure you do that," she says as I end the call.

Wincing as my temples begin to ache, I rub the sides of my head. Without looking or acknowledging Ty, I head down the hall and enter the bedroom. I pop a couple of pain relievers without even a drink, sucking them down dry.

I've never felt this way in my life. It's a mixture of terror and anxiety, yet in the midst of the chaos, there's a smidgen of calm.

Inhaling a deep breath, the air is filled with his cologne. The scent takes me back to another time, and as I sense his proximity to me, knowing he's standing at the door watching me, I would give virtually anything to open my eyes and have this entire part of my life erased. I would go back to the day he signed up at Blackwater Coal and forbid him from working there.

That's what caused this. His injury. Things were never the same after that.

"Elin?"

His voice brings me back to the bedroom and the current situation. I don't answer because I don't trust my voice. I also don't respond because I don't know how to deal with the emotion in his. It's not anger and it's not fury, it's something else. Something so much more real that I don't have a default answer for.

"Did you file for divorce today?" he asks.

"I found out what I have to do and how much it's going to cost," I whisper.

"What the hell, Elin?"

There's a drip of franticness in his tone now too that stirs up the same feeling inside me.

"Aren't ya going to say anything?" he asks. He moves closer behind me, within touching distance, but he doesn't reach out, and I'm glad for that.

"What is there to say?" I reply simply, looking at the picture of a landscape over the bed.

"Oh, I don't know. Maybe . . . why? Why you thought you

should end our marriage and not even say something to me first? I was here last night and you didn't say anything. Hell, Elin. We were *together* last night."

Shrugging, I turn slowly to face him. His eyes are wild, his hands laced together at the back of his neck—maybe to keep from reaching out for me, I don't know. But it's a good idea, so I stick mine in the pockets of my jeans for the same reason.

"I just got it over with," I say. "It was inevitable."

He looks at me like I've lost my mind. "You're fucking crazy."

"I'm fucking crazy? I've been right here, Tyler. Where have you been?"

"Damn it, Elin," he groans, pacing a circle in the middle of the bedroom floor.

"*Damn it, Elin?*" I repeat. His words stoke some life back into me, diffuse some of the numbness I'd begun to feel.

"I never said I wanted a divorce from you!" he booms.

"Sometimes actions speak louder than words."

"Yeah, you're right—they fucking do! What was last night? Was that my way of asking you to see about a divorce? You think I came over here and held you in my arms so you'd get the picture I didn't want to be with you anymore? Don't lie to yourself, Elin, and don't lie to me either."

"Ugh," I huff, walking around him and into the hall. Ignoring his shouts for me to come back, I enter the living room. I need to put some distance between us. Scurrying to the far end of the sofa, I clench the armrest as he walks in.

"I couldn't divorce you," he says, positioning himself against the other side of the sofa.

"As soon as I can save the money, I'll file. You don't have to do it," I whisper. Even as the words come out of my mouth, I want to fall to the floor and sob. I know, in the bottom of my gut, that I don't want it to be over. I want to love this man for the rest of my life. But I don't want the relationship he and I have now. It's not . . . us.

We've agreed to stop the fights dozens of times, promised each other we'd do better. Yet, we're still here.

His jaw ticks, his knuckles turning white as he re-grips the couch. "The hell you will." Running his hands through his hair, his eyes never leave mine. "I'll tear up every set of papers they send me. I'll put up a fight at every turn, Elin. I'm not letting you do this to us."

"I don't have another answer!"

"The answer is right fucking here!" he shouts back, holding his arms out to his sides.

Tears burn my skin as they flow down my face. He notices them, watches them cascade to the floor, before he looks me in the eye again. When he does, I see the pain he's in, and as much as I hate to admit it, it breaks my heart.

I just want this over.

"Please," I gasp, "just let me go."

"Let you go?" he asks, his voice starting to break. "Like it's something I can just laugh about and keep going?" He leans towards me, his eyes burning into mine. "You're everything to me, Elin. You're my lover, my best friend, my partner in everything, the mother of my children someday."

My chest heaves with my sobs. I can't even see him in front of me anymore. It's all a blur, a watery vision of colors and fuzzy shapes.

"If you take *you* away from me, you take *everything*. Don't you understand?" he says, just loud enough for me to hear over myself. "You're everything to me, Elin Whitt. You're my entire world."

"You don't get to say that after you just vanish! That's not how this works!"

"Is that what this is?" he asks, starting to come around the couch. I back away in the opposite direction and he stops. "Are you punishing me for leaving? Fine, make me feel the pain you felt when I left—"

My hand trembles as I put it in the air to silence him. My body shakes with fury as I think back on the night I lost our baby. "You could *never* feel the pain I felt. I could never, *ever* do that to you, even if I wanted to. You have no idea," I seethe.

"I didn't know what else to do. I—"

"You didn't know what to do? About what, Ty? What in your fucking life was so bad?" My hand shakes as I point a finger at him. "You don't get to just come and go as you please. You don't get to get sick of being married and—"

"That's not what happened!"

"I don't even care!" I scream, my temples throbbing as blood rushes through my body. "I don't even care," I say again, wiping my nose with the back of my hand.

"Yes, you do."

"It doesn't matter," I laugh sadly. "How can I ever trust you not to just walk away when things get hard or boring?"

"Is that what you think I did?" he asks, astonished. "You think I just got sick of this life and walked out?"

"Yup."

"How could you think that?"

"What am I supposed to think? You leaving was a new low, Ty, a new bottom. You've never even thought about leaving me before and all it took was one little—"

"You asked me to."

My hands throw in the air. "Yeah, I did. You're right. So you just decide a few weeks of not talking to me at all was the right answer?"

"My phone broke. I—"

"What if I needed you?"

The heft of my question cuts him off, his mouth still open. Slowly, his head cocks to the side. "Did you?"

I only look at him. No smile, no smirk, no staring daggers his way. Just a somber look that has him thrown off balance.

"Elin . . ."

"Do I even want to know what you were doing?"

He still hasn't recovered from my insinuation. Gathering all the courage I can gather, I go for it. I ask the one question that, depending on the answer, will answer every other one.

"Was it another woman, Tyler?"

"No!"

"Do you have any idea the reasons I've came up with to try to make myself feel better about this? Did you have any idea the hysteria I'd feel not knowing if you were alive? Then I hear from Pettis that you are alive and well and everything becomes clear that it's probably another woman—"

He lurches forward. "It was not another woman!"

"How do I know?" I ask breathlessly.

He runs his hands through his hair, tugging at the roots. "Do you want to know why I left?"

"It doesn't matter now," I reply, not sure that's true.

He starts to speak and then stops a few times, like he's gathering the courage to share whatever secret he's kept to himself. The longer it takes him to come forward with the truth, the more confident I feel that I don't want to hear it.

"Save it," I say, starting back to the kitchen. If he won't leave, I will.

"I felt emasculated."

The room stills, an eerie silence dropping over the space. He doesn't speak and neither do I as he waits for some sort of reaction.

"I did," he shrugs, looking at the floor. "Here I am, the man of the house. I can't work and I'm sitting here all fucking day, watching you kill yourself at work and taking care of the house and me and paying the bills while I do nothing."

"You were hurt," I say in disbelief.

"And then," he continues, like he got a second wind, "all I hear about is the baby stuff. When we can have sex, when we can't. What's wrong with you, what could be wrong with me."

"Well, I'm sorry for wanting to have your child!" I burst out.

"I want you to have my child. I want you to have a fucking dozen of them!" he booms. "But my God, Elin. That's all it was about. I felt like I couldn't perform, like I was shooting blanks and you were judging me for it, and I swear to all that's holy, I don't believe there's anything wrong with us but the fucking pressure."

I blink back salty tears as the truth lingers on my tongue. Before I can find the courage to tell him about the baby, he speaks again and I'm relieved.

"You were pissed all the time and that made me frustrated and it was just one thing after another. Every time one of us opened our mouths—"

"We'd fight," we say in unison. Exchanging a sad smile, I bow my head.

"I wasn't with another woman. I wasn't on drugs, no matter what Pettis told you. Yes, I took that money to buy them, but I didn't."

Looking up at him, I hold my breath. "But you were going to?"

"Yeah. I won't lie to you. I was just taking what I was pre-scribed, basically, although I went through that last script in about half the time. I was going to buy more and just keep the numbness I had going on to block everything out." He takes a step towards me. "But I didn't."

"Where's the money now?"

"I used it to live. Food, gas, whatever." His face falls. "I pussed out. You asked me to go and I did. I just . . . I wanted a break from all the fighting. I thought we could take some time apart and really clear our heads, you know? Why come back if it's the same thing?"

I want to tell him because I needed him, because I was silently pleading for him to return, but I don't because that would require an explanation I'm not ready to give him. I cross my arms across my chest, both as an outward expression to keep him away . . . and to keep myself for reaching for him.

"Where did you go?" I ask.

"Kruger Farms. I stayed over there in the top of a barn of a farmer that my dad used to know." He chews his bottom lip, watch-ing me.

"And I'm supposed to believe that?"

"Yeah, baby, you are. You can call them and ask them, if you want." He forces a swallow before squaring his shoulders to me. "I wasn't an addict, or I don't think I was. But the first few days of being there, I had to get off the pain meds. I was sick. It was worse than I thought it was going to be, but I did it. And if I went through all of that in front of you, you'd never look at me the same way again," he smiles sadly. "I hit rock bottom, E."

My chest heaves as the weight of his words falls on me. I had no idea things were this serious with him. A part of me wants to hold him, to ask him why, and another part of me wants to slap him for being so stupid.

More than ever, I'm looking at a man that, on the surface, I know better than anyone. But do I even know him at all?

"How do I know you won't do that again?" I ask. "Do you want pills now?"

He smiles the most honest grin I've seen since he's been back. "I have no interest. I only want you."

My mind reels. "Why didn't you come to me? Why didn't you let me help you?"

"That's why I left, so maybe there would be some hope that we could fix this. That I could fix this. There was no way I could let you see me like that. It would taint you."

"It still tainted me. It ruined our marriage."

His features harden again. "Our marriage is *not* ruined."

"There's no way to fix this, Ty. Not like you want. Not like I'd want. I don't even know you. I mean, drugs, Ty?"

"I'm clean. I swear to God. I wasn't an addict or something, just starting down that road, but thank fuck I caught it. Or maybe you caught it by catching me. I don't know," he sighs. "I'll fix this, Elin."

"How do you think you're going to fix the damage you caused when you don't even know what that all entails?"

"Tell me," he says earnestly.

I shake my head.

His eyes cloud, his voice wavering. "I need you, Elin."

Looking down the hall, my chest tightens. I remember sitting in the bathroom that's not fifteen steps from where we are, watching the toilet water turn pink after my doctor's appointment. Feeling a part of me leave my body, a part of my heart ripping away.

I look at Ty. "Yeah, well, I needed you too."

Fifteen

TY

PAIN IS STREAKED across her face, her anguish on display for the world, for me, to see.

I can't take it.

If there's one thing in this world I've wanted more than any other, it's Elin Watson. From the moment I saw her at her locker, her body in a pair of jean shorts and a yellow top that fell off her right shoulder nibbling on a red sucker, I had to have her.

And I finally got her. I promised to take care of her, protect her, love her. Standing here, seeing the fallout from not doing those things destroys me from the inside out.

She watches me from across the room.

"Do you remember the first day I kissed you?" I ask, watching her face soften as the memory pops in her head. "I'd wanted to kiss you for days, but I was afraid to push too hard."

"I remember Lindsay telling me to be careful around you. That all the girls liked you and you were a player," she remembers.

"All the girls did like me," I say, trying to bring her back to me. Trying to remind her that I'm the kid she fell in love with. "But I liked *you*."

"Everyone said it was just because I was the new girl," she says.

"Well, I've known you for a long damn time, and I want you more today than I did that day in the hallway outside of math lab."

She looks out the window, a faint smile on her lips. "I told you no the first time you asked me out. Everyone knew you around town, everyone liked you. It was overwhelming."

"It doesn't help that on your first day, I kind of stalked you, huh?"

Elin starts to come around. The tension eases from her face, the lines weaken around her eyes as a hint of the sparkle comes back. "When you made Pettis get up from beside me at lunch, I was scared to death. I couldn't figure out what you wanted from me."

"I think we both know what I wanted from you," I wink. "Your ass in those shorts . . ."

She laughs, the sound music to my ears. "You ended up getting it."

Taking a step closer to her, she doesn't move away. I breathe a sigh of relief. It's a small victory I'm too happy to take. "Do you know what I want from you now?"

"Ty . . ."

"I just want my wife back, E. I want my life back."

"You can't just have it back," she whispers. "Things were burned." She looks at me through her thick lashes. "*I was burned.*"

"*I'm sorry.*"

She blows out a breath and glances quickly down the hallway. Swallowing roughly, she hesitates a long moment. When she looks at me again, something has changed. Her bottom lip quivers, her brows pull together in a concerted effort to maybe hold herself together.

"I could've helped you, Tyler. If you would've told me how you felt, what you were going through, we could've fixed it. But you didn't trust me, and I can't . . ."

Tears well up again and I reach for her. My heart cracking in my chest, she bats my hands away.

"Stop," she says, her voice void of any strength.

"You want me to stand here and watch you cry and not want to comfort you?"

Smiling through the tears, she breaks my heart even more. "You can go, and I'll cry by myself. I've gotten pretty good at it lately."

"Damn it, Elin. What do we have if we don't have each other? Everything we've ever wanted—every dream, hope, every idea of a family and a future—are tied together. You can't just walk away from that."

"I didn't," she says, finally breaking her silence. "You did."

"I did not. I walked away to protect you."

"Funny, I'm walking away to protect me too."

Her voice cracks, and I don't care anymore. I grab her and pull her into me, and she, surprisingly, lets me.

She doesn't make an effort to embrace me, but I don't care. I just hold her for dear life.

"Our future is in front of us," I whisper, brushing the hair off her shoulder. "We can figure this out. I'll get a new job, which you'll love, because I know you hated the mine, and we can start a family." I press a kiss to the top of her head. "I can't wait to see your belly swollen with my baby."

Her body shakes. I rub my hands down her back, not sure if she's laughing or crying.

"We'll paint the nursery and stay up late trying to figure out how to put together the bed and all the baby—"

"Stop," she begs, her head buried in my shirt. "Please. Stop."

Squeezing her tighter, I feel her emotionally backing away from me. She's building some sort of barrier to keep me out, and I have to figure out how to tear it down quick.

"I swear to you, I'll be everything you need. I'll—"

She pulls back, her lips forming a thin line. "You were always everything I needed," she says quietly. "I can't imagine being with another man."

"It's a good fucking thing, because you won't be with another man," I point out. "I'll kill him."

"You aren't the problem, Ty. It's just . . ." She struggles, looking at the floor.

She's all over the place tonight, both physically and mental-ly, and I can't figure out what's causing all of this vacillating. One minute she's in my arms and the next she's telling me she wants me to leave and never come back.

What the fuck?

A sick feeling crawls through my veins. "I think there's more to this than you're letting on."

She gulps and turns her back on me, walking into the kitchen. I follow.

"Elin?"

"You need to go," she says, her voice steady.

"I *need* to find out what in the hell happened while I was gone."

She pops open the back door and leans against it. She looks at me with no feeling, void of any sadness, anger . . . or love. "Doesn't matter, Ty."

"That's bullshit," I scoff at her blatant lie. Her eyes go wide as I stand tall in front of her, the next words out of my mouth ones I don't want to say, yet I have to. "You weren't with someone else were you?"

"God, no!" she says, shocked. It's obvious the idea is new to her, and that has me sighing in relief.

"Thank fuck."

"Go, please, before I call Jiggs."

"What's he gonna do?" I chuckle.

She doesn't flinch. "Go, Ty."

My blood starts to boil, my fists curling at my sides. If she thinks this is over just like that, she's out of her damn mind.

Her gaze is fire, her sadness turned to fury. I feel the fight begin, the switch we are all too familiar with.

"This isn't over, you know that, right?" I say, heading to the door. "I'm just leaving so we don't get into some huge argument and say things we can't take back."

She watches me hit the threshold, and I pause, waiting for her to change her mind. She doesn't.

"I'll call you tomorrow," I say, watching her eyes widen.

"Don't," she whispers. "I'll file papers when I get the—"

My laugh cuts her off. Bending down so we're eye to eye, I

make things crystal clear. "I won't be signing any fucking papers, Elin. Ever."

She sucks in a hasty breath, and I give her time to process my words.

"You are mine. You will always be mine," I tell her. "Get that through your beautiful fucking head."

"Leave," she says, on the cusp of crying.

"I'm leaving, but get one thing straight," I warn. "I'm leaving this house because *you asked me to* and because whatever comes out of my mouth from here on out isn't going to do either of us any good." I clear my throat, trying to get the rest of the words out over the lump lodged there. "I'm leaving the house, E. I'm not leaving you. And I will be back."

Sixteen

ELIN

THE DOOR GROANS as my husband walks out. I hold my breath, half hoping he bursts back in, half hoping I hear his truck start.

In a few moments, the latter happens and I exhale. It's shaky, wobbly, and I try to stay as quiet as possible as I listen to him back down the driveway and take off down the street.

Glancing around the room, his energy is still here. Although I told him to go, although he needed to go because him staying here would only make things harder in the long run, I miss him immediately.

My skin still sings from his touch. His cologne lingers on my shirt, the air kissed by his presence. This is going to be much, much harder than I even thought.

My phone chirps beside me and I pick it up.

"Hey," I say, clearing my throat.

"Hey, Elin. It's Cord."

I smile at the sound of my friend's voice. "What's up?"

"I was with Ty when he heard what Pettis had to say. I figured I'd drive by and see if he was there. You know, make sure he's not going to get arrested tonight or anything," he says as lightly as he can. "I saw him just pull out of your driveway but he won't answer his cell."

Gulping back a sob, I don't know what to say. "Ty's fine."

"How are *you*?"

"I don't know," I whisper.

"I'm in front of your house. Do you want me to stop?"

His headlights shine through the living room window and instant relief washes over me. "Yeah, why don't you?"

The call ends and within a few seconds, he raps on the front door. I venture to the living room and let him in.

Cord steps inside, wearing a pair of dark denim jeans, a white t-shirt, and a brown fleece jacket. He looks like the requisite boy-next-door with his clean cut good looks and simple, easy nature. "How are you?" he asks, shrugging off his flannel jacket. "Damn, it's hot in here."

"I keep it warm," I say, glancing at the thermostat. "Ty always kept it cooler . . ."

My eyes wet at the sound of his name. I remember all the arguments we'd have over the thermostat, how one of us would change it and the other would change it right back. It was really one of the only things we just couldn't agree on.

Cord watches me carefully. "Did you really file for divorce today?"

I slump on the sofa. "No. I just went to see how to do it."

"That's pretty big," he comments, sitting in the chair across the room. "Did you mean it?"

"I did it, didn't I?"

"That doesn't mean you wanted to."

My head in my hands, I feel a bone-crushing exhaustion settle in.

"I'm going to be honest," Cord says, interrupting my thoughts. "You don't look like a woman that just did something she believes in."

"I did what I had to do, Cord."

"Nah, I don't think so."

"What in the world do you know about my marriage? How do you know what I did or didn't have to do?" I ask, annoyed.

"Because no one has a gun pointed to your head telling you to talk to an attorney or they're pulling the trigger," he says, completely unaffected by the look I'm shooting him. "You saw someone about a divorce. That's no small thing."

"No shit," I mock, shaking my head.

Cord sighs and sits back in the chair. "I hate this."

"Yeah, well, join the crowd."

His brows shoot to the ceiling.

"Of course I hate this," I whisper, flopping back against the cushions. "Do you think this was the way I saw my life going?"

"Then let's hold up here and figure out a way around it."

"There is no way around it, Cord," I snip.

The corner of his lip turns up and he narrows his eyes. "Then you aren't the lady I thought you were."

"Excuse me?"

He shrugs. "I gave you way too much credit, Elin."

"What?" I lean up, flabbergasted. "You gave me too much credit? Fuck you, Cord."

He laughs and that only makes me madder.

"So I'm the bad guy in this?" I fire. "Somehow I'm the asshole because I want to know my options? Ty can take the liberty to do whatever the hell he wants while I'm here losing our b—"

I clamp my mouth shut right before spilling my secret. A storm rolls across his features as his eyes draw to my hands on my stomach and then back up to me.

"Don't," I war, my voice teetering as I await his response.

He exhales, the breath whistling between his teeth. "Things are starting to get a little clearer."

"I'm happy for you. Now you can go and take all that extra credit you threw my way with you. And keep your mouth shut about . . . whatever it is you think you've figured out," I warn as angrily as I can, shoving my hands in my pockets and away from my stomach.

He doesn't move, just watches me. "I still think I gave you too much credit," he says finally.

My arms fly in the air. "Cord, I'm about two seconds from punching you in the face."

"Thank you," he snickers. "You just proved my point."

"And how's that?"

"You *are* a fighter," he says, leaning his elbows on his knees. "Always have been. Do you remember the time Gabrielle Donaldson got suspended for fighting back when that new girl jumped her in the hallway? And then three days later, the center for the basketball team got into a fight and didn't get shit because it was Sectional week?"

"Yeah," I laugh. "I went to the office and called bullshit. I about got myself suspended over that. Principal Mackey is an idiot. It's why I give him hell now with the boys. Payback."

"Exactly. You've always been the person to go to bat for someone when you feel something's not right. You do it for the kids in the school, you went to Mackey this year when James got in trouble, remember that?"

I nod, not seeing where this is heading. "Cut to the chase."

"Look, you fight for everyone and everything. Why aren't you fighting for your marriage?"

"Don't even come at me with that!" I shout, rising up off the couch.

"I'm coming at you with this because it's what you need to hear, darlin'."

"You have no idea what I need to hear!" My blood soars past my ears, my jaw clenching so hard it hurts. "You can't come in here and tell me what I should do or how I should feel. You don't know what I've been through!"

I can't look him in the eye and see the pity. The weight of his stare is enough to let me know that he does know, or has a very good idea, of what I've been through.

Cord is standing in front of me, drawing me to his chest before I know it. His hug is simple, a platonic act that I need more than I even realized. When he pulls back and smiles at me, I'm a little steadier.

"I'm not judging you," he says, his rich voice soft. "I'm just telling you that you should've trusted your gut."

"How do you know what my gut says?"

"Will you stop answering me with questions?" he chuckles. "Elin . . ."

He walks in a circle before stopping by the entertainment center. He lifts a framed photograph of all of us—me, him, Ty, Jiggs, and Lindsay—a couple of weeks after graduation. We are at the lake, huge smiles and peace signs flipped up for the camera.

"I know how easy it is to get drawn into your head," he says. "It's easy as hell to sit around and think about everything that's wrong and think of a way out because you're desperate for the pain to end."

He looks at me again, his eyes somber. "Graduation was hard on me. Everyone was so happy, planning their lives, you know?" He forces a swallow, his hand holding the photograph dropping to his side. He twists it back and forth and back again. "I just kept thinking how I was officially on my own."

"Cord, that wasn't true," I say hurriedly.

"No, it was. My foster parents made it clear they were taking on another kid and I needed to find a place to go. They didn't get the check from the state after that and they needed that income. I get it, I mean, that was their job, but I had a week to find a way to take care of myself."

"Fostering a child shouldn't be a job," I say, my heart rate spiking. "You should take a child in because you love them. Not for a paycheck."

His shoulders rise and drop. "It was what it was. I don't know why I thought they'd be there after that. I guess because I was with them the longest out of all the foster homes I was in. It was my mistake."

"Cord—"

He cuts me off with the wave of his hand. "So we were at the lake that day, all of us, and you were all going on about your plans and all that, and I just kept thinking how fucked I was. I didn't know where I was gonna sleep in a few days. You all were having these huge parties thrown for you by your families, and I had a week to get out of my family's house."

"Oh, Cord," I say, reaching for his hand.

He smiles, but doesn't take it.

"That night," he says, his voice gruff, "I went out to Dugger Lake. The same place I had sat with my mom when she visited me the only time in my life. I sat on the old railroad tracks that go over the water and thought about what options I had. The more I thought about it, the worse I felt."

"Rightfully so," I say, taking his hand in mine, even though he tries to pull it back. "Cord, you couldn't help what your parents or what your foster family did to you. You had every right to feel bad about that! You were eighteen years old."

"Did you know Jiggs and Ty found me that night?"

I look deep into his eyes, darker than I've ever seen them. A cold chill rips through me.

"No," I say. "I don't remember them saying anything."

He slips his hand out of mine and sets the picture back on the shelf. "Well, they did. To this day, I don't know if it was happenstance or if they were looking for me, but they caught me about thirty seconds from jumping off those tracks."

"You would've died!"

"That was the point."

"Cord!" I gasp, my hand flying to my mouth.

"I know," he says simply. "Crazy, right? But at that moment in my life, everything looked hopeless and I was on the brink of making an *insane decision*. I just wanted the hurt to stop. I wanted the decisions made. I wanted to stop being different. If they hadn't come when they did . . ." He turns and touches me on the nose. "I wouldn't be here."

Stunned, I walk backwards until the backs of my legs hit the sofa and I fall onto the cushions.

"That man of yours and your brother saved my life, Elin."

A plethora of memories overtakes me and everything falls into place. "That's why you stayed with us right after that."

"Yeah," he smiles. "And why your dad got me on at the mine, because Jiggs begged him to help me."

"How did I never know this?"

"It's not something you want broadcast," he laughs. "You and Lindsay have always been so sweet to me. Good girls, the both of you. You have no clue how many times in my life you've made me smile, and it was the only time I felt happy some days."

Words fail me. There's no way to respond to that.

"You guys have been the only consistent thing in my life. Y'all have never turned your backs on me."

"We're your friends, Cord," I choke out.

"Fuck that. You're my family. The only family I have."

His words are crisp and clear and they fall hard on my heart.

"That's why I'm here. Because I can't sit back and watch you make this mistake. You all have pulled me up many times in my life, and I have to try to pull you up now."

"Whoa," I say, still trying to come to terms with Cord's story. "My marriage and what happened to you are two different things."

"Not really," he says easily. "You and I both got sunk by a set of circumstances and made decisions in the throes of the moment. Neither of which were good, clear-headed decisions."

"What do you want me to do, Cord?" I sigh. "Everything is broken. I can't trust him. I can't tell him . . . things," I gulp, "that a woman should want to tell her husband."

"You should tell him about . . . that."

"Why? Help him feel better about his decision? That I have some fatal flaw and can never give him what he wants?"

Both hands on his hips, he shakes his head. "You know there isn't a lot of difference between what you say Ty did to you and what you did to him."

Flabbergasted, my jaw drops to the floor. "*Ty left me*, Cord. He. Left. Me. He took off out of here, on fucking drugs from what I hear, and left everyone that loved him. I can't just brush that under the rug."

"He was trying to deal with things. He made a decision in the middle of a bunch of shit, just like I did, and just like you are doing. See how stupid that is?"

I start to talk, but he waves me off.

"And as far as you not doing anything to him . . ."

He looks at my stomach for a long moment. I flinch under his scrutiny, his observation piercing me to the point it almost hurts.

Covering my belly with my hand, to somehow protect my secret and my pride, I can't respond to his insinuations. I'm terrified to go there.

He nods, tearing his eyes away from mine. "I'm sorry, Elin."

A single tear drips down my cheek, the simple words the first time anyone has had the chance to comfort me since the loss besides Lindsay. The words are almost a warm blanket over my torn soul, soothing the ragged, lonely edges from losing something so precious.

I watch my friend watch me and we don't say anything; he doesn't muddy the moment by expressing his undying sorrow for me or by telling me it will be okay. He does what Cord does and just knows that his presence is enough. He's there.

Sniffling, I stand again, this time my legs swaying a bit. A weight has been lifted somehow, just by someone else knowing what happened. But at the same time, a jut of fear begins to work its way into my gut.

"Cord," I say, sniffling again, "please don't say anything."

"It's not my place to tell. But Elin, you should tell your husband."

The fact he calls Ty "my husband" doesn't go without notice.

"I called him to tell him, but he wouldn't answer," I say sadly.

"He still deserves to know."

"I'll decide what he deserves to know," I counter. "I had to go through losing that baby by myself. That was, by far, the hardest day of my life—harder than watching him leave or hearing the phone not pick up for days and days or asking about a divorce. And I did it alone. So I'm pretty sure I can decide how much of anything I want to do alone from here on out."

He shakes his head, clearly not entertained by my little speech. "He shouldn't have left, I agree. Most of the reasons he did it were completely selfish. But he was also trying to protect you."

"Don't go there with me, Cord," I boom.

"Even if he wasn't a full-blown addict, that shit fucks up your brain. I get that he didn't want to go off it in front of you. Even if he'd just been taking it a few weeks straight, he'd have some bad days. He knew that and didn't want you seeing it. That would've fucked *you* up." He furrows his brows. "You don't think if he knew about the miscarriage he wouldn't have come back? Because I guarantee you that boy would've been here. *Guarantee it.*"

I wipe the tears away that are coming fast and hard now. "I didn't want him back to comfort me if he didn't want to be here, and he clearly didn't."

"You aren't being fair."

"Life's not fair, Cord. Don't we both know that?"

He swipes his coat off the chair and heads to the door, his temple pulsing. With his hand on the knob, he turns to look at me.

"Don't make decisions because you just want to end the pain. Don't lose Ty because you're mad or hurt or confused. Be the smart girl I know you to be."

The door twists open and the cool night air hits me in the face. I'm not sure if it's the chill in the breeze or the stark reality of Cord's words that has me shivering.

Seventeen

TY

THE GYM DOOR is propped open with a large trash can. It's Jason's doing. The kid practices so hard he pukes almost every night. Within an hour of the start of drills, he runs to the door and loses his dinner in the can.

Every. Night.

He works his tail off, not just because he has colleges looking at him for scholarships, potentially giving him a way out of this town when he couldn't afford it otherwise. But his jump shot also has given him a sort of fame in the area. Everyone knows his name, knows "Jason from Jackson," just like once upon a time they knew a Ty from here too. The only difference is I'll do everything in my power to see him do more than just mine coal ten years from now.

And that starts with walking in here tonight.

The moon hangs bright above, the sound of balls hitting the rubberized gym floor echoing across the parking lot. I tighten my jacket over me, trying to fill the hollowness in my chest as much as I'm trying to keep the cool air out.

I'm empty. I'm a shell, a ghost of a life that I once lived so vibrantly. But the difference tonight as opposed to the many nights before is this: I can feel *me* somewhere inside my body. The spark I used to feel when I woke up and looked at my day—at spending the morning mining coal next to Jiggs and Cord, dinner with Elin before practice later—is back. It's flickering, growing, starting to burn as my confidence, the realization that I'm going to have to take my life back by the horns or watch it slip away becomes ever apparent.

And I'm not about to watch Elin or these boys drift away.

As much as I hate that Elin met with Parker, and I hate even more that I had to hear it from Pettis, it was exactly what I needed to get my shit straight.

The halogen bulbs glitter as I enter the gymnasium. Sneakers squeak against the floor as Reynolds' whistle screams.

"Nice work!" he shouts.

I round the corner and pause by the bleachers. Dustin marches across the floor and stops inches from the coach's face. They go at it, fingers in chests, veins popping.

"Hit the showers, Dustin!" I boom.

All heads turn to me. Jaws hit the floor. My eyes stay trained on my player.

"You heard him," Reynolds says, his chest rising and falling from the exchange.

"He's not the coach," Dustin growls, turning to Reynolds. "You are."

Reynolds doesn't back down. "This is his team. You know that. Now hit the showers like you were told."

No one utters a word as I traverse the room. When I reach Dustin, his eyes are wide. He's only seen this look on my face a couple of times and neither has ended well for him.

I love this kid. I've even had him over for supper a few times and Elin keeps an eye on him academically. But his attitude can be something fierce, something I try to handle when it erupts at me because I get where it's coming from. His parents left town while he was at a friend's house when he was seven years old. He's been in foster care ever since, moving from house to house, school to school. He's been in Jackson for five years now, part of the team for two. I've heard enough stories, seen enough of his strained life, to have empathy for the boy. Yet, it's my job to teach him to manage his anger and act like the man he's going to be, hard life or not.

"Apologize to him," I say through gritted teeth.

"He had us running suicides for the last twenty minutes!"

"I don't give a shit if he had you running them all practice. You do not disrespect your coach like that. Apologize or get the hell out of here."

A flicker of something dashes through his eyes and I make note of it.

"Everyone, come here," I say.

The boys gather around, balls on their hips, sweat dripping off their chins. They watch me with a mixture of trepidation and respect that makes me pause.

This team, all fifteen athletes standing in front of me, are my responsibility. They're my boys, my team, my group of kids to inspire and encourage, even if I did officially resign. I can't let them down any more than I already have.

Taking a deep breath, I face them all.

"How are ya?" I ask.

They nod, mumble their typical "fine," "okay," "all right" and wait for me to continue.

"Look, guys, I want to say I'm sorry."

"No, Coach, it's fine—" Jason begins, but I wave him off.

"You know what? It's not fine," I say, looking him in the eye.

"No, it's not," Dustin says, squaring his shoulders.

"Where have you been?" Pauly asks, a tall kid with blonde hair.

"Yeah, Coach . . ." Their questions come at me in a flurry, some asking out of concern, other voices on the cusp of an outburst.

I take a deep breath. "Guys, give me a minute." I run my hand through my hair. "Look, I get why you're mad. You have every right to be. If any of you want to talk one-on-one, let me know and we can meet up after practice or do some fishing this weekend and get it all worked out, okay?"

The energy in the room stills, lowering a few notches. I breathe a little easier.

"You all give me one hundred percent every night on this court," I continue. "Some of you have done that now for four years.

WRITTEN IN THE *Scars*   125

And I resigned and didn't respect you enough to give you a heads-up. I was wrong to do that."

Holding out my hands, Jason passes me a ball. I flip him a smile and he returns it.

"I love basketball," I say, passing the ball between my hands. "It's good competition, a fun way to pass some time. But you know what else it is, what it teaches?"

"Teamwork," Jason says quietly, unsure if it was a rhetorical question.

"Exactly. It teaches us to rely on the guys around you. So when James has a bad night and can't hit the broad side of a barn—"

"Hey!" he interjects to the laughs of his friends.

"When that happens," I smile, "we have Dustin or Pauly or Matt that can pick up the slack. It's not just you, individually, out there, taking on the opponent. It's all of you."

I bounce the ball a few times, trying to get my thoughts together, when the silence is broken by Jason.

"You know, Coach," he says, clearing his throat, "There aren't just fifteen of us. There's seventeen. There's Reynolds and you too."

I smile at my starting forward.

"Whatever happened to you, we would've been there for you too. Just like on the court. If you were missing your shots, we would've had your back," Jason says.

"But you stopped playing," Dustin challenges, clearly the most affected by my departure. "You just walked off the team."

"And I was wrong," I say, turning to face him. "I got all caught up in myself and forgot about my team. I forgot a lot of things. Sometimes . . ." I pull my gaze to the floor. "Sometimes it's easier to run off and try to deal with things on your own because you don't want people to see you struggle. But all that does is—"

"It lets your team down," Dustin chimes in.

"Yeah," I shrug, looking at him pointedly. "It lets your team down and I let a lot of people down on the notion that I was doing them a favor. Guys," I say, looking across the line of them, "I let you down. I hope you'll accept my apology."

"Of course," Jason says immediately.

Looking down the row of teenaged faces, they all nod their heads.

"Teams only work when we respect each other, when we are open with each other when we struggle. This team doesn't stop being a team when the whistle blows. I forgot that. Let's all learn from my mistake."

I glance at Dustin out of the corner of my eye. He toes the black line on the floor with his sneaker before looking up at Reynolds. "Hey, man. I'm sorry."

Reynolds grabs his shoulder and shakes it. "It's okay. It's been a rough week around here."

"Are you back, Coach?" Jason asks.

Looking at Reynolds, he waits for me to respond. I shrug and he laughs.

"Let's hope he's back," Reynolds sighs, sticking his whistle in his mouth. "I'm too old for this shit. You boys are killing me."

A series of laughs fills the gym and I sigh in relief. This. This is what I do, who I am and it feels fucking amazing to be back and remembering it.

"Looks like you have been turned over to me. Get a drink and let's see what kind of shape you're in," I tell them.

They all take off to the coolers, except Dustin. His brows pulled together, he takes the ball from my hands.

"You good, Coach?"

"Getting there," I wink. "Feels better being back here though, I'll tell ya that."

He nods and chews his bottom lip. "I saw Mrs. Whitt today."

"Did you?" I ask, trying not to let the fact that the mention of her threw me a little.

"She said she hoped you'd be here tonight."

"Yeah, well, here I am."

The ball goes between his hands, his nervous tell that something's the matter.

"What's wrong, Dustin?"

"I . . . um . . ." He takes a deep breath. "I got into some trouble last week, Coach."

"What happened?"

"Nothing, really. I mean, I didn't do anything. I was accused of sending a few emails to a teacher that I didn't send. I wouldn't do that," he says, shaking his head. "The principal wouldn't even look into it, even when I told him that teacher has it in for me. Just suspended me for three days."

"What?" I say, my jaw tensing. "Are you still suspended? When was this?"

I curse myself for not being there for him. Dustin wouldn't do that; it's not the kind of kid he is. And if he gets suspended, it will ruin his scholarship chances, which means his entire future will be gone. He'll end up . . . like me.

"It was last week. But relax," he says, smiling at the look of panic on my face. "Mrs. Whitt saw me in the parking lot. She was coming to the high school for an IT class or something and asked why I wasn't in class. I told her I was leaving because of what happened, and she took my elbow and marched me back into the office."

My chest swells at the thought that my wife did this for Dustin. This is my forever, the woman I love. The little pit bull shoved into this angelic body that fights for what she wants. She's ready to throw the towel in on us. What's that say about me?

My shoulders slump and he notices.

"Don't worry," he says, misreading my reaction. "Mrs. Whitt got them to look at the server and realize it wasn't me. I'm still on the team, Coach."

"Good. That's good, buddy."

"Yeah, so . . ." He takes a step back to give me some room. "I'll just go get warmed back up. Okay?"

I nod encouragingly, but my head isn't there. Neither is my heart. Both are back on County Road 211 in a little white house with black shutters.

Eighteen

ELIN

MY BAG HITS the table with a smack.

I wince, shaking my hand to give it back some life. My tote is overflowing with papers to grade and art pieces to put stickers on, and I'm dead tired. That's probably because I didn't sleep last night and the ten cups of coffee I guzzled today are wearing off, leaving me with a late afternoon slump.

Damn Ty.

All day, my mind wandered like the wind. It flowed from the past, to memories of Ty, to the future and what it would be like without him. The latter rolls my stomach. It creates an inherent need to crouch in a corner and close my eyes and play dead. Because that's what I feel when I think of life without him: dead.

Everything is just so muddled.

Every part of my life is touched by Ty, wrapped around him, incorporated in him in some way—all the way back to junior high. Every memory I have, he's in it. It's his face I see when I'm scared, it's his voice I hear when I need comfort, it's his touch I crave when I feel lonely.

"You realize you're doing to Ty the very same thing you're pissed at him for, right?"

Cord's insinuation rang through my head all day, poking me when I least expected it. Is that what I'm doing? Yes, I'm withholding information, but it's something he would've known if he hadn't left. That's different.

I think.

I head into my bedroom. I slip off my dress and boots from work and throw on a pair of sweats and a hoodie. It's all done on auto-pilot. My body goes through the motions while my head and heart have an argument of their own.

My brain thinks I should be logical and fair and tell Ty about the miscarriage. My heart knows I can't make it through that conversation and feels the need to protect me. My mouth doesn't want to take sides and spill the wrong way.

I'm scared, plain and simple.

When I enter the kitchen again, I see my phone blinking on the counter with a voice message.

"Hello, Elin. It's Parker. I wanted to let you know that your husband was in the office this afternoon. He advised me he won't be cooperating with the divorce, should it go forward. I'm sure you know that, but I wanted to see if your mind had changed in any way. Please give me a call back tomorrow."

"Ugh," I groan, dropping the phone onto the counter. Burying my head in my hands, I lean against the wall. "Why do you have to be so damn stubborn?"

A smile touches my lips, even though I fight it. Something about him wanting to fight for us, for me, feels good. Even though it would be easier if he would just let me go, let us end, a part of me deep in the shadows of my gut delights in the fact that he won't.

Gravel crunches outside and I look out the window. Ty's truck is sitting behind my car and he's climbing out.

My breath hitches in my throat. No matter how many times I've seen him in my life, he still makes it hard to breathe.

He doesn't look towards the house. Instead, he walks around the back of his truck. I can hear him banging on something and the tailgate closing.

I wait, but he doesn't come to the door. I wait still, but nothing.

Slipping on a pair of rubber boots, I head outside. My heart thumps in my chest in a mixture of excitement and dread. Seeing him is going to make tonight a long, lonely night.

Rounding the corner, I see him in the middle of the yard with a rake. There's a pile next to him of old clothes and I stop in my tracks. He looks up, but keeps raking, a little hint of a smile on his lips. "How was your day?"

His shoulders flex under the brown thermal shirt as he works the rake back and forth. His thighs fill out his jeans, and I pray he doesn't turn around because I don't want to see his ass. Not in those jeans. Dear Lord.

"Cat got your tongue?" he teases, dropping the rake. He heads to the pile and grabs a pair of corduroy jeans we bought together at Goodwill almost ten years ago.

"What are you doing, Ty?"

"What do you think I'm doing?"

He ignores me and shoves leaves down the leg of the pants. I just watch with amazement that after everything that's happening, he's here. Doing this. Like we've done for the last decade. Together.

Finally, he looks up. "You gonna stand there or you gonna come over here and help me make this scarecrow?"

"I . . ." I'm speechless. I shouldn't help him. I should make him leave. But I find myself walking across the lawn and grabbing the pants. I'm rewarded with a mega-watt smile.

"I think the rain that's supposed to come this weekend will put an end to the scarecrow days. I figured we better get it up today before it's too late," he says, working on the second leg.

I watch him, my brows pulled together. "Why are you doing this?"

"Because it's what we do," he says, pulling rubber bands out of his pocket and fastening them around the leg holes.

"Ty," I protest as he takes the pants from me and hands me the shirt. "You have to stop this."

"Stop what?"

"Stop *this*."

He rises and looks at me. Bits of broken leaves are splattered across his shirt and in his hair. I want to reach out and brush them off, touch his cheek, but I resist. Barely.

"You can't come by here anymore and do these things. They aren't our thing anymore."

"We've been through this," he mutters. His arms reach into the pile and he pulls up a heap of brown leaves, shoving them into the shirt with more force than necessary. I pull away.

He sighs, releasing a breath that sounds like he's been holding forever. "I'm not letting you walk away from me. If I have to spend the next ten years winning you back, I will. I'm prepared to do that."

The sincerity in his eyes causes my bottom lip to tremble. "I promised you for better or worse, until death do us part. This is the worse part. I'm aiming for the better now."

"Ty . . ." The words are stolen by the look on his face.

"Even if it takes me until the death part, I'll try. I love you, Elin. I'm going to remind you of that until you believe it."

"It could take a long time," I say, my words kissed by a sniffle. "I don't think your patience would last very long."

"Probably not. So you should just give in now," he laughs, pulling his hand away from the side of my face.

He fills the shirt and then grabs a bale of straw and a pumpkin and builds the scarecrow by the road while I watch, lending a hand when I see he needs it.

There's a calm between us, an ease rooted in a comfort between two people that has been built over a lifetime. This is something I won't have with anyone else.

My cheeks heat as I realize he's watching me. He grins and I grin back without thinking.

"What are we naming him this year?" he asks, tugging a hat over the top of the pumpkin.

"How about Docken?"

"Docken?" he laughs. "Where'd you get that?"

"A little girl in my class named her puppy that. It's just the first thing I thought of," I shrug.

"Docken it is. But take that off the potential baby name list. It definitely sounds like a dog's name," he laughs easily.

I look away.

"Hey," he says, nudging me with his shoulder. "I was kidding. If you like it, it can stay on the list. Maybe a middle name."

"We're done here," I say, changing the subject and taking a step away from him. "I'm going in. I have a lot of papers to grade."

"Need help?"

I look at him and can't help but laugh. "You are not coming inside and helping me grade papers."

"You love how I help grade papers," he laughs, wiggling his eyebrows.

"You are not coming in and . . ."

"Eating your pussy? That's how grading papers with me usually ends, and I do believe I get an A-plus."

"Damn it, Ty!" I say, turning away so he doesn't see my face. "Go home."

"I am home, beautiful."

I hate that I'm on the brink of breaking, that he makes me forget why I'm mad.

Heading into the house, I hear him toss his things into the truck. "Wanna go to dinner?" he asks.

"Nope," I call out over my shoulder.

"Want me to make you dinner while you grade papers?"

"Nope."

"Want me to have you for dinner?"

I shake my head and turn to face him. My hand on my hip doesn't take away from the smile on my face. "Ty? Enough."

"That wasn't a no."

"You are impossible. I'm mad at you."

"I figured that out. You can stop being mad now."

"No, I can't."

"Then think of how much fun it'll be being mad at me when I'm in the same house. You can be mean to me all day and night. It would be much more cathartic for you."

My laugh dances out of my mouth before I can stop it.

"And think of the makeup sex when I convince you to stop being mad." His eyes twinkle in the sunset. "But I'll tell ya something, E. I don't think I can wait very long to get inside you again."

"Stop," I breathe, watching him cut the distance between us in half.

As much as I want to fight it, it just feels like it would take way more energy than I have. Plus, I like the playful smile on his face and feeling the hole in my heart being filled a little.

Softening quicker than I anticipated, I choose to give in. Just for a little while. It'll end in an argument, anyway.

"Can I take you to dinner?" he asks.

Before I can talk myself out of it, I throw my hands up in the air and head towards the house. "I'm going in to eat leftovers. You can come if you want."

"Only if you come first," he chuckles.

I hear his footsteps behind me, and I smile all the way to the back door.

TY

I FOLLOW HER inside and into the kitchen. She never looks at me over her shoulder, never really acknowledges that I'm here.

She does this every time she's mad. It's her version of the silent treatment, although she's not usually completely quiet. She'll answer questions with a word or two, but she's so easy to break. You can goad her right into a full blown conversation. I've often thought she would choose another form of being pissed if she knew just how damn adorable she was like this.

Slipping off her boots by the table, she heads to the sink to wash her hands. Just being in the same room with her, even if she's not looking or speaking to me, is pretty damn close to heaven.

I figure the best way to go about this evening is to pretend everything is normal, that I've just come home from the mine and she's pissed I moved the thermostat. Be natural. Normal. Married.

Opening the refrigerator, I'm pleasantly surprised to see a bottle of my favorite beer in the drawer on the bottom. She doesn't drink this and I ponder the thought of why she kept it as I pop the tab.

I catch her looking at me as I bring the bottle to my lips. She rolls her eyes, knowing what I'm thinking, and I laugh, nearly choking on the brew.

"Move," she huffs, bumping me with her hip.

I step out of the way and watch her rummage through the fridge. "So, what's for dinner?"

"I have taco meat in here from a couple of days ago," she says, pulling out a plastic tub.

"It's not even Tuesday."

She glares at me. "You are more than welcome to leave."

I smile back. "Tacos are great any day of the week. Can I help?"

"Ugh," she groans, marching by me. She goes about heating the meat in a skillet and getting out the toppings and shells.

I just watch her work. She seems angry, but it's a front. The tremor in her hand as she cuts the lettuce is her giveaway. She's trying to stay mad, but why?

"How's your class?" I ask, sitting at the table.

"Good."

"Dustin said you got him out of some trouble last week."

"He was just going to take it," she says, looking at me over her shoulder. "He didn't do it and they weren't going to look into it because they'd already tried and convicted him in their minds. But I marched him back in the office and had a sit down with the Principal, the tapes were reviewed, and his name was cleared."

"One of the many reasons I love you."

Her hand stills mid-chop.

"You know what we need?" I ask, trying to keep her relaxed. "A puppy."

"We do not need a puppy, Ty."

"Think about it. When I'm at work, it would keep you company. You could take it on your walks and—"

She turns around and leans against the counter.

"We aren't getting—"

"A puppy," I cut her off. "Let's run up to Terre Haute this weekend and check the pound."

"Ty," she whines, clearly frustrated.

"What, baby? Would you rather have a kitten?"

She tosses the knife on the counter and sighs. "This was a bad idea."

"Well," I say, smirking, "if you don't want a pet and want to go straight for the baby, I'm game to try. Just come over here."

In a flash, her back is to me. Her shoulders are stiff, her spine ramrod straight.

Without thinking, I get to my feet and cross the kitchen and stand behind her. "What did I say?" I ask, letting my hand rest on her shoulder. She nearly jumps at the contact.

"Nothing."

"Oh, I said something, but I don't know what."

She blows out a breath and shakes my hand off her shoulder. Busying herself with dinner, she leaves me standing while she takes everything to the table.

Our eyes never meet, our bodies never touch. There's an awkwardness that's wedged itself between us that I can't budge. Only when she's sitting at the table does she look at me, still standing where she left me at the stove.

"You coming?" she asks.

I sit across from her and watch her make her plate. "Elin, whatever I said, I'm sorry."

"It's fine."

It's not fine. That much is clear. But I don't know why.

I make a taco and take a bite, relishing in the taste of home-cooked food. "I heard from Murphy," I tell her, breaking the silence. "He said the word is the mine will be opening back up soon."

"You aren't seriously considering going back to work there." Her eyes are wide, the fork in her hand falling slowly to the table.

"What else am I supposed to do?"

"Apply at the power plant, the electric company. Go back to school and teach," she says hurriedly.

"I've applied to all of those places. The plant has two slots open and ninety-four candidates. I have to be realistic."

Reaching across the table, I place my hand on top of hers. She stares at them, her chest rising and falling.

"You can't go back there," she chokes out.

Her words spear my heart. She cares. I knew she did, but to hear it encourages me. Somewhere through her anger, despite her filing for divorce, she still wants me. And maybe, just maybe, it's not buried as deep as I feared.

"Baby, listen to me. There's no other option to make that kind of money."

"Life's not about money."

"No, but there are bills to pay." I swallow hard. "And we have a lot less money because of me. I have to be able to give you a decent life, and the best way for me to do that right now is the mine. If something else opens, fuck yeah, I'll take it. But we have to be real, E."

I watch her beautiful face crease with worry, and while I secretly love it, I don't want to waste our night talking about work.

"They've not officially reopened anyway," I point out, "so this is a discussion for another day. Let's talk about the puppy."

She smiles. "No puppies."

"Kittens?"

"Their pee stinks."

"All right," I sigh, shoving away from the table. "Babies it is."

Standing abruptly, she swipes her plate from the table and dumps it in the trash. "I need to grade those papers."

"Want me to help?"

She spins on her heels and gives me a look.

"No, really," I say. "Do you want my help? I have nothing better to do and I can put them in stacks or something?"

A faint smile tickles her lips, but she fights it back.

Pushing to my feet, I start her way. Much to my surprise, she doesn't back away or stop me. Not to press my luck, I stop inches from her.

I don't want to leave. I want to pick her up and carry her into our bedroom and show her how much I love her. Brushing a lock of hair out of her face, I touch her for a moment longer than necessary because I need it. I think she does too—maybe more than me.

"You really want me to leave?"

Her nod is almost nonexistent.

I swallow back all the words I really want to say. "I'll go. But I don't want to."

"I need you to," she whispers, holding on to my wrist.

Her words and actions are at odds and it rips me apart.

"Why?" I ask. "Elin, something's going on with you and I want to know what it is."

"You know what it is," she says, but it's not what she means. I can see the other reason, something darker, right behind her green eyes.

"Yet you're asking me to leave you again."

Her gaze hits the floor. I lift her chin so she's looking at me.

"Tell me what's wrong. What are you hiding in there?"

She drags in a long, deep breath that shakes her chest. Her eyes grow wide, her hand clamping on my wrist. "I . . ."

My phone rings in my pocket, and the sound shakes her out of the moment.

"You should get that," she says, clearing her throat. She releases my wrist and steps away from my touch.

Growling, I pull the offender from my pocket and see Jiggs' name. "It's your brother."

"Go," she says, grabbing her bag off the floor beside the table. Her voice is clear now, the moment of truth far behind us. "I need to get to this anyway."

"You sure you don't wanna talk?"

With the bag on her shoulder, she turns on her heel. A look of resolution is stretched across her face. "I'm sure."

It's clear I'm not going to get anywhere now, just dig myself in a deeper hole. I head for the door but stop beside her.

Not giving her a chance to object, I slide her against me and press a kiss to the top of her head. "I love you. This bullshit is gonna stop soon, one way or the other. My patience is running thin. So figure out how you're gonna deal when I come home for good because it's happening."

And then I leave, the door squealing behind me.

Nineteen

ELIN

"HELLO?" I SQUINT against the late afternoon sun and toggle the phone against my ear.

"Where have you been?"

"Hang on," I mumble, getting the phone situated before I pull out onto the highway. "Okay. That's better. How are you, Linds?"

"Oh, I'm good. Just sitting over here, wondering why my best friend hasn't answered my calls in two freaking days. Just peachy."

Rolling my eyes, I smile. "I'm sorry. I just have a lot going on and need some space to think."

"Space? From me? Sorry, my friend. You don't get that."

I laugh, squeezing my car in between two trucks and barreling down the road towards my house.

It's been a long day full of addition and the letters S and T. Of course, half of the kids in the class that had to bring something that started with a T brought a tie. And every time I said "tie," I was thinking "Ty," and my heart hurt a little. Or a lot. Definitely more than was fair.

"Things are just weird," I tell her. "I have a lot on my mind."

"Jiggs said that Ty's been coming around to see you."

"I've seen him a couple of times," I admit.

She sighs. "Is that a good thing or a bad thing?"

"I don't know. One minute I think one thing and the next . . ."

"Did he tell you where he went? Did he explain things?"

"Yeah."

She pauses and waits for me to continue. I don't. As much as I love her, Ty's problems are his to tell. I won't betray that, not even for her.

"So . . ." she leads.

"So he explained it and I understand."

"What's the hold-up then?" she asks.

I flip my turn signal on and make a left onto my road. "I just want to make sure it's the right thing to do. I love him and I know he loves me. But, really, our problems aren't resolved. We are just kind of in limbo right this second."

"So you just don't want to jump right back into it?"

"Exactly."

She takes a deep breath. "Did you tell him about the baby?"

My chest squeezes. "No, I haven't. It's gonna break his heart and it's going to be devastating to me to tell him. And, really, I'm not sure if it matters."

"Of course it fucking matters!" she says. "I will always take your side in an argument publicly, but if you don't tell him about this, and soon, you are wrong, Elin."

I fill my lungs with air and blow it out slowly. This is something I've been pondering, something I know is true. I need to tell him. I need to let him know the truth. He deserves it. I just can't bring myself to bring it up.

"Tell me about the baby," I say, changing the subject. "How do you feel?"

"Gosh, I feel pretty good, actually," she nearly sings. "I've been a little sick, but nothing I can complain about. I go to the doctor again in two weeks and I think we'll be able to hear the heartbeat!"

I swallow past a lump in my throat. "I'd like to go with you. I mean, if you don't mind."

"I'd love that, Elin."

"I'm pulling into the house," I say as I hook a right onto the driveway. "But let's get together this weekend and have lunch.

Sound good?"

"Absolutely. And call me if you need anything. Please. Whatever you're going through, you don't have to do it alone." She hesitates. "You know what, call me even if you don't need anything. Call me because I'm a needy friend and you know I'll bitch if I don't hear your voice."

I grab my bag off the passenger's seat and head to the back door, chuckling. "I love you. I'll call you soon."

"Night, chickie."

Popping the door open, I'm met with a chill. The air isn't warm like I expect after leaving it set on 74-degrees. I flip on lights, set my bag down, and check the thermostat. It's on but not running.

"Shit," I say out loud, looking at the ceiling.

The furnace does this each start to winter. There's some trick to it that Ty figured out the second year we lived here. A trick I don't know.

I eye the basement door on the other side of the kitchen. It mocks me with its hidden shadows and bugs and damp crevices. Shivering, I wonder if Jiggs could get it working or if I'm going to have to call my husband.

My lip twitches at the thought of seeing him again, and I try to kick myself for it, but I don't. Wanting to see him is as natural to me as breathing or sleeping or craving soda.

Slumping against the wall, I can feel my heart thumping against my ribs. A decision is going to have to be made. I've known it since he left after taco night.

I'm going to have to either be firm and end this for good or I'm going to have to tell him my truths and try to work this out. The latter is something I don't think I can survive.

Taking a deep breath, I head through the kitchen and place my hand on the knob to the basement door.

I can do this.

TY

"I'M FUCKING BEAT." I toss my gloves in the back of the truck, looking over the bed at Jiggs.

He laughs. "I told you before we got here this morning that this was going to suck."

"Thanks though for the hookup today."

My leg cramps, the muscle still not fully rehabilitated. It hurts like a motherfucker. Still, it's money I can give to Elin to put back in savings. I'll do it every day for the rest of my life if I have to. I want to if that means I can make things right. If I can get one step closer to having a full house and family again.

"He said he didn't know how much longer he'd have work for us, but if Murphy can get us back to mining in the next couple of weeks, it should work out."

"Let's fucking hope."

Jiggs digs around in his lunch box and pulls out a giant pickle. "So how's my sister?" he asks, taking a snap off the cured cucumber.

"Watching you eat that is like watching you eat a dick. I can't."

"Fuck off," he laughs, swallowing. But he doesn't take another bite.

"Elin's . . . Elin," I shrug. "I'm trying to see her without pushing her because I'm scared as hell to go right back to screaming matches again. But fuck, Jiggs, I'm tired of not being home. I'm sick of not seeing her every day."

"You think she's coming around at all?"

"I got papers in the mail when I went by Cord's at lunch," I laugh. "Not divorce papers, just a set from Parker explaining the process and what he would suggest. So I guess not."

He whistles between his teeth. "She'll be all right. Just give her a little space. Let her come to you."

"She—" I'm cut off by my phone ringing. I grab it out of my pocket to see Elin's face. "It's her," I grin, swiping the screen. "Hey, E!"

"Hi," she says, irritation thick in her voice. "What's the trick to the furnace?"

"The trick to the furnace?" I laugh. "Why? What's it doing?"

"That damn thing it does every winter. I have no idea what I'm looking at and it's cold in here."

"Want me to come fix it?" I grin, looking at Jiggs.

She sighs. "Just tell me how to fix it and I'll do it. Or I'll call my brother."

"But I was your first call. I like that," I laugh.

"Forget it. I'll call Jiggs."

"He's standing right here, and he knows nothing about furnaces, right, Jiggs?"

"I got nothing, Elin!" he shouts as I hold the phone up in the air.

"See?" I say. "You better let me help you."

She yelps in the phone, making me laugh.

"Are you in the basement?" I ask, trying to imagine her in the place she's deemed the scariest place on earth.

"Yes," she whines.

"Don't look on the north windowsill. The spider that lives in that web is as big as my hand."

"Fuck you," she says, her voice wavering.

"And the snake that lives—"

"Forget it!" she screams.

Her feet pounding against the stairs leading to the kitchen has me laughing out loud. "Elin, calm down. I was only kidding."

"Just come fix it. Please," she begs as the basement door shuts and locks behind her.

"You don't have to ask me twice. Be there in a second."

I give a quick salute to Jiggs and hop in my truck. Racing the 8.2 miles across town to the house, I get there in half the time it should take.

Jogging to the back door, my breath billowing in front of me, I rap against the door quickly before pushing it open. She's standing in front of the stove, a sweater wrapped around her shoulders.

"Hey," I say, noticing how the sunlight streaming in from the window makes her look like she has a halo.

"Hey," she says, looking defeated.

"What's wrong?" I ask.

She shrugs, her shoulders slumping.

"You didn't want to call me, huh?" I laugh.

The sound eases her posture and she stands straight and smiles. "No, but I'm freezing, so I didn't have a choice."

"Thank God for small favors." I toss the envelope from her attorney on the counter. "You can have that."

Turning to head to the basement door, I hear her pick up the envelope.

"No, that's your copy to read," she says from behind me.

"Already told you," I say, opening the door, "I'm not participating in this madness."

I leave her, jaw hanging wide, as I barrel down the rickety stairs and work my magic on the furnace. In less than three minutes, it's up and running. Elin cheers from the kitchen.

Bounding back up the steps, her smiling face is waiting on me.

"Thank you," she says earnestly. "I know you didn't have to come over here and do that."

"Of course I did."

She frowns, but doesn't argue. Progress.

"You know," I say, trying to figure out how to delay my inevitable departure, "it's warmer outside than it is in here."

"Hopefully it doesn't take long to heat up."

"Let's go outside," I say, trying to hide the fact that I'm scheming ways to stay with her.

"For what?"

"To not freeze to death," I say like she's silly, and wrap my arm around the small of her back. She lets me guide her outside. She feels so good against my arm that I have half a notion to keep walking and walking until we are at the sea.

The sky is a ripple of pinks and purples and oranges as it begins its drop over the horizon and I tuck her into my side as we watch the colors bleed together.

"Thank you for helping me," she whispers, not taking her eyes off the sunset. "I was scared to call you."

"Why would you be scared to call me?"

"I was afraid you wouldn't answer."

When she looks at me, her eyes are full of some unnamed emotion. It sparks a desire in me to fight whatever demon has put that look there. I lift her chin. Her skin is so soft under my touch. My thumb strokes her cheek as I gaze into her eyes.

"Never be scared to call me. Don't hesitate to ask me for what you need, what you want. I know I walked out," I say, gulping, "but it wasn't walking out on you. And I will never do that to you again. I swear to God."

"I know you won't."

"What?" I say in disbelief. "I mean, you're right, I won't, but you know that? You believe me?"

She nods, turning her head to kiss my palm. Her lips tremble against the rough skin on my hand, her hand shaking ever-so-slightly as she holds it.

"I do believe you," she says softly. "But that doesn't fix everything."

I pull her into me, trying to put her, me, our life back together with my embrace. Her arms find my waist, and I hold her in the middle of the driveway, swaying back and forth in a moment I'll never, ever forget. The feeling of my world careening back into focus, into the places it should be, nearly drops me to my knees with my girl in my arms.

"I should go in," she says, looking up at me.

"It's cold in there."

She shrugs and I see her start to slip away from me again. Frantic, I struggle to find a way to stop it.

"Let's go for a drive," I suggest.

She looks at me warily.

"It's just a drive," I promise. "The house can warm up and then I'll drop you back off, if that's what you want. What can it hurt?"

"You won't try to make out with me or anything, right?" she teases. "Because I know that look in your eye, Tyler Whitt."

"Only if you ask," I wink, opening the door to my truck and watching her climb in. Before I shut it, I lean in and whisper into her ear. "Hey, E."

"Yeah?"

"Please ask."

Twenty

ELIN

IT'S LIKE YOUR favorite sweater on a crisp winter day or the smell of your grandmother's apple pie at Sunday dinner. It's walking into your childhood bedroom, even though you haven't been in there for ten years, and knowing exactly where your possessions are because that's your space. That's your room. That's home.

Being in Ty's truck as we drive out of town and hit a back road, dust flying off the tires as the asphalt turns into gravel, is the same thing. My heart finds a rhythm that's eluded me, my body releasing the rigidity that's stretched over my shoulders. I can breathe, here, with him, in this old truck.

I glance over my shoulder. He has one hand on the steering wheel, the other on his thigh. His hair is a mussed up mess, the dark locks sticking up everywhere. It's reminiscent of how it looks in the morning when he rolls out of bed, and I have a hard time keeping my hands to myself. Watching him get dressed and undressed used to be the best part of my day.

The ice around my heart, the wall I've so carefully constructed, is crumbling. I feel it. As much as I want it to be there to protect me, I like the feeling of . . . this. It's the warmth of being me, of being part of a relationship that's a once-in-a-lifetime type of thing. Even though things have been rocky, this is my life. I know it. I feel it. I want it.

He catches me checking him out and smiles, reaching across the console and taking my hand in his. Flipping my hand over, he rubs his thumb across my palm and focuses his attention back on the road.

"You wanna know something?" he asks, his voice deep and crackly.

"Sure," I say, watching his eyes squint as he turns the truck up the lane to Moon Mountain, a hill that overlooks Dugger Lake. It's our favorite parking spot, one that we've used countless times since Ty got his license. "I said no making out!" I laugh, taking my hand away from his.

"You did not. You asked if I was going to try and I said not unless you ask. I'm hoping if I set the mood right, you'll ask," he smirks.

The truck hits the top of the hill just as the final rays of sunlight stream from the sky. The lake that the hill overlooks ripples in the breeze, the green cattle fields surrounding it shining with the dew that's beginning to settle.

"It's so beautiful up here," I say as Ty turns off the ignition. It's silent, absolutely still, and I pop open my door and hop out.

The air is clean yet chilly, but I don't have time to take in the cold. Ty opens the tailgate and picks me up and sets me on it, settling between my legs with a hesitant smile on his lips.

"You are so beautiful," he says, stroking my cheek.

"Charmer," I giggle, unable to resist the handsome face in front of me.

He laughs and takes his place beside me, his knee touching mine as our legs swing off the end.

"Feels like we've done this a time or two," he points out.

"Because we've done this a time or a hundred. So many memories up here."

I look around the land below. I know what this looks like at dusk, like now, and also as the morning sun rises behind me. I know what it looks like at midnight when the world sleeps and what it looks like at six a.m. when only a few trucks pass along the road below as people begin to come to life and head off for their day.

"We've celebrated birthdays up here. Remember when you and Jiggs turned twenty-one and he decided he was going to try to swim that lake to celebrate?" Ty laughs.

"Yeah, in January! He almost got hypothermia," I remember. "Or when Cord started a fire that one night after you won the basketball Sectional and it got away from him and almost burned that field?"

"I forgot about that," Ty laughs. "I think he threw gas on the fire to start it. He really should've tried Boy Scouts as a kid or something."

"What about when my parents passed away and I couldn't stop crying? You brought me here then, remember? And let me just have my tears and screams away from everyone?"

"Yeah," he says, nodding. He looks at me over his shoulder, his dark eyes peering at me. "Remember when we celebrated our first anniversary in this very spot? We were too poor to go to dinner, so we packed bologna and cheese sandwiches and came here instead?"

My heart fills in my chest at the memory of our sandwiches and cherry flavored drinks in paper cups, the best we could do. "You know," I say, "I think that's my favorite anniversary."

"Mine, too," he grins. "It was really simple then."

"When did everything get so complicated, Ty?"

He shrugs, his face falling. "I don't know. But it sure as shit did."

The wedge that's been between us starts to slice its way down, parting us in an invisible trench. Sometimes it makes me feel safe and I'm thankful for it. But now? I'm clamoring to make it go away.

"Ty?"

"Yeah?"

"What are we doing?"

His mouth falls, his eyes leaving mine and heading across the lake to some place, some memory, some thought I'm not privy to. He slips off the back of the truck and faces the lake for a long minute. When he turns to me, he's resigned to a decision.

"I tell the boys on my team that we don't quit," he says, his tone steady. "I'm always reminding them that we set our eyes on a prize and we work our tails off until we get there. Regardless of how painful, even though it might hurt, we get to the finish line."

"Sounds like good logic," I say, swallowing a lump that's suddenly lodged in my throat.

"It is. In theory. But I'm rethinking it now." He shoves his hands in his pockets and squares his shoulders up to me. "Sometimes you have to let things go. Just because you start on a path, even if you're balls-to-the-wall at first, doesn't mean you should stay on it. It's less quitting, I guess, and more adjusting. Moving on to the next thing you think you want."

He knows I'm dying for him to expound, that I'm terrified that he means he's decided my recent rhetoric is right. Even though that's what I've asked him to do, I can't bear to hear it come out of his mouth. He knows this, yet he doesn't go on. He waits for me to respond.

With a voice shakier than I'd like, I give in. "What are you moving on from now?"

Slowly, inch-by-inch, the corner of his mouth upturns. With every movement, every flinch, my heartbeat picks up.

"I quit pretending like I don't know what we're doing," he says. "I've tried to ease back into this because I think that's what you want. I've slept on that fucking futon in Cord's room with that stupid dog licking me in the face every morning long enough." He smirks, cocking a brow. "Baby, I'm coming home. If you don't like it, too damn bad."

"Ty . . ."

"Don't 'Ty' me," he snickers, walking towards me. With each step, a flutter ripples through my belly. "All this shit will only make us stronger, like a scar that has healed over. That skin is stronger than the area around it. It's been to war and won. That's us."

My heart skips a beat as he takes my hand.

"I won't even bring this up five years from now and remind you how silly you were thinking you were going to divorce me. I'm yours, E. You're mine. We are two people that get it right most of the time, but, on occasion, we fuck up. I'll take full responsibility for causing this, but I'm also taking responsibility for ending it. Honesty, transparency from here on out, but there is a *here on out*, Elin, because I'm done living without you."

Tears wet my eyes and I blink them back as quickly as they form. This is it—do or die. I either accept this and tell him my secret or I push back. And I know if I choose the latter, that might really be it.

"It's not that simple," I sniffle, wiping my nose on the sleeve of my shirt.

"Yeah, it is."

I shake my head, my hair swishing around my shoulders. Looking into his face, his devilishly handsome features and silky hair, the face I love, I don't know if I can tell him.

My heart shatters. The force of it shaking my body, my shoulders slumping forward. My lungs fill and empty of air more quickly than I mean to, and I suddenly can't get enough oxygen despite the rate of my breathing.

Ty is touching me in a half a second, brushing my hair off my face and examining me for what's wrong. He'll never see it. You can't see the scars I bear.

"What's wrong?" he asks, his voice tender. "Elin, you gotta talk to me."

Lifting my chin, my teeth nearly chattering for fear or anticipation or a mixture of both, I can barely open my mouth to speak.

My words are going to slice him, tear him apart. And me all over again.

TY

MY GUT IS a twisted, tense knot as I watch Elin come to grips with telling me whatever it is that's been on her mind. I knew there was something. I could see it in her eyes when she'd start to laugh at something I said or find herself warming up to me before remembering whatever this is and scurrying away again.

I figured it was that she took another job or broke something of mine when I left—something small and stupid she thinks I'd be mad about. Right now, watching her go through the hoops of actually telling me makes me think this isn't a broken fishing rod or misplaced playbook.

"Talk to me."

"I can't," she says, the tears flowing steadily down her cheeks. She looks at me through the liquid filling her eyes. The sadness and fear is palpable.

"Hey," I say, trying to soothe her. "You can talk to me about anything."

"Not this."

"Especially this," I promise. "If something is bothering you this much, this is the thing you need to tell me. Trust me."

She doesn't move, doesn't open her mouth, doesn't attempt to spill the secret she's holding safe.

I rest my hands on her knees, peering at her. "Regardless of what it is, we can work it out."

Tears pool again as her eyes widen. "Ty . . ." she whispers, choking back a sob.

Pulling her head against my chest, I try to tell her with my body that I'm here. That I'm not going anywhere, despite what she has to say.

"We have to trust each other, lean on each other, communicate with each other. We're no different than a team. We *are* a team," I say. "If we don't talk, if we sit the bench and refuse to play, we can't win. And, Elin, baby," I say, squeezing her for good measure, "if I don't have you, there's nothing to play for."

Her cries soften, her back not shaking as badly as before. I hold her as the moon becomes bright above and the fireflies begin to light up around us.

"The fireflies are out," I say. "Do you remember the time Jiggs caught a bunch and took off the glow part and put it in his hair?" I ask. The memory makes me chuckle and it's not long before I can feel her ease too. "The fucker glowed all night. Your brother is such a weirdo."

She pulls away and looks up at me in the way someone only can that knows you and your memories inside out.

"I believe you did that too," she grins, drying her cheeks.

"I don't remember that."

"I'm sure you don't, either from choice or from the whiskey," she says, all out laughing now.

Stroking her cheek, I nearly beam at her turn-around. "There's my girl."

Her head rests against my palm and I place my other on the other side. Tilting her to look straight at me, I bend so we're at eye-level. She tries to look away, but I won't let her. Holding her head in place, I plant a gentle kiss to the middle of her lips. When I pull back, I see her wheels turning.

"I don't know how to tell you this," she says, rubbing her eyes.

"Just open your mouth and say it and be done."

When she pulls her hands away, the wateriness is back. Her gaze is heavy on mine, like she's trying to tell me without words.

I can't look away. Not that I want to, but if I did, I couldn't.

"Ty," she says before her voice breaks and the tears stream again. I don't reach for her, not this time. I'm pinned in place, frozen to the spot on the ground just a foot or so in front of her. "I . . . I . . ." She presses her lips together, her face turning a warm shade of pink. "I was pregnant. And I lost the baby."

Everything stops.

Everything except the steady flow of tears down her beautiful, pink cheeks and the drop of my stomach into an abyss that's more bottomless than I ever imagined.

I'm sure I misheard her, something about her miscarrying a baby? Does she mean the one we lost a few years ago?

Looking into her tear-stained face, I know that's not the case.

I think I'm going to be sick.

"What?" I ask, taking a short step back in case I spew my dinner at her feet. "What did you say?"

She doesn't answer me, but she doesn't have to. The pained look on her face, the sadness that is smeared across her features, the devastation I can see plain as day written all over her tells me all I have to know. My hand shakes as I draw it over my eyes, trying to break the numbness settling over me.

"I . . ." Words are on the tip of my tongue, yet evade me. "When? How did I not know this?"

"I'm sorry," she says before a full-blown sob breaks the night air.

Her cries are muffled as I press her against me, unable to do anything but hold her. Her agony rips from her body and into mine, shredding the fibers of my soul. It's a slow, agonizing torture listening to her grieve for a child I didn't know existed, a life I can't yet bring myself to believe was real.

"I called to tell you . . ." she says into my shirt. "So many times. You didn't answer."

My mind spins like a top, trying to grab something to work from. "When did you find out?"

"A few days after you left. I went to the doctor because I thought I was having a nervous breakdown and found out that I had been pregnant."

Coughing back the vomit that creeps up my throat, I squeeze my eyes shut.

"I'm sorry," she cries again, her word as broken as my heart. "I'm so sorry, Ty."

"My God, Elin. Don't apologize," I scoff, fighting back the first set of tears I've felt since my father passed away.

Her hands twist in my shirt, her knuckles pressing into my back. They shake as she unfurls the suffering she's been holding in.

Kissing the top of her head, I take a deep breath and try to calm my nerves. "I don't know what to say."

She places a single kiss to my sternum before letting me go. Her face is streaked with mascara, her lips swollen. "There's nothing for you to say, nothing you *can* say. I lost the baby. I'm sorry."

"Stop saying you're sorry!" I say gruffly, my throat clenching shut. "Damn it, Elin. This is not your fault." I pace a circle, my sneakers stomping against the brown grass. "I just . . . I should've fucking been there for you. Damn it!"

"I needed you."

My mouth opens in an attempt to respond, but nothing comes out. They say the truth hurts. That's not true. The truth blisters, and I feel it in every cell in my body.

"There's nothing I can say right now that will tell you how sorry I am," I choke out. "I should've been there for you." I look at her stomach.

Would it have been different had I stayed? Did I cause this? If so . . .

"I needed you so much, prayed so hard you'd come home and help me," she whimpers. "I was so scared, and I just felt like I'd failed. First I couldn't get pregnant, and then I couldn't keep it. I was so scared." Her words are cut with an agony I've never heard before, a sound I'd give anything to make go away.

"No," I insist, shaking my head. "Don't go there. Don't *even* go there, Elin."

Tugging at my hair, feeling the pull of my roots stinging as they rip away from my scalp, devastation hits me full-force.

"If I'd known, I would've been here. I swear to God I would've." I bite back a surge of emotions I can't explain. "Were you alone?"

"I had Lindsay," she whispers. "I was just dealing with this, sitting on the bed with Lindsay and feeling . . . ripped apart, I guess. Destroyed. As time went on, I got madder at you for not being there. All the sadness just consumed me, Ty. I was so—*I am so*—angry. Bitter, even."

My hand finds her shoulder and I pull her into me before she can fight it. "I can't handle the idea that you experienced that without me."

"Me either," she breathes. "I don't know if I ever will. It's like this entire process is now stained, every piece of it just another terrible memory."

"I get that," I say softly, "I do. But it's not a good enough reason to end us."

She nuzzles into my chest, her arms clasping around my waist. "You had a right to know, and I was wrong for not telling you."

"You should've given me a chance to come home. To help you. To . . . go through this with you."

"I didn't want you to come home because of a tragedy. I never want to be that girl, the one the guy stays with out of pity. If you didn't want me . . ."

I grab her shoulders and look her squarely in the eye. "I have wanted you since the moment I saw you at your locker in eighth grade. From the moment I asked if you had any gum because I wanted to hear the voice of the girl that took my breath away. I've wanted you since that exact second, and I've never stopped."

An image of what that must've looked like, what she must've felt like, what she must've gone through, rumbles through my mind. Abandoned by me, losing a child she didn't even know she had.

If only I'd stayed.

A humiliation as deep as I've ever known swamps me. "I'm sorry," I say as the unfamiliar feeling of tears dropping past my lashes begins. It's like a dam—once it's breached, it's uncontrollable.

My body shakes against her as I cry for being a failure. I cry for the loss of a child I didn't know existed, for not being there for my best friend at the one time of her life she needed me more than ever.

I cry for not paying attention at work, letting myself get lazy and not watching the beam that fell on me and smashing my leg. I cry for my weakness of needing the pills to feel better and not rehabbing it, working harder at it, and needing an easy way out.

I cry for all those things for a long time. Elin holds me, our roles reversed, as she, the victim, becomes the strong one. And that makes me feel even fucking worse.

When I look at her again, she smiles in a way that shows what she would've looked like as a mother. It's the way she looks when she talks about her students, about Dustin when he got into trouble, the way she looked when she called 911 when she found a baby deer struck by a car on the side of the road as a teenager.

"Now you know," she whispers, rubbing her thumb against my lips.

"This is why you've been pushing me away?"

She nods as we reach for each other, the only other person that feels the pain we do, the only other person that can heal us from that very hurt.

The chill in the air dances across my bare skin and I shiver as my body comes down from the adrenaline.

"You ready to go?" she asks.

"Yeah."

"Ty?"

"Yeah?"

She reaches for me with a shaky hand. "Will you kiss me?"

In the midst of the fireflies, under the bright fall moon, I kiss my wife with everything I have.

Twenty-One

TY

TAKE MY eyes off the road just long enough to glance at her sleeping beside me, her head resting on my shoulder. I just look at her face and think back to what this little pit bull, as Cord calls her, has been through. Alone. It's enough to break the strongest man.

My teeth ache from being ground against one another in order to keep from going crazy. I need to yell, need to vent, need to make something feel the pain I feel.

She stirs beside me as I pull into the driveway. Killing the engine, I sit and try to gather my thoughts.

The only sound is her faint breathing, and while I want to talk to her, apologize, try to find some comfort in her, I'm glad for the quiet. It's like a bubble in the truck, she and I insulated from the world.

Elin loves me. And for that, I'm the luckiest fucker on the face of the planet. And that she still loves me after all of this? It's a blessing I can't fathom, but one I won't fail to acknowledge every day for the rest of my life.

Scooting my seat back to the farthest position, I pull her onto my lap. She curls up against me, her arms going around my neck and her head against my shoulder. I kiss her forehead before opening the door and carrying her towards the house.

"What's going on?" she asks sleepily as I push the back door open, the squeaking waking her. "Where are we?"

"Home," I say, kicking the door closed behind us.

"I can walk."

"Shh," I whisper, finding my way through the darkness like the back of my hand. "Let me carry you."

"You don't have to."

"I know I don't. I want to. Let me, please."

"Okay," she says softly, her cheek finding my chest again.

Padding down the hallway, I enter our bedroom. The moonlight streams through the window, giving me enough light to see our bed. The blue sheets are her favorite, the cream comforter in a messy heap at the bottom. She never makes the bed and seeing it like that, the same as always, makes me smile.

I lay her against the sheets. She smiles up at me, a soft, knowing smile, and kicks off her shoes and socks. "Grab your t-shirt off the dresser, please," she asks, wiggling out of her jeans. I grab the shirt and turn back to face her and she's sitting naked on the center of the bed.

I should say something—compliment her body or tell her how beautiful she looks, but with the truths of the night, it all seems wrong. I don't know what to say. Maybe she's right and there is nothing to say.

"Shirt?" she asks, holding out her hand.

Tossing her the shirt, she slips it over her head and slithers down in the blankets.

Her hair spilling against the sheets, she peers up at me. Propping herself up on her elbows, we stare at each other, a husband and a wife trying to find the steps to a dance that once came so naturally.

"If I tell you something, promise you won't laugh at me?" she asks.

"No. But I'll try not to."

She smiles and snuggles further into the blankets. "I remember one night I couldn't sleep. I felt like everything I wanted had been robbed from me and I was just beyond sad. Beyond angry. Just almost numb, I guess. And I got out of bed for the first time in a couple of days and walked into the living room and laid on the couch. I turned the television on and flipped through the channels and landed on some two a.m. preacher. He was talking about love, naturally, and how we should use every experience in our life to build love and how that's a test in this world. How can you take your darkest moments and find a way to love more?"

I watch her eyes twinkle in the moonlight and I know she's getting ready to amaze me. She never fails.

"I start crying," she continues, "even though I'm certain there are no tears left. And I'm sure there's no way I can find love in this mess. I loved you and you left. I loved this baby and it was taken from me. How can I be expected to find love in that? It was laughable."

"I see your point."

"But then I fall asleep and I have this dream, Ty. Not about you," she adds, pointing a finger at me. "You were still on the black list. It was about the baby. I didn't see it or anything, but the feeling of being pregnant, this . . . this . . . it's a fullness. A warmth. Like you're rounded out or something. I can't explain it. And that's the thing," she said, propping back up on her elbows again. "Even though I was losing the baby, that feeling was there, just like the first time. I felt it. Maybe for a few hours or a day, but I felt it."

"Elin . . ." The rest of the sentence catches in my throat, despite the simple smile on her face.

"I loved that baby," she says, her voice breaking. "And if I never get pregnant again, I have an inkling of what it would've been like and I'm grateful for that."

I climb across the bed and gather her in my arms. She lays across me, her hair spilling over my elbow and her eyes looking up at me so intently.

"You amaze me," I whisper. "You are the strongest person I know."

She laughs, a sweet, gentle giggle. "I don't know about that. But I made it through losing you and losing a baby at the same time, so I'm pretty sure I can make it through anything."

"You didn't lose me," I scoff.

"Well, it sure as hell felt like it."

"I will never leave you again, regardless of why or how. I will always come back."

"Promise me?"

"Absolutely."

She presses her lips against mine before climbing off me. She lies beside me and waits for me to make a move.

I slip off my clothes, down to my boxers, and then unfold beside her. "I'm making an executive decision to sleep in my bed," I say, pulling her against my side.

"I suppose I'll go along with that." Her hand drapes over my side and traces the scars on my back. "Even though you're here, I don't want you to think this means I want to jump back to where we left off. And I have questions for you still . . ."

"Fire away. Whenever you're ready."

She kisses the center of my chest and sighs. "I've missed this."

"Not as much as me. I've been sleeping on couches for the past few months. My back is aching like a motherfucker."

She laughs. "I'm glad you were miserable, and I'm not even sorry."

"Sadist."

"Realist." Her leg wraps over mine like it does before she falls asleep. "Does this mean you are moving back in?"

"I think it's time for the rest of me to come home," I say, kissing the top of her head.

She yawns, her heartbeat evening out. "The rest of you?"

"My heart was always here," I whisper.

Smiling as she pulls me tighter, her voice is full of sleep when she finally speaks. "I'm still mad at you."

"I can live with that," I whisper as we both fall asleep.

Twenty-Two

ELIN

THE SUN IS too bright. My eyes fight to open against the assault blazing through the windows. Glancing at the clock, I see it's almost noon and I struggle to determine that it is Saturday and I haven't overslept.

My body feels deliciously rested, my brain cozy from getting hours of uninterrupted sleep. It's confusing considering my lack of any real sleep lately . . . and then I look to the vertical pillow beside me and see Ty's clothes on the floor.

Closing my eyes, I smile. He's home both because he wants to be and I want him to be. Maybe he did always want to be?

The load off my shoulders is a giant relief as I remember telling him about the pregnancy.

My feet are cold against the floor, my body chilling because either the furnace is broken again or he's turned down the thermostat. I don't even care.

Aiming for the kitchen, I pad down the hall but stop when I notice the nursery door scooted open. My fingertips find the wooden edge and I press it forward slowly.

Ty is standing near the windows in his boxers, looking at the big oak tree outside. He glances over his shoulder, his morning hair all crazy in the most perfect way.

"Good morning," I say, coming up behind him. I wrap my arms

around his fit waist and lay my head on his back.

"Morning," he says, his hands resting on my threaded ones at his front. "I tried to sneak out so I didn't wake you."

"You didn't. I slept better than I have in months."

"Me too."

Our bodies sway, a comfortable lull that could put me to sleep again. I press a kiss in the center of his back and walk around to his side. "How are you today?" I ask. "Hungry?"

He keeps his vision trained on something out the window. "You know what you said last night about finding love in tough situations?"

"Yeah."

"I've been thinking about that." He angles his head to the side and looks at me. "A lot of things happened, a lot of things I won't forget. Like what it's like to feel your body crunch beneath the weight of a timber trapping you underground. All the things your mind considers when you contemplate you might not make it to the surface before you die.

"I know what it's like to crave a release from pain and I know what it's like to suffer the humiliation of knowing you've let everyone around you down," he says, swallowing hard. "But the one thing I don't think I'll be able to really make peace with is not being here for you."

"I struggle with that too. Maybe it's unfair—"

"No, it's not," he gruffs. "I'm the one that slammed my phone and broke it in pieces. I didn't replace it. It was me that thought you would be fine with Jiggs, but I was wrong. It was my place, my role."

I start to disagree, but can't. He's right. We both know it.

"Do you think we can fix this?" I say instead.

"We are going to find the love. We are going to love each other so fucking much that we either forget the pain or we can't feel it anymore. That doesn't mean we forget the baby," he says, a shake to his head, "but it means we honor it by loving each other."

I can't breathe, can't respond to his words because it's the most beautiful thing I've ever heard.

"Day by day," he says, "we take it easy. We have no rush. No pressure. No calendars and stupid ass internal temperatures. It's me and you. I want to date you all over again."

Giggling, I press a soft kiss to his lips. "I hope you're out of practice dating people, Coach."

"It's a damn good thing I have a playbook full of practice techniques then, isn't it?"

He squeezes my ass, making me yelp as he carries me out of the room, melting me into a pile of goo with his decadent smirk.

ELIN

THE MUSIC IS streaming overhead, scents of oregano and tomato sauce wafting through the door as I clutch Ty's hand as he leads me into Thoroughbreds. He glances at me over his shoulder, his eyes sparkling in the halogen lights, as the doors chime shut behind us.

I squeeze his hand; it's met with a gentle clasping of his own.

I can't stop smiling. I haven't stopped since we came up for air a few hours ago. Not that he has either, nor has he stopped touching me in some way, like he's afraid I won't be there if he breaks contact. There have been no objections from me.

"Now that's a sight for sore eyes!" Jiggs shouts, tipping a beer bottle our way.

Our friends are at our usual table in the corner. The looks on their faces make Ty and I laugh as they see us together, our fingers interlocked.

"All is right in the world!" Lindsay says, standing up and hugging me. I return the embrace with one hand because Ty won't let go of my other.

"Yeah, we are getting there."

"Excuse me," she says, clearing her throat. "You do remember me, right? I'm Lindsay Watson, married to a man that you grew up with. You remember Jiggs?"

"Shut up," I laugh. "I've been . . . busy."

She looks at my husband and giggles. "Oh, I bet you have. How are ya, Ty?"

"Much better these days," he winks.

A hand touches my shoulder and I jump, as does Ty. We turn to see Cord beaming behind us, one hand on each of us.

"Finally," he laughs. "My God, I thought the two of you were gonna kill me. Hard-headed bastards."

"Yeah, she is," Ty says, laughing as I knock him with my shoulder.

"Come on, let's play some pool," Jiggs says.

Ty kisses me, letting his lips linger much longer than necessary, before joining my brother at the table in front of us. "Cord, wanna play?" he asks.

"Nope. I suck."

"Which is why we want you to play," Ty jokes. "So we can kick your ass."

We watch them rack the balls and then Jiggs break. We all feel it, I know we do, the feeling of our tribe being back together. It's the way things should be.

"I have to say," Lindsay says, "seeing you walk in here with him made my day. Did you get everything figured out?"

"Some things just have to be shelved and hope that time heals like it's supposed to. I'm trying to let things go."

"You will," Lindsay says, standing up. "I gotta pee. I'm sorry. I'm drinking all this water because I literally crave water all day. All night. But then I have to pee constantly," she laughs, hand on her belly, and makes a beeline for the restroom.

Turning to my right, Cord is watching me. He takes a long draw of his beer and settles back in his chair with a smirk.

"What?" I ask, taking my drink from the server. "Why are you looking at me like that?"

"No reason," he says, the dimple in his cheek settling in.

I sip my cola and watch my friend make fun of me without making fun of me. His adorableness making me roll my eyes. "Oh, there's a reason," I say. "You're just scared to tell me what it is."

"Hell, yeah, I am. You're not known as the pit bull for nothing."

"Oh, shut up!" I laugh, tossing a napkin at him. "That nickname is so unwarranted."

"Whatever. I've seen you in action, babe." He leans forward and peers at me. "So, you took my advice, I see."

"Yes, I took your advice," I say. "It was good advice. What can I say?"

"You could say, 'Wow, Cord, you're a genius.' Or tell me how handsome I am or how I just saved your life. Any of those would be sufficient."

Laughing, I watch Ty's ass in his jeans as he bends over the table to take a shot. "Cord, I love you. And you're handsome and you might've saved my marriage. But you being a genius and saving my actual life are stretching it."

"Fair enough," he admits, shrugging his shoulders. "You know, maybe I should've been a psychiatrist. I could charge big money for this shit."

"Don't do that. Then you'll be all expensive and book up for a year at a time and I won't get free help."

"Ah, I'd never charge you. Even if I become the next big thing, you'll still have total access to me for no charge."

"Good to know," I laugh, placing my drink on a napkin and look at him. I toss him a grin and he blanches.

"That look on your face scares me," he says, pointing his finger at me.

"Let's talk about you," I say sweetly, buttering him up.

He groans, rolling his eyes. "Let's not."

My excitement is all over my face. I know this because of Cord's reaction, which makes me laugh. "We need to get you a girl."

"Nah."

"Come on, McCurry. It's time you step out of this bachelor role and settle down."

He leans back in his chair, his eyes darkening. His fingers lace together, planted on his lap. "I have no intentions of settling down."

"And why not?"

"Pushy much?" he laughs.

"You know this about me," I giggle. "We need you to get a girl and be happy."

"Maybe I'm happy the way I am."

"How could you be?" I sigh. "Everyone needs someone to love, someone to relax with and have fun with."

"I have Yogi."

"Cord . . ."

Leaning forward, his eyes peer into mine. "Look, Elin. I appreciate you trying to do what you think is best for me. I do. But not everyone is built the way you are."

"Not everyone is built . . . awesome?"

"Try . . . built to settle down." He releases a heavy breath. "I don't have the capacity to love like you do, Elin."

I blanch, my brows pulling together. "What the hell are you talking about?"

"I don't," he says, shaking his head. "I've never felt love like you have with Ty or like you had with your parents. It's always just been . . . me."

"You saying you don't love me?" I tease.

"You know what I mean," he chuckles. "I don't know how to give that kind of love or feel it, even, I guess. It's not something I know."

He smiles, tries to play it off for me, but my heart cracks at the idea. How can this man, one of the sweetest men I know, feel this way?

"Cord, buddy, you love all of us. Think about it." I bite my tongue, trying to choose my words carefully. I know this is all because his mother didn't want him and I hate her for that. But I'm not sure saying that will help right now. "You just haven't met the right girl yet, maybe."

"Maybe. I'll just keep the friends-with-benefits thing going awhile. But that motherfucker," he says, looking over my shoulder, "isn't one of my friends."

I turn to see what he's referring to. Pettis is approaching our table, his cousin, Sharp, by his side.

"Oh, shit," I mutter, looking up at Ty. He's leaned against the table, not missing a thing.

"How are you fine folks this evening?" Pettis asks, his grin that of a movie villain.

Before we can respond, Becca walks up beside Pettis. "Can I get you guys anything else?" She scans the group, picking up on the awkwardness, before her gaze lands on Cord.

Without thinking, she brushes her hair off her shoulder and smiles wide. "Need anything, Cord?"

"I think I'm good, Becca. Thank you," he drawls, a kind smile flashing her way while holding on to the fury aimed at Pettis.

Pettis laughs. "I could use a beer."

"I'll grab it," Becca says, tearing her eyes away from Cord. "Anything in particular?"

Pettis scans her up and down and grins. "Wanna do something after you get off?"

Cord stands, shocking everyone with his quick movement. "Nah, she doesn't."

"I'm pretty sure she can answer for herself," Pettis says.

Becca's eyes go wide, as do mine, as she watches Cord's reaction. His All-American look just took a turn to the dark side and it's intriguing. His jaw sets tight as he peers down at Pettis.

"Tell him, Becca. We're going out tonight."

"Um," she stumbles, her cheeks heating as she obviously scrambles to stay on top of whatever it is Cord's playing. "Yeah. Um, Cord asked me to go out later. Sorry."

Jumping to my feet to take the attention off Becca, I flash Pettis a cheesy smile as Sharp laughs from his side.

"You're Whitt's old lady, aren't ya?" he asks, taking a step to me.

"Fuck off, Sharp," I say, holding my ground. There's a twist of anxiety in my gut, but I override it. "No one wants you here." I can feel Ty behind me, his energy bouncing off me.

"You might not, but what about you, Whitt?" Sharp asks, his words as piercing as his name. "Since we're taking orders here tonight, you need anything?"

"Get out of here, Sharp," Ty growls, moving me to the side. "This isn't the time or the place for this."

"What?" Pettis laughs. "You don't want your wifey here to know you and Sharp are buds. That you were buying a little something-something off him while she was taking care of the kids at school?"

"That's enough," Cord rumbles, making Becca take a step back towards Jiggs.

Sharp and Pettis laugh, their voices as dirty as the fibers of the shirts covering their needle-pricked skin. "It's hard to tell the wives sometimes, especially when you have that pretty boy image you got going on, that you are just like the rest of us."

"Fuck you, Sharp. I never bought a fucking thing from you."

He shrugs, a dopey grin on his face. "But you were going to. You called me. Remember that? Or is that wiped out now that princess here took you back?"

Pettis laughs again, his voice rolling through the pub. "You always thought you were better than the rest of us. The Golden Boy from Jackson, can do no wrong. I'm telling ya, kids, the golden boy has fallen from grace. Does she know about you and that redhead in Rockville, Ty?"

"What?" I gasp, looking at Ty. My attention isn't there for long because Cord lurches forward.

"Well, I never had grace to start with," Cord says as his fist flies through the air between them.

The sound of Cord's hand smashing against Pettis' face ricochets through the room. His head flops back, blood trickling from his nose, as he stumbles to stay on his feet. Sharp grabs his shoulder and steadies him.

"I warned you," Cord says, his fists clenching at his sides.

"Hey!" Bob Gurley, the owner of the pub, says as he rushes our way. "What's happening over here?"

"These guys were starting trouble," Becca says, looking at Pettis and Sharp over her shoulder. "And someone put them in their place." Her gaze flutters to Cord and he gives her a small smile.

"Get out of here, Pettis," Bob says. "I warned you the last time you were in here all hopped up on God knows what to stay out of my business."

"This is a free country," Pettis says, grabbing a napkin off the table and wiping his nose.

"And this is a private business," Bob says. "Get out."

Pettis shoots us a dirty look as he turns on his heel and heads for the door. Before he leaves he looks over his shoulder. "You've opened a can of worms, McCurry. Be ready."

"Fuck him," Cord says, falling back in his chair. He shakes his hand before inspecting it for damage.

Ty tries to take my hand, but I shake him off. Everyone but the two of us seems oblivious to Pettis' statement.

"I kind of stole your glory," Cord laughs, looking at my husband. "But I warned him once. I had to follow through."

"A man of your word," Ty laughs.

Becca rushes up with a towel full of ice. Bending down, she takes Cord's hand from me and lays the bundle gently on top. I take a few steps away from Ty, my head reeling.

Redhead? In Rockville? Who was that? I look at Ty and his face is pale. *Let this be one of Pettis' games. Please.*

"Does this hurt?" Becca asks Cord, her elbow accidentally brushing me in the thigh.

"Feels the best it's felt in a long time," Cord responds.

Becca blushes, her hand shaking just a bit. "I know you didn't mean the date was for real, but thank you for intervening there."

"What do you mean the date wasn't for real?" Cord asks, smirking. "I was hoping you would do something with me tonight. Or tomorrow. Whatever you can swing."

"Really? I'd like that."

Ty takes my hand and starts to tug me to the door. Jerking my hand away, not ready to hear something that could ruin everything,

I start around the chairs and to the pool table with Jiggs and Lindsay.

Lindsay giggles. "I knew there was chemistry there," she says, nodding at Cord and Becca. "Or that there would be. I could feel it."

"I hope so," I say, watching Becca blush.

"Has your friend here told you what she wants to do?" Jiggs asks me.

Glancing at my brother, I can see the line of irritation just below the surface. It's the same look I see in the mirror when I'm trying desperately to not lose my cool, when I'm playing something off.

"What's that?" I ask, switching my gaze to Lindsay.

She fumbles with a straw from her glass of water. "You want to do this again, Jiggs?" she sighs.

"No, I don't want to do anything. I'm pretty certain I made that clear."

"What are you two talking about?" Ty asks, his hand finding my waist.

"Lindsay wants to move to Florida."

My stomach flip-flops. "You're still talking about this? You can't be serious."

"She's serious," Jiggs says, a little too loud so his voice overrides hers. "I had an email this morning from a realtor in Sarasota. Apparently my wife has asked them to find a house near her parents and they wanted to know if a pool was a definite no."

"Lindsay!" My jaw hits the floor as Jiggs watches me. "You can't leave. Your life is here."

A heavy breath escapes her lips. It's obvious she's been through this conversation a few times before, and it's not one she wants to revisit.

"What is there for us here? For any of us?" Lindsay asks. "We are having a baby. What can we offer it here?"

"A family," I scoff. "You could offer it a family here."

"And Jiggs' family is here," Ty says, squeezing my hips with his large hands. "You can't just expect him to walk away from Elin. Me. Cord."

She smiles, but it's not real. It's a stretching of her lips, a physical, put-on gesture that has no substance behind it. "We can all go. Let's leave this place for something more . . . stable."

Imploring her with every nonverbal cue I can manage, I ask her to stop being crazy. To not throw things in a tizzy right when they're being worked out. But she doesn't take them. I can see it on her face.

"I expect him to do what's best for our child," she says matter-of-factly. "You would do the same thing, Elin."

"I . . ." There are so many ways to take her statement that I can't land on one to respond to. I just stand there and stare at her, feeling the weight of Ty and Jiggs' eyes on me.

"I'm ready to go," she says, looking at my brother. "You ready?"

"Sure."

Lindsay gives me a hug that lacks any warmth to it at all. "See you later."

She sidesteps me and then her voice drifts my way as she says goodbye to Cord, leaving me looking at Jiggs.

"Ty, give me a minute with my brother," I say. He kisses me on the cheek, but I pull away from it. Once he's gone, I give Jiggs a half-hearted smile. "She's just hormonal. She won't go through with it."

His shoulders sag and I can't take it. Wrapping him in my arms, I squeeze him as tightly as I can.

"I love ya," Jiggs whispers against my ear. "We'll work it out."

"I know," I say, pulling back. "Keep your chin up."

He tilts it in the air, taking my words at face value, and I laugh.

"Let me ask you something," I say so only he can hear. "Do you think Ty would cheat on me? Even if he had drugs in his system? Even if he was mad?"

"Absolutely not." There's no hesitation in Jiggs' reply. "You know I'd tell you the truth. And if I thought that was even true, I'd kill the motherfucker. But he's not capable of that, Elin. He's not built that way."

He waits to see if I'm going to ask anything else and when it's apparent I'm not, he clasps my shoulder and leaves.

"Let's go," Ty says, nodding towards the door.

My jaw clenches, steeling myself for the possibility of something I don't want to hear, I nod.

He takes my hand so I can't pull it away and laces our fingers together. "Mr. McCurry, we are out of here."

"You just got here," he objects.

"Well, you have a hot date to keep your eye on," I point out. "You don't need us."

"I do, indeed," Cord grins. "I'll catch you tomorrow."

"Come by in the afternoon. Bring Becca. I'll make food."

"Don't have to tell me twice," Cord says.

Before I can respond, Ty's dragging me out of the restaurant.

THE DOOR SLAMS, vibrating Ty's sunglasses off the dashboard. The key goes in the ignition just as forcefully before we speed out of the parking lot.

"Want to tell me Pettis is full of shit?" I ask, my arms folded over my chest. Leaning away from the middle console, as far out of arm's reach as I can get, I look straight ahead.

He blows out a breath, worry lines creasing his forehead. "I didn't see Pettis while I was gone."

"Okay, well, that's really good to know," I bite out, "but that's not the part I'm worried about."

"He's such a fucking asshole."

"Right now, you're looking like the asshole."

Ty starts to glare at me out of the corner of his eye, but catches himself. "Elin, it's not what you think."

"Then fucking start talking, Tyler. Because you said you weren't with someone else. Remember that? Remember me telling you that was the one thing I couldn't handle?"

"I wasn't with her!"

Flinching, my arms smack against my legs. "Her? So there *is* a her?"

"Not like that."

"I don't care what it was like. If she exists, this is over."

"She's the granddaughter of Kruger, all right? I can't even figure out how Pettis saw us together," he laments.

"Fuck you!" I gasp. "You fucking cheat!"

"I didn't cheat on you!" He flips the radio off, even though it could barely be heard over the blood soaring through my veins. "I was with her a couple of times getting shit for the Kruger's. I was never with her like that. Not like Pettis implied."

There are no tears. Watching the passing landscape, I try to process this.

"Elin, I swear to you . . ."

"Don't you see?" I say, whipping my head to his. "None of this would even be discussed had you not left."

"What do you want me to do?" he booms. "I fucked up, Elin. All right, you got me. You win."

"I win? What the hell are you talking about?"

"Is this what you want? You want to ruin everything we've started to figure out because Pettis is a dick? Because you let what he says fucking matter?"

"What he says doesn't matter," I seethe. "What matters is you being a liar."

The chuckle rumbling through the cab of the truck is ominous. "You know what? You think what you want. If you really think I'd do that, then you don't know me at all." The truck takes the turn into our driveway at an acute angle, gravel flying every direction. The engine is cut and he looks at me, his eyes blazing. "This one is up to you. Believe me. If you don't, you can be the one to run away from everything this time."

ELIN

"TY!" I SHOUT, my steps pounding down the sidewalk after him. "Wait."

He doesn't, but he does leave the back door open. When I step inside, he's leaning against the stove, waiting for me. His mouth is set in a firm line, not like a man hiding something. But like a man that's been accused of something heinous.

"He's not capable of that, Elin. He's not built that way."

"You swear you weren't having an affair?" I gulp. My hands are twisting in front of me as I try to read even the most minute pieces of his body language.

"I swear."

No effort is made to come towards me; the ball is left in my court. I'm not sure what to do with it.

"You promise?" I ask again.

He shoves off the appliance, his lips twitching. "You already asked me that."

"So?"

"You want me to pinkie swear?" he teases. "Want to call Kruger and ask him if his granddaughter and I went into town for supplies a time or two? Maybe you'd like to call her, but I'd have to call Kruger first to get her number and being that Nila—that's her name—is getting married in a couple of weeks, I'm going to guess he won't be pleased."

Biting my lip, I watch him take a step towards me. Then another. Before I know it, his lips are at my ear. "Why in the world would I ever want another woman when I have you?"

I melt into him, both from his words and the relief of knowing he's telling me the truth. "Ty," I breathe, walking until my back hits the cabinets. "I don't want to tell you to stop . . ." Moaning as his kisses turn into soft bites against the skin at the base of my neck, my hands find his back and press him into me.

Grabbing the cabinet on either side of me, he touches his lips to mine. Working my lips over with his soft, smooth mouth, I nearly turn into a pile of mush on the floor.

My jaw slacks and he wastes no time taking full advantage. His tongue swipes the inside of my bottom lip before leisurely dragging over mine.

My hands thread together at the back of his neck. I press him towards me, wanting—needing—this connection.

He presses against me, and I feel his solidness against my belly. My core flames, an intense burst with no build-up, just a red-hot fire that flows into the apex of my thighs.

With no warning, he stills. His mouth pulls from mine, his body retracting.

"Ty?" I ask, panting. "What the hell?"

Shoving off the cabinet, he reaches behind me. I follow his hand as he draws an envelope in front of my face.

The corner of his lip is upturned, his brows shooting upwards as well. "Let's take care of this first."

"The envelope from Parker?" I ask incredulously, grabbing at his hips.

"I can't focus if I know it's sitting on the counter."

He's toying with me, but I'm not in the mood. I reach out and jerk the envelope from him. My eyes meeting his and holding the envelope mid-air, the tearing sound rips through the room as I split it in half.

His smile grows as does the slash in the papers. I don't smile, don't frown, just keep pulling until there is one piece in each hand.

"They no longer exist," I say, handing him both halves. "Now fuck me."

Laughing, he tosses the envelope in the trash and is standing in front of me before I realize it.

"Are you sure you can handle more?" he teases, his fingers playing with the hem of my dress. "You took a lot of dick this morning."

I gasp as his fingers skim over the tops of my thighs and work their way so, so slowly upwards.

"Maybe you're out of shape," I counter, trying to keep my voice calm. "Maybe you can't deliver again."

His chest rumbles as he releases a low, sexy chuckle. "I can deliver. Don't you worry about that."

"What are you waiting for?" I tilt my hips, brushing my pussy over his hand. "Feel how wet I am?"

"You're dripping down my hand," he growls, placing his palm on my pubic bone. Applying pressure there, two fingers spread lower, over my clit, and dip into my wetness.

I hiss a breath, widening my stance, feeling his touch right where I need it.

"You like that?" he asks, knowing good and well that I do.

"Does it feel like I do?"

"It feels like you do," he says, strumming my clit with the pad of his finger. "It feels like you want more than this."

"Ah," I groan, grinding my body against his hand. "I need you, Ty. I need you now."

His mouth captures mine, his tongue commanding mine in a display of ownership, creating a blissful sensation from head to toe.

Before I know what's happening, he drops to his knees. He motions for my legs to widen before his fingers drag from my ass all that way to my clit.

His eyes never leave mine, his free hand biting into my hip and holding me in place.

"My God, Ty," I moan, my head falling back. "Ah!" I yelp as his face presses into me. His tongue rolls my swollen bud before pressing then flicking it, working me into a frenzy.

A finger, then two, enter my opening—in and out in the most wonderful form of torture I can imagine.

Just as I begin to see a flurry of colors, my body starting to lift off to bliss, he pulls away.

His hands digging into my hips, he dots kisses against the insides of my thighs, leaving a trail of assaulted skin behind as he stands.

Breathless, we gasp for air. I grab the button of his pants and work furiously to undo it. The zipper sounds as I tug it down and push his jeans and boxers over his hips. They pool on the floor.

His cock is solid and heavy as I take it in my hand. Stroking the length, a dot of pre-cum glistens at the tip. I fall to my knees and smile as Ty's eyes eagerly meet mine.

My tongue flicks against the top, the softness meeting the hard. Ty hisses a breath as I lick the liquid from the tip of his cock.

I take the head in my mouth and roll my tongue around it. My free hand cups his balls, and squeezing them gently as I stroke his shaft, I watch my husband's face coat with pleasure.

Licking around the head before letting my tongue draw down his length and around the base, I drag it back to the top along the underside.

His hips thrust forward, his hands embedding in my hair, as I take his cock into my mouth. Pumping him tightly, just the way he likes it, I feel the smoothness of his skin inside my mouth.

"Fuck, E," he moans. His hands on my head urge me on, the head of his cock beginning to swell further.

Keeping the pace, I work him higher, feeling myself grow wetter with each passing second. Angling forward to take more of his size into my mouth, I look him in the eye.

His greens are filled with unbridled lust and I smile, flicking my tongue against his tip. I find the spot just behind his balls and press two fingertips against it with unrelenting pressure. His entire body shivers, his eyes flutter closed as a hiss escapes his throat.

"Feels good, doesn't it?" I ask, massaging that spot with the pads of my fingers.

I take him into my mouth again and roll the tip around like a sucker. The suction pops as I release it. "You should feel how wet I am. My pussy is begging for you."

I'm pulled to my feet instantly and am led across the kitchen to the table.

"Your pussy will never have to beg for long," he says, standing behind me.

Leaning over the table and grabbing the other side, I glance at him over my shoulder. His cock in his hand, his chest now bare, he looks at me like he's about to devour me.

I shake my ass side to side and grin. "What are you waiting for?"

"Just enjoying the sight," he says.

The tip of his cock swirls around my opening before I feel it part me. He enters me slowly, yet with enough force that it's blissfully uncomfortable. Once he's all the way in, he pauses, running his fingers down my spine. Then he begins to move and I lose all contact with reality.

I PEEK UNDER the foil. The cheese is the perfect golden color and the spaghetti sauce is bubbling beneath. Sticking the pan of garlic knots on the rack below, I close the oven.

Wiping my hands off, I toss the towel on the table as I pull open the kitchen door. The sky is a beautiful shade of orange and blue as the sun begins its descent below the horizon.

It's a peaceful evening, a great ending to a pretty good day. After the fight and amazing makeup between Ty and myself, today was a little touch-and-go to start. As the day wore on, I realized being mad at Ty for something Pettis said wasn't worth it. I have to trust him and I do. I'm trusting my gut.

My lungs pull in the crisp air as I walk down the sidewalk and to the sound of a hammer in front.

Rounding the corner, I see Ty nailing up a loose board on the garage. Wearing a pair of jeans with a hole in the knee, a long-sleeved white thermal shirt, and his Arrows cap, he looks edible.

He glances up at me. "What are you looking at?" he laughs.

"Just wondering if the sexy man working on my garage wants to go in for dinner?"

"Does he get you for dessert?"

"That could be arranged."

He stands and puts his tools back in the bag and disappears to the side. As he puts his stuff away, I spy a basketball lying beneath the hoop. I pick it up and take a couple of shots, missing both.

I hear his laugh before I see him. "It's hard to imagine you're the wife of a basketball coach with a jump shot like that."

"My husband doesn't teach me how to shoot," I pout.

"What a dick he must be," Ty smirks. Extending his hands to the front, I toss him the ball. He shoots from where he's standing, barely jumping or trying, and the ball swishes through the net. "That turns you on, doesn't it?"

Rolling my eyes, I shoot again. And miss.

"That turns me on," he says, retrieving my shot. "That's why I haven't taught you to shoot. I just like watching your boobs bounce like that when you miss."

"You're an asshole," I tease, catching the ball.

He follows the ball and presses a kiss to my lips. "Play me a game."

"Why would I do that?"

"I'll make it worth your while."

Tilting my head to the side, I sigh. "And how's that?"

"If you win," he says, "I'll do dishes for a week. And if I win . . . I'll eat your pussy every night for a week."

Laughing, I shoot him a look. "That doesn't seem like you win either way."

"How do you figure? If I do dishes, you'll be happy and that makes me happy. If I'm eating your pussy—and let's face it, that's gonna be the end result of this—we're both happy."

"Silly boy," I say.

Throwing the ball towards the net, I'm shocked that it goes through. Ty rebounds and takes my place, easily swishing the ball through the net.

I shoot again and miss. He shoots and drains it from the edge of the driveway.

"Damn it," I say, putting my feet where his were. "There's no way I'll make that."

"Nope, there isn't," he laughs. "I'm all about watching your body. So, you know, go ahead and shoot."

I do and it doesn't come close.

"That's an H," he says, draining another one from the other side.

Before I can shoot, Jiggs' truck rumbles down the road and into the driveway. I flinch as his headlights shine in my eyes until he flips them off.

The door to his truck whines as he opens it and climbs out. "What are you two doin'?" he asks, motioning for me to toss him the ball. I do and he shoots and makes it.

"Playing HORSE," Ty informs him. "I just won."

I start to object, to point out the game isn't over, but he flashes me a look so sinful I nearly melt into the driveway.

"I made baked spaghetti," I say instead. "Where's Lindsay?"

"Home. She's not feeling good." His eyes settle on me and I read between the lines.

"Did you two fight all night?"

"More or less," he sighs.

Before he can expound, Cord's truck hits the gravel and comes to a stop next to Jiggs'. Yogi stands in the back, takes in the scene, before lying back down as Cord and Becca get out of the truck.

I wait for a smile, a grin, but they don't come. Flashing Becca a questioning glance, she shrugs.

"Hey," Ty greets them. "You guys hungry?"

"I hear you're a great cook," Becca says, pulling me into a quick hug. "Do you have a bathroom I can use?"

"Sure," I say, taking in the worry lines around her eyes. "It's through the door to the right. Want me to walk you in?"

"No, that's okay," she says and heads off. I get the distinct feeling she wants a few minutes alone, so I let her go.

The boys are in the midst of a conversation when I turn around. Jiggs looks at Ty, and I see his Adam's apple bob in his throat. He doesn't look at me, and it's clear he's making a concerted effort not to.

"What are you talking about?" I ask, my eyes trained on my brother because I know he'll break way before my husband.

Ty turns his back to me, his head twisting back and forth. "Damn it, Jiggs. You could've called me instead."

"How was I supposed to know you hadn't told her? This isn't a bad thing, you know."

"What in the world are you talking about?" I demand. Although I know the answer, I want to hear it from them.

I want to hear it from Ty.

I watch his back tense, his shoulders stiffen, his lungs drawing in a deep breath before he turns to face me. His eyes are dark, his jaw set firmly in place. "Blackwater called. The mine is reopening this week."

Goose bumps ripple across my skin as I begin to shuffle backwards. "You aren't going though, right?" I look from Ty, to Jiggs, to Cord, and back to Ty. My mouth goes dry as they fail to respond.

"E . . ."

I fire a look at Jiggs. "Are you going back?"

"Of course," my brother says. "I'm a miner, Elin. My wife is having a baby. I need a job."

"Are you going, Cord?"

"Yes," he sighs and places a hand on my shoulder. "It's normal to be worried. The last time you dealt with that place, your husband came out on a stretcher."

"He was almost killed!" I say, pointing to Ty. He's watching me, a wariness settling over him.

"Do you have any idea what I felt when they called and told me you'd been hit by that timber? That you were on your way to the emergency room and they didn't know how bad it was?" I ask, tears burning my eyes. "I thought, 'This is it. This is the accident we all wait for. The one my mom waited for when my dad mined, the one my grandmother prayed to avoid every morning when Grandpa left for the fields. It's happened to me.'"

I squeeze my eyes closed. "I got there and they wouldn't let me see you. They said you were in surgery, and I kept thinking that I didn't get to tell you goodbye that morning. You left without waking me up, do you remember that?"

He nods, reaching for me. I take his hand and let him pull me to his side. His arm stretches around my shoulder, holding me close.

I look at Jiggs. "You guys can't go back down there. You just can't." Glancing from Ty to Cord and back to Jiggs, I reiterate it again. "None of you can go back there."

"We get it, Elin, we do," Jiggs says. "We were down there when that thing fell on him. I was scared to beat all hell. There are no other jobs here."

"You could go back to school. You could—"

"And go into debt? And get a degree that we can never use? And how are we going to pay the bills while we are doing that?" Ty asks.

I'm too numb for the tears to fall. My shoulders slump, my mind vaguely remembering the spaghetti in the oven, but I can't even bother to mention it.

"We've applied everywhere," Jiggs says, shrugging. "No one is hiring. For every opening, there's fifty applicants. This is all we have, not to mention my wife is wanting me to move to fucking Florida over the job market. This is a good thing, Elin. This is what we've been hoping for."

Burying my head in my hands, I breathe as deeply and slowly as I can. I'm acting irrational. I know that.

We watch each other, a crackle in the air between us. Ty draws me in with this sincerity, with the look of love and protection in his eyes. I place my hand on his chest and feel his heart beat strongly, passionately.

"I was going to talk to you about it tonight," he says, his voice low enough for just me to hear.

"After you beat me in HORSE?" I say, blinking back my tears.

"I was going to beat you, take you inside, take my winnings, and then figure out how to discuss this."

"So," I say, wiping my eyes, "you were going to lick me senseless and use that to weaken me?"

"Shut. Up," Jiggs groans.

"Exactly," Ty laughs, the warmth in his tone making me smile.

I pull myself as close to him as possible. "Promise me you'll come home every night."

"Of course," he says. "Promise me you'll be home every night when I get here."

I grin up at my husband. "I will. Because you have a bet to make good on."

"Yes, I fucking do."

"Enough," Jiggs groans. "I'm going inside. You said something about spaghetti."

Jiggs and Ty walk away. As I start to follow them, I look around for Cord. He's standing at his truck, his elbows on the tailgate, scratching Yogi behind her ears.

Heading his direction, I smack him on the back as I near. "What's wrong with you?"

"Not much."

"Liar."

He glances at me over his shoulder, shaking his head. "You're a pain in my ass, you know that?"

"I do. Now 'fess up, McCurry."

He looks towards the house and gives a little wave to Becca through the window. She smiles back, but doesn't come out to us.

"Did something happen with her?" I ask, petting the dog.

A small laugh rumbles out of him. "Not really. She's a good girl."

"So? I don't see the problem."

He gives Yogi one final nuzzle before facing me. Taking a deep breath, he speaks. "My phone rang this morning."

"My phone rings all the time."

"Smartass," he laughs. "So do you pick yours up and it happens to be the woman that gave birth to you that gave you up for adoption that you've met once in your life?"

The gasp I emit is quick and shaky. My eyes are bulging, my hand going to my mouth. "You're kidding me."

The color of his eyes, usually so playful and clear, are dirtied with unnamed emotion. He doesn't look like the Cord I'm used to seeing: sharp, fun, smart. He reminds me of one of the kids in my class that is in trouble and afraid.

His head shakes side to side. "She's incarcerated somewhere in Kansas."

"What's she want you to do about it?" I say that, but then realize that's not even what I'm thinking. "Why would she even call you about that? What the hell, Cord?"

"I don't know," he sighs, clearly torn about his predicament.

"So, how does that conversation go?" I ask, starting to see red as I watch Cord fight with the situation this callous and despicable woman put him in. "Hey, I'm the lady that hasn't cared about you for your entire life. But I need help so come help me?"

"Basically." He leans against the truck, his head in his hands. Yogi comes up and licks his forehead.

"Fuck her, Cord. You don't owe her anything."

"The jail said she was arrested for drug trafficking. If I bail her out, I'd be responsible for her—"

"Oh, no," I say, pulling his hands down so he'll look at me. "You aren't bailing her out. I can see on your face that you feel responsible for this somehow, like because she called you that you should run and help her, but you aren't."

Shoving away from the vehicle, he crosses his arms over his chest. "I know that. I do. I'm not stupid, Elin."

"I know," I say, my hand resting on his bicep. "But I hate seeing her put you in this spot."

"I don't even know how she got my number."

"She can lose it," I say, squeezing his arm before letting go.

"She's nothing to you. We are your family."

The words wash over his face, inch by inch, until they begin to lift the corners of his lips. "Thank you."

Waving my hand in the air, I snort. "No thanks needed. You know I love telling you what to do."

"No shit," he laughs, wrapping an arm around my shoulder and starting towards my house. "I don't think this thing with Becca is going to work out though."

"Why?" I ask, stopping in my tracks. "I thought it was going good."

"We hung out last night and today a little. She's a great girl."

I nod, an exaggerated up and down, agreeing with him. He laughs at my antics, but the heaviness is back in his eyes.

"She needs someone that is ready to give her a house and a family. That guy's not me, Elin."

"He could be you!"

"He's not," he laughs. "My life turns into a mess every time I think about trying to make something out of it."

Huffing, I nearly stomp my foot. "That's not true."

"It is. And it's okay." His arm goes back over my shoulders again and we hit the stairs to the house. "I'm just the sidekick, the guy that wanders aimlessly around. I'm okay with that."

He pulls the door open and waits for me to go inside. Before I do, I study his face long and hard. "Everyone has a purpose in life. Even you."

"I wish I could figure it out," he groans as I walk by.

"You will. I promise."

Starting inside, I'm stopped by the sound of a phone ringing behind me. Looking over my shoulder, I see Ty's phone on the lawn chair by the basketball net.

Jogging down the driveway, I snag it. Swiping the screen on, I answer it. "Hello?" I say breathlessly.

"Hello," a female voice responds. "Is Ty there?"

"Um, who is this?"

"Tell him it's Nila."

Red. Instantly, I see explosions of red-hot fury. My hand trembles, almost dropping the phone, as I catch myself from telling her off. Instead, I give her what she wants. I'll get what I want at the same time—the truth.

"Just a second," I say, heading towards the house.

Before I hit the steps to the patio, Ty pokes his head outside. He starts to say something, but reads my face first.

"You have a call." I extend my hand, the phone lying in my palm like a dead fish. "It's Nila."

Stepping gingerly towards me, the door shutting behind him, he takes the phone.

"Answer it," I demand.

"This is Ty." He listens to the voice on the other side, smiling easily. "Yeah, I'm good. How are you?"

My blood pressure soars sky-high, my body shaking with fury as I listen to him banter so effortlessly with Nila—whoever the hell she is.

"No, I didn't," Ty says. "I'll look for it though." He turns his back to me. "You're joking?"

I listen as he whistles through his teeth, taking off his baseball hat and rubbing the top of his head. "Wow, Nila. I don't know what to say . . ."

"I do," I mutter. The sound of my voice has Ty spinning around to face me. I glare. He laughs. I flip him off. He grabs my wrist and holds me in place.

"If not, I'll swing up that way and see ya. I'll let you know. Thanks for calling," he says, his voice super sweet. He tosses me a wink as I jerk my hand away from his. "It was good to see you too. Tell your Grandpa thanks again for me."

As soon as the call is ended, my finger is in his chest. "You lied to me!"

"Calm down," he scoffs, clearly entertained by my reaction.

"I'm not calming down! She called you. The girl that you didn't do anything with."

I start to march to the door, but his arm is around my waist, dragging me into his arms. "Will you stop acting like this?" he laughs. "What's wrong with you?"

My arms pinned to my sides, I struggle to break free. "You are what's wrong with me."

"Tell you what," he says, resting his head on the top of my head. "Let's make a deal."

"I don't deal with liars."

"I don't normally deal with lunatics, either, but I'm making an exception tonight, so I guess you can too."

The complete lack of fear or frustration in his voice calms me a little. I stop fighting to pull away.

"Let's go in and have dinner with our friends. Then we can go to bed and I will tell you everything you want to know about Nila Kruger." He plants a kiss to the back of my head. "And if you're a good girl, I'll let you have my cock after we're done talking."

"I doubt I'll want it," I sigh, trying to not succumb to him.

"There you go, lying again," he laughs. Swatting me on my ass towards the house, I reach for his hand. He laces our fingers together and we head inside.

Twenty-Five

TY

HER FINGERS SKIRT over the scars on my back, drifting delicately over the raised skin. Her arm is draped over my side, her cheek pressed into my chest, as we lie in silence.

She's still mad. I don't think she would be if she knew how adorable she is when she's mad over nothing. It's been entertaining to watch.

Warmth surrounds me, and not just from her naked body or the blankets on our bed or the fact that she has the thermostat set on seventy-six. It's a contentedness, a satisfied, relaxed peace that I'm not sure I've ever felt before.

"What are you thinking?" she whispers, her tone thick with sleep.

"Just how much I love you."

She presses a kiss to my sternum.

"What are you thinking?" I ask, closing my eyes and feeling her touch.

Her chest rises and falls against mine before she looks up at me. "I don't know how to put it, exactly."

Wrapping my arms around her, feeling her silky skin beneath me, I release a heavy breath. "Things feel different between us, don't you think?"

"In what way?"

"Like . . ." I shrug. "I don't know. Like we made it through all this shit and now we're on the other side. We fought the fight and now we're here with the scars to prove it. Nothing could ever get between us now."

"Except secrets," she says warily. Her hand wallops my chest as I start laughing. "I'm trying, Ty. I'm trying to believe you but you're making it really hard."

Taking her hand, I move it to my cock. "You can say that again."

She huffs, still irritated and wanting me to cut to the chase. She's not about to ask—her pride won't let her. But she'll dance around the topic all night if I let her. I might.

"The two of us," I sigh.

"What?"

"How do you feel about it being the two of us? I mean, with everything that's happened?" I angle myself so I can see her eyes. "Do you want it to be the three of us someday? Or four? Or five?"

"Maybe once we work things out," she whispers. "Once we're in a better position financially, we can make another appointment and see."

Swallowing hard, she tries to look away, but I don't let her. Finances are one thing, but that's not what's bothering her. I capture her chin with my fingers and hold it in place.

"What if I lose another baby?" she asks, fear dripping off each word.

I suck in a breath to steady my words before I release them into the universe. "Then *we* do. Because whatever happens is you and me, not you alone. Got it?"

Her lips tilt in a soft grin, and I kiss her in response.

"Whatever happens in either of our lives—we do together. We've proven we don't do well alone," I laugh.

"No, we don't," she chuckles.

"I can handle whatever happens in my life as long as you're by my side, Elin. And I'll be there, holding your hand, as you go through yours. And at night, we will end up here, in bed, together, and we'll laugh about our day and plan the next. Sound like a plan?"

Her leg lies over mine and she holds my face in her hands. The smile on her face has mine mirroring it. "When did you know you loved me?" she asks.

I think back, trying to remember the exact moment. I remember the first day I saw her at her locker and the way my heart fluttered in my chest. I recall listening to her in Spanish class, trying to sound out the words and being obsessed with the way she rolled her r's. The way she laughed in the cafeteria, how her locker was always organized, and the way she redid her ponytail a hundred times after gym class made me love her more.

"Ty?" she asks, touching the tip of my nose, bringing me out of my memories.

"You know," I say, smiling at her, "I don't think there was a time I didn't love you."

She beams, rolling me on my back and lying on my chest. I love the way she feels against me, her weight reinforcing her presence in my life.

"It's true," I say, cupping her ass cheeks in my hands. "I think I loved you from the minute I saw you. I know I was obsessed with you since then, but it just morphed into love as I grew older and could understand it."

"Do you remember the time you got in a fight with the boy at my softball game in high school?" she laughs. "I was mortified!"

I shrug, watching her relive the memory. "He was flirting with you from the sidelines. And then he had his buddy come up to me and tell me he was going to fuck you that weekend. I made sure to get the point across."

"You did," she says, shaking her head. "You were insane."

"No, I was marking my territory. Besides, he shouldn't have talked about you like that. I should've hit him harder."

Her head tosses back as she laughs. I wait for her to settle, my hand falling off the side of the bed and beneath the mattress. Pulling out an envelope, I lay it on my chest.

"What's this?" she asks.

"It's something for you."

She struggles to sit up and, with a heavy dose of anticipation, she takes the envelope and opens it. After reading the short letter from Mrs. Kruger, she looks inside the envelope again.

Her breath catches in her throat as she sees the check. "What is this?"

"It's two thousand dollars."

With wide, beautiful eyes, she looks at me. "Ty . . ."

"That's why Nila called. She wanted to make sure I got it because they lost the tracking and sent it a week ago."

Elin's eyes light up, the stress of the situation evaporated.

"You can apologize now," I chuckle.

"Two thousand dollars?" she asks, looking at the check again in disbelief.

"What can I say? I'm a hell of a worker, especially when I'm working for something specific."

She eyes me curiously. I pick her up and sit her on top of me, so she's straddling me.

"This will catch up on our bills," she says. "It's a godsend."

"No."

"No?" she laughs.

"No." I look as deeply as I can into her eyes. "My paychecks from Blackwater Coal will catch up on our bills. This money is for *you*."

Her throat moves as she forces as swallow. "What do you mean?"

"I mean, I don't want to wait to move on with our lives. We've wasted enough time stressing, saving money, waiting until the time is right."

"You mean . . ."

"If you still think we need to see a fertility doctor, make the appointment. Use that money for the co-pays and whatever."

"Really?" she gasps. "Are you sure? I don't know if it's logical, Ty. We could use it on other things right now."

"It makes perfect sense if this is what you want."

I rise up and palm the back of her head and bring her mouth to mine. She moans against my lips as I flip her to her back and hover above her.

"I want to put a baby inside you," I whisper into her mouth. She shivers, arching her hips so her bare pussy brushes my cock.

"Do it," she moans, reaching down and stroking my length.

I bite my lip as she squeezes my dick. "I'm so fucking hard," I say through gritted teeth.

Releasing me, I feel her hand beneath me. Looking down, I see her fingers gliding through her wetness.

Her eyes on me, she smiles devilishly as she brings her fingers to my lips. "I'm so wet for you it's ridiculous," she breathes, swiping the moisture over my bottom lip.

I suck her fingertips into my mouth and watch her eyes grow wide. My cock pulses against her opening so hard it hurts.

"How do you want it?" I ask, taking a nipple into my mouth. I suck it, rolling it with my tongue, as my other hand cups her other breast.

She moans at the contact, raising her hips to meet mine again. "Just give it to me," she begs, arching her back further.

I flip her onto her belly and flatten my palm right above her pussy, raising her ass up in the air. She looks at me over her shoulder, a glimmer in her eye that goes straight to my cock.

"Hold on, baby," I say, touching the tip of my dick against the opening of her pussy. "This is gonna be one helluva ride."

Twenty-Six

TY

PULLING UP TO the Bath House, the little building miners use to change from street clothes to work clothes, I flip off the lights to the truck and sit in the spot marked "Second Shift Boss" without getting out.

My breath billows in front of me, hitting the quickly chilling windows and causing them to fog up.

There's a sense of familiarity in the routine of doing this, my first day back to work. I've done it for years, after all. But the last time I saw this place I was being carted out in an ambulance. Even though I know it'll be fine and I really do believe everything I said to Elin, it still has my stomach a little twisted.

I watch as a car pulls up a few spots down and Pettis climbs out. He walks in front of my truck, never looking up at me, and enters the House. The light streams out the door, cutting a slice of halogen-induced sunshine over the mine mud that saturates the ground.

"How'd I get so fucking lucky?" I mutter to myself, grabbing my lunchbox off the passenger's seat. I get out and lock up and head inside the Bath House. The atmosphere is somber as I enter, my twelve-man crew, counting me, all present.

The walls are a dingy yellow color that looks like piss. The floor is cement, chipped and stained and probably grey when it was poured decades ago. With the years of coal mud being trekked over it, it's now the color of tobacco spit.

Cord looks up and smiles, fastening the last snap of his bibs. The mine tape that lays horizontally across the material reflects the lights above. "About time you showed up," he jokes. "Someone's gonna have to play nice with Pettis. They don't pay me enough for that."

"Fuck off," I say, swallowing hard. I stick my lunch in my locker and start going through my gear.

"The Pre-Shift Report is in your inbox," Jiggs says, testing the batteries on his flashlight and helmet. They last one ten-hour shift, maybe a little more. We learned the hard way to make sure they're good and bright before you head to the shaft, otherwise you're fighting a shitty light for ten hours in a place that's as dark and damp as your worst childhood nightmare.

I nod, acknowledging the existence of the report, and step into my bibs. The guys chatter around me, easing into a role we've played most of our adult lives, good naturedly ribbing each other, and I say a little prayer that it holds. Pettis isn't usually on our crew and I'm not sure why he is this time. He's a poison to every team he's on, and nearly every Foreman, myself included, has demanded he be removed at one point or another.

"How long is he gonna make it?" Jiggs mumbles as he walks by. I shrug, knowing he means Pettis, but I don't know. I wonder the same thing. After this shit at Thoroughbreds, there's no way I'm keeping him with me.

The crackle of my radio breaks my concentration. It brings a bolt of realism to the moment.

"Whitt, this is Percora. You get the report?"

"Yeah," I say into the radio. I swipe it out of my box and scan it quickly. "I see the equipment locations. Ceilings are bolted for the first half mile. We're mining the top and south ends."

"Yup," Percora confirms. "Good to have ya back, Whitt. Try not to get crushed tonight, will ya?"

"Go to hell, Percora," I say, shaking my head.

The radio falls silent and I grab my flashlight. "You boys ready?"

WRITTEN IN THE $\mathscr{S}cars$ 197

A chorus of mumbles rings out and we all make our way to the door. The wind picks up, a cold undertone to the breeze shearing across the parking lot as we head to the opening of the slope.

Cord takes a big breath of air. "Ah, there's nothing like the smell of shit in the evening."

Jiggs laughs. "The smell of that direct deposit next Friday is gonna be worth it."

"The things we do for money," Pettis chimes in.

"Pettis," Cord says, looking at me and waiting for some indication that he should be quiet. I don't give it to him. "The next ten hours are gonna go a whole lot fuckin' easier if you shut the fuck up."

"I didn't say anything to you, McCurry," Pettis fires back.

"See, that's the thing," Cord says, standing tall over Pettis. "It doesn't matter if you speak to me. Just hearing your voice is enough to make me want to break you in half. So until Ty figures out how to get you off this crew, let's operate under the understanding that I have no problem busting you in the face. Again. And you won't do shit back."

Pettis straightens his shoulders, but wobbles. "What the fuck did I do to you?"

"Think about it," Cord winks. "I'm sure somewhere inside that dense head of yours, you'll figure it out."

The air around us sizzles, the mood changing. The mine does that to you. Something about staring down a black abyss that leads you hundreds of feet beneath the surface of the earth in a slot just big enough to stand in will sober up the goofiest of men. Doesn't matter how many times you do it. Repetition does not help. It's an unnatural motion, a trip to hell every damn time.

"You okay?" I ask Cord. His outburst was a little over-the-top, even being that it was directed at Pettis.

"Yeah. Just a lot of shit I'm thinking about. You know how it goes."

"What about you?" I ask Jiggs. "Your head on straight?"

"I haven't slept in two nights. I've fought with my wife for about fifty-two hours straight. Yeah, I'm great."

"Is she still talking about moving?"

"Fuck, she's on the phone with realtors, her mom, going through ads trying to find me a job down there. I just can't get through to her."

"Her heart is in the right place," I say.

"I know," he mutters, his head hanging. "I just feel like everything is falling apart."

The rails of the buggy scream as it hits the top. We greet the first four men to make it out before we look at each other. As foreman, I go first. Cord, Jiggs, and Grunt, a guy that doesn't speak in words, just grunts, join me in the buggy.

No one says a word, not that we could hear it anyway. With every foot we fall below the surface of the ground, my chest tightens a little more. The air gets a little damper. The darkness more suffocating. The sound of the equipment below louder.

The shaft is narrow and low, just big enough for equipment to get in and out. It feels like it shrinks as we sink farther into the Earth.

I close my eyes and picture Elin, wondering what she's doing. In my mind, she's curled up on our bed, her reading glasses covering her eyes, a stack of papers on her lap. She looks up at me and smiles, her hair falling over her shoulders.

The equipment is still running, barking and howling, a hellish sound that makes perfect sense for the setting, once we hit bottom. Reluctantly, I part my eyes and let them adjust to the absence of light.

Climbing out of the cart, I nod to the next four to leave from the first shift, my boots sinking in the mud. It squishes around my weight, sliding up the bottom of my bibs.

"Fuck," I hiss, looking up to the Yoder, the foreman just getting off. "It's wetter than fuck down here."

"Yeah," he says, his face so black from the soot and mud that I can only see the whites of his eyes. "It's really fuckin' damp. I called up a few hours ago because I've not seen a hole this damn wet in my whole life."

I pick up a boot and the mud falls off in globs. "This is gonna be fun."

"But hey," Yoder says, smacking me on the back, "we're back to work."

"Yeah," I say, letting out a half-laugh, "we're back to fuckin' work."

Yoder goes off to wait for the buggy to come back down to pick up him and the last three guys. I find the Dinner Shack—a picnic table on a sled—and lay out my report. Ignoring the shrill of the machines and the dim light and the putrid smell of coal, I study our objective.

"It's gonna be hell," Jiggs says, clasping my shoulder with his hand. "You ready for this, Bossman?"

I just nod. Because there's no other way to put it: four-hundred feet below ground is a hell all of its own.

Twenty-Seven

ELIN

FORTY-EIGHT.

Forty-nine.

Fifty.

I watch as each minute ticks by, the clock primed to roll over to four a.m. My lids are heavy, my eyes burn, but they refuse to close.

It's adrenaline, I'm sure. Ty didn't call once he left the house, although I was sure he would. He'd usually send a text from the Bath House before they went down. But tonight, he didn't.

I went to Lindsay's earlier in the evening and she made nachos and we ate them in the nursery while we chose a paint color. I was surprised she is going to do a nursery with the way she's been talking about Florida. But I needed the distraction so I didn't ask questions. Jiggs has no opinion on decoration, only that the baby has a framed photo of his baseball hero, Lincoln Landry, on the wall somewhere in the room.

We chose a really pretty dove grey and a pale yellow that will be beautiful whether it's a boy or a girl and easily accented with blue or pink, as required.

"I love this," I say, holding the winning color sample against the wall. "It's going to be perfect."

"I love it too." She brushes a strand of hair off her shoulder. "I know I've been a little crazy about moving and stuff."

"Yeah, you have. Why, Linds?"

She shrugs, her lips dipping. "I just want what's best for this baby. I don't want to leave you . . ." Tears well in her eyes. "I don't want to leave Blown or Ty or Cord. But I'm afraid we'll stay here and not be able to put food on the table and we can't afford to take risks like that. Not anymore."

"Will you just think about it? For my brother?"

She smiles through the tears glittering down her cheeks. "I will. I just feel like this is what I have to do. You understand, don't you?"

I smile back, but don't answer because even though I get it, I don't.

A smile touches my lips as I think of how Lindsay's belly is beginning to round. She's slathering on cocoa butter and praying for no stretch marks and I just laughed. But, in reality, I'd give anything for them.

I think to how Ty and I might've done our nursey and how big my belly would've been. I wonder what names we'd choose and if Ty would've rubbed my feet every night the way Jiggs does Lindsay's, even when they're fighting.

"Maybe someday," I whisper, rolling onto my side and closing my eyes.

Twenty-Eight

TY

"**Y**OU DON'T KNOW half the shit you think you know," I laugh, tipping my beer at Jiggs.

"Well, that's half again more than you, fucker," he jokes.

Cord shakes his head. "If either of you two knew anything, that truck would be fixed. How long y'all been working on it?"

"Too damn long," Jiggs groans.

Cord and Jiggs get into the details of the truck in the barn out back. I bow out of the conversation and settle into the recliner in the middle of Jiggs' living room.

Elin and Lindsay sit in the kitchen, hovered over a computer screen. A pile of brownies sit in front of them, the whole house smelling like baked goods.

This is how it should be. My friends giving each other shit about life, a game on the television, and my wife sitting at the table with her best friend, talking babies while she wears my shirt and her hair is still ruffled from the quick make-out session we had in the garage. Every once in a while she looks over her shoulder at me and catches me staring at her. We share a smile, one of those that half promises something more later, because fuck if she's not the prettiest girl I've ever seen and half makes me feel like a teenager scoping out my crush.

Taking a sip of my beer, I hear my name spoken beside me and I glance over at Jiggs.

"Did ya hear any of that?" he asks me.

"Nope."

"Cord wonders if there's a fuse that's bad."

I glance at Cord. "Maybe. We didn't check that yet."

"Now ya got me wondering," Jiggs says, standing up. I follow suit.

"I'm gonna take a piss," Cord says, "then I'll meet ya both out there." He disappears down the hall. I grab my jacket off the back of the couch while Jiggs heads to the coat closet by the door.

Slipping on my coat, I head over to Elin. The computer is lit up with row after row of things I can't imagine a baby would ever need. Ever.

"What in the hell is that thing?" I ask, gathering my wife's hair back in one hand. The strands are silky in my palm.

"It's a breastfeeding cushion," Lindsay starts to say before her phone rings. She glances down at it. "That's my mom. Do you mind if I answer?"

"Go," Elin tells her before tipping her head back so she's looking up at me. "You heading to the barn?"

"Yeah, just for a bit. You ready to go?"

She yawns. "Yeah, I'm tired."

"You just wanna go to bed with me," I tease.

"Always."

"Ready?" Jiggs yells from the entryway.

I kiss Elin on the forehead and make my way to the front of the house.

ELIN

I SCROLL THROUGH the website and add a few things to the favorites list for Lindsay to check out. Clicking one last baby bib that says, "My Aunt Rocks," I smile as I shut the lid to the computer.

Stretching my arms over my head, I yawn again.

"Hey," a voice drawls out from behind me.

I jump at the intrusion and twist in my seat. "Cord! You scared me. I thought you went to the barn."

"Sorry," he laughs, shrugging on his jacket. He eyes me curiously. "What's going on with you these days?"

"Um," I say, lifting and dropping my shoulders, "nothing new. What about you?"

"Nothing new over here."

"Ran into Becca lately?" I hint.

"No," he chuckles. "I told you that wasn't going to happen." He pulls a chair out across from me and sits, shaking his head.

I watch him as he dazes off, his mind clearly somewhere else.

"Hey," I say. "You okay?"

"Yeah." He drops his hands on the table, the sound making a thud. "I just . . . I feel . . . lost."

His words spear me, and instinctively, I place my hand on top of his. A small smile graces his lips at the contact and I wish I could jump up and hug him, but I'm afraid it would break the moment.

"Why do you feel that way?"

"You know how you said you always knew you were going to be a teacher? And how Ty just falls into coaching like it's what he was born to do? Or the way Lindsay smiles the whole time she's cuttin' your hair? Or the way Jiggs never stops trying to work on cars, even though we all know he can't fix them for shit?"

"Yeah," I laugh, watching the twinkle grow in his eyes.

"I don't have that. Y'all have this passion for something, this . . ." He runs his hands through the air, like he's trying to grab words. "Something you were born to do. Something that was in your blood the day you were brought to this world. You all have a toolbox for life. I don't."

"First of all," I say, tucking a leg under me and settling in for the long haul with this conversation, "I believe you know how much of a mess my life has been. And I do believe it was you that set me straight. It was your tools I borrowed."

"Life makes no sense to me."

"Life doesn't make sense to any of us, Cord."

"No, I mean it really doesn't make sense to me. Nothing I've ever done seems like the right thing. I've never felt like I fit in, except with you guys. I've never felt a connection with a girl that's deeper than a fuck. No job or place feels like that's what I should do. Does that make sense?"

Sighing, I reach my other hand across the table and place it over his. "Look, maybe you just haven't found your path yet. But you have time to figure out what you were put on this Earth to do and who you're supposed to love. You'll get it."

He narrows his eyes, a smirk on his lips. "Ya think?"

"I *know*," I say, squeezing his hands before sitting back in my chair.

He studies me for a long minute, then two, before leaning against the table. The light hanging above us shines on his face and catches on the watch on his wrist.

"What else do you know?" he asks, raising his brow.

"As in?"

"Don't use your teacher voice with me," he laughs.

"Well, it's what I use when I'm not understanding what you mean," I giggle.

"As in, do you have any secrets or news you'd like to share with the class?"

Laughing, I yawn yet again. "No. Not that I know of. Why? Do you know something I should know?"

He peers at me through his long lashes. "Excuse me for asking, but since you're so in my business, I'll jump into yours. Are you pregnant?"

"What?" I gasp, sitting up straight. "No. Of course not. Why would you ask me that?"

"You've yawned all night."

"I'm tired! I can't sleep when Ty's at work."

"Your face is flushed."

"It's hot as hell in here."

"And," he says, "you didn't touch your dinner tonight."

"Because the hamburger was pink and I can't eat it when it's mooing at me," I say with a huff, as I rise from the table.

I start to say something else. That I'd rather not discuss the topic of pregnancy with him. It dredges up things I'd rather not think about. But the more I think about it, the more a little bubble of uncertainty sits in the middle of my stomach.

I race through a calendar in my head, trying to figure out when to expect my period. It's never exactly on time and with the stress of everything, I haven't paid a lot of attention.

My heartbeat starts to quicken and I feel my cheeks heat further.

Cord's chair pushes out, the legs dragging against the floor. I look up at him and he smiles.

"Cord . . ." My mouth goes dry before I can say anything else.

"Reading people is a remnant of being a foster kid. You learn to read people, notice little things because if you don't, you'll get your ass kicked," he shrugs. "If you are, congratulations. And if you're not . . . it *will* happen," he says, tossing the hood of his jacket over his head. "Now I'm going to go show those boys how to work on a truck."

He winks and heads out the front door, leaving me in the kitchen with my jaw hanging wide open.

Twenty-Nine

ELIN

"WHAT?" I LOOK up as Lindsay rounds the corner. Her hand still holds her phone, as her face mars with confusion. "What?" she asks again.

I laugh, a sound of disbelief married with anxiety. "I'm not sure."

"Dude, you're scaring me," she says, coming towards me. "What's the matter, Elin?"

My hand trembles as I raise it from my side. The bangle bracelets on my wrist rustle prettily together. As if on auto-pilot, it heads to my stomach but I stop it, hesitate, before it lands. With a deep breath, I watch my palm meet my stomach.

My eyes fly to hers. "Linds?"

"Yeah?"

"Um, I don't know if this is even possible. I mean it's possible, technically," I say hurriedly, the brownie I ate starting to creep up my throat, "but I'm not sure . . ."

"Elin?" She closes the distance between us, her eyes drifting to my hand on my stomach.

I giggle nervously. "I'm probably not," I say. "I mean, I never thought about it. But maybe?"

"Oh my God," she breathes, her eyes flying wide. "Seriously? You think so?"

"I don't know. I don't even know if I want to know."

"Of course you do!" she says, dragging me down the hall. "I mean, I do, so you do. Oh my God! This would be the best thing ever!"

My heart squeezes, nearly cutting off my oxygen. Knowing that it would be the best thing ever for the both of us to have babies with the men we love, but also knowing that if things had worked out, we already would be on that path, makes a hot set of tears sting my eyes.

We reach the bathroom door, the one where I ran into Ty at the night of the bonfire. Lindsay spins me around to face her.

"Do you want to know?" she demands. "I mean, you'll have to know sooner or later. And I want to force you in there to take a test, but I also know how personal this is and maybe you want to wait and do it with Ty?"

I imagine his face if it turns out I'm not. Looking down at my stomach for a few moments before up at my friend again, I say, "Let's do it."

Lindsay lets out a squeal and flips on the light. She rummages through a cabinet. No words may come out of my mouth, but a million emotions swirl together in my body creating a beautiful, dangerous chaos that I'm not sure I can navigate.

"Ta-da!" she exclaims, standing up and wielding a little box. It rattles as she shakes it. "I knew I had an extra!"

She extends her hand, offering me the device that will either change my world or ruin an excitement that, despite my best efforts, has already started to take root.

"Am I really going to do this?" I ask, taking the box.

"Yes, you are. I have to know."

"Well, get out of here and let me pee on the stick."

Lindsay laughs, bouncing on the balls of her feet. "Okay, but I want to watch it turn with you. Okay? I mean, I don't even care if that's gross."

"Out," I laugh, shoving her towards the door gently. Once she's gone, I shut it and lock it for good measure.

The package ripped open, I toss the box and directions away. Forcing a swallow, I study the little white gadget.

"Be good to me," I whisper, pulling down my pants.

It takes forever to actually urinate, and I try to guide the thin piece of plastic into the stream. Finishing up and getting myself together, I sit it on the counter and refuse to look at it.

I can't.

A ball sits in my throat as I open the door and face my friend. I think I might pass out.

"Well?" she asks.

I press my lips together and fight to hold back tears. Even though I didn't expect this situation, now that I'm in it, I want it. Oh, dear Lord, do I want it. I've never wanted anything more than this.

"Let's look," she whispers, laying a hand along my shoulders.

In unison, we turn. Together, we suck in a hasty breath. At the same time, we fall into each other's arms, tears dotting our faces.

"It's positive," Lindsay gushes in my hair.

A reply won't come past the sobs racking my body. My knees shake, a smile etched across my cheeks as I grab at the counter to hold myself up. I place both hands on my belly and look down.

It looks the same as it always does, Ty's shirt hanging loosely over the round curve from the Freshman Fifteen I never lost. Still, I feel it. A sense of wonder, a feeling of fullness that it's not just me right now. It's . . . us.

A baby.

"I'm pregnant," I whisper, not to anyone in particular. My head snaps up. "When was the last time I drank?"

Lindsay laughs and places her hand on my belly too. "They'll grow up together. Just a few months apart. My girl and your boy."

"What?" I laugh.

She shrugs. "Ty would be awesome with a boy. When are you telling him?"

I want to tell him now. I want to run to the barn and jump on him, kissing him senseless as I try to put this into words. But Jiggs is there and Cord too, and after everything . . .

My stomach flip-flops as ice water fills my veins, and I shiver at the thought of losing yet another baby.

"They're off after tomorrow," I say, thinking of their schedule. "They'll be home for two days."

"You want to wait till then? Can you manage to keep it a secret for another whole twenty-four hours?"

I imagine seeing him in bed, his early morning hair all ruffled. I'll come in with his coffee and watch him give me his sleepy smile. I'll climb in bed beside him and nuzzle against his solid chest and give him the news. Just the two of us.

Besides, it'll give me time to get my head wrapped around this and to convince myself it's going to be okay.

"I'll try," I say. "I really want it to be special. Maybe I'll play a game or something, I don't know. But I want it to be something we remember. Maybe if I do it different, we'll have different results."

Lindsay makes a face at my insinuation, but chooses to disregard it. "So I have to keep it a secret?" she moans instead. "I'm so bad at that!"

"Don't you dare tell a soul. Not even Jiggs," I warn her, my finger wagging in her face. "I mean it, Linds."

"I won't," she says, rolling her eyes. "Of course I won't. But, Elin, *you're pregnant!*"

"I'm pregnant," I whisper.

The door opens and closes, the sound echoing through the house. We look at each other as Lindsay heads for the bathroom door.

"I'll go stall them. Clean up your face or Ty's gonna know something is wrong," Lindsay instructs.

"Lindsay!"

"What?" she hisses.

"You are so not moving to Florida."

She gives me a look, one I'm not totally convinced means she's going to stop the push for the move, but I'm too amped up to think about it. It's a conversation for another day.

I splash some water on my face and pat it dry. Tucking the test in toilet paper, I stash it in a cabinet and make a mental note to come back and get it later.

I head down the hall, trying not to touch my stomach and not smile like the loon I feel. Everyone is standing in the kitchen when I arrive.

"You okay?" Ty asks immediately, reaching for me. His brows are pulled together.

"I'm good. Lindsay was just, um, telling me about the baby and I just got a little worked up. It's so exciting, you know."

I glance at my brother and he's oblivious, devouring the rest of the brownies on the plate. But when I look at Cord, he's grinning.

As subtly as I can, I nod. He winks, his cheeks breaking into a wide smile.

"Ready to go?" Ty asks, pulling me into his side.

I place a hand on his back, feeling his raised scar through the material of his shirt.

He's here. I'm here. And, maybe, finally, so is our baby.

Thirty

TY

SLATE-COLORED CLOUDS ROLL overhead, a low rumble of thunder noticeable every few minutes. The ground sloshes beneath my boots as I make my way to the entrance of the mine alongside Jiggs and Cord.

"Not a bad first week back," Jiggs notes, swinging his lunchbox beside him. "We met goal. Nothing broke down—"

"And I didn't kill Pettis," Cord laughs.

"I reported his bullshit from last night," I note, thinking back to twelve hours before. "No miner can go any farther than we've prepped for. Fucker has a death wish, and while I'm not entirely brokenhearted about *that*, I kinda wanna live."

"Me too," Jiggs snorts. "I got a kid on the way. Would like to be around to teach him how to make a jump shot like his dad."

"Better let Uncle Ty teach him that if you want him to be the best," I joke as I spy Pettis and Grunt up ahead. "I have a feeling Pettis is going to get fired tonight once we're done. When I reported him this morning, Percora said he'd take care of it. You know what it'll look like if something goes wrong right after we re-open."

"It'll close us down and we'll go without a paycheck again," Cord says, tinkering with his flashlight. "I think this thing has a loose cable or something. It keeps going off." He shakes it in the air and mutters under his breath.

"Shit's breaking already," Jiggs laughs as we approach Pettis and Grunt. "You boys ready?"

Grunt makes the sound he makes that means yes, no, and maybe. Pettis nods, eyeing us all warily.

I watch the cart come up the ramp. Grunt and Pettis get in first and descend into the darkness.

"Let's do this and go home for a couple of days."

ELIN

"DON'T FORGET YOUR gloves!" I rush to the door and hand a pair of bright red gloves to one of my favorite students. "It's getting cold out there, big guy. You'll need these."

"Thanks, Mrs. Whitt," he grins a wide, toothy smile.

I ruffle his hair before he turns and joins the line to head out to recess.

Closing the door softly behind me, I let out a long, tired breath. I tossed and turned last night, finally just getting up around one in the morning. I sat in the living room and planned out how to tell Ty about the baby. It was the excitement of knowing that kept me up. But by the time I fell asleep and woke up, the adrenaline had worn off and I was sluggish.

When I realized Ty wasn't home yet, the adrenaline kicked back in.

Turns out his crew was working over, which isn't out of the ordinary. A simple call to the Blackwater Office, something I've done a number of times over the years, answered that. Still, it started my day off wobbly and the rollercoaster of highs and lows is taking its toll.

"Ouch," I mutter, stopping in my tracks. One hand goes onto a student's desk as I bed forward and squeeze my eyes shut. A rumble, not quite a cramp but not *not* a cramp either, tightens in my belly. "Breathe," I tell myself, concentrating on the rising and falling of my chest.

My heartbeat races as much as I try to steady it. "No," I whisper. "No, no, no."

I need my husband. I need to hear his voice.

Quick steps lead me to my purse in my bottom desk drawer. Shaky hands tug at the zipper and retrieve my cell.

"Let him be home," I whisper as another tug rips through my insides. "Please. Let him be home."

Tears build in the corner of my eyes as I unlock my screen to see no missed calls and no texts. It's ten o'clock, seven minutes past, to be exact, and I can't fight the flicker in the back of my mind that it's odd I haven't heard from him at all.

I tell myself he's probably just exhausted and grabbed a shower and fell asleep as I find his name in my favorites list. My finger is on his picture, "My Love" printed across the top, ready to drop and place the call when a knock reverberates through my classroom.

Thirty-One

ELIN

MY HAND HOVERS over his name and I teeter on the verge of not answering the door and going through with the call. That answer is made for me.

It pushes open and Mr. Walters, the elementary school principal, pokes his head around it. "Elin?"

Blowing out a hasty breath, I sit the phone down. "Yes, I'm sorry, Mr. Walters. Can I help you?"

He steps through the opening.

I suck in a soft breath.

Gloom is written all over his tight features. He clears his throat and stands tall. "I don't really know how to say this, Elin, but can you get your things and come with me, please?"

"Um, sure. Is . . . is everything all right?"

A million thoughts run through my head—have I been fired? Has someone filed a report against me?

"Blackwater Coal called the office a few minutes ago and asked that you come to their headquarters immediately," he says softly.

"Why would they do that?"

I'm afraid to ask, but even more terrified of the answer. When Ty got hurt, they called my phone and asked me to meet the ambulance at the hospital. My phone hasn't rung today. I check it again. No missed calls.

Why would they call the school?

It occurs to me, just as a slight quiver to Mr. Walters' composure sets in, that I might prefer that question to remain unanswered. My legs go numb, as do my hands that reach furiously for my things.

He's talking, but I'm mentally removed from this moment. It's some sort of survival mechanism, I'm sure. If I can just come up with a decent reason, it will make it all right.

Maybe Ty tested positive for drugs and I need to pick him up?

Instantly, I'm relieved at the idea. That we can deal with.

Yes, I'll pick him up and rip him a new asshole and make him get professional help this time. Real help, not some self-detox in the—

" . . . accident, Elin."

My head jerks to the front of the room.

"What did you say?"

He's watching me like you look at the family standing beside a casket, like you want to seem all warm and familial, yet you're afraid in their current state they may completely melt down. It's a look that's friendly, yet mixed with sadness, and one I hate. It's also one I can't process at the moment because my mind is stuck on that one little word.

"Accident?" I ask, my voice too loud for the room. "What accident? Who's been in an accident?"

"I'm honestly not sure," he says and I believe him. The lines on his face soften. "They just asked that you arrive as quickly as possible. Can I give you a ride?"

THE CAR FLIES down the highway, past the fields now waiting on spring to arrive for the next crop. Nothing looks out of the ordinary, nothing feels different than any other Thursday morning, except I'm in Mr. Walters' car going a wild rate of speed as I try to get ahold of Lindsay.

Every time it rings, it goes dead.

"Shit!" I say, ending yet another failed attempt at getting

through. "I can't take this."

My head falls in my hands and I force air in then out of my lungs. My heart is beating violently in my chest as every worst-case scenario fires through my brain.

"Elin, if it was anything incredibly wrong, don't you think we'd have heard it on the radio? Or gotten some wind of it in the media?" His hand lands on my knee and I stare at it. It feels heavy, the weight of it sitting awkwardly on my leg. He withdraws it quickly.

"I don't know," I reply, wishing he'd shut up. I know he's trying to help, but I need to think. I scroll to Ty's name and call his number for the hundredth time.

Straight to voice mail.

My hand shakes uncontrollably as I concentrate on my breathing and I try to convince myself this is going to be okay.

Feeling my phone buzz in my hand, I jump. "Hey!" I say as soon as I swipe it on. "Lindsay? Where are you?"

"Heading to Blackwater."

The one word etched with a sob so deep, so distressing, it shatters what's left of my nerves.

It must be Jiggs. They wouldn't call her if something happened to Ty.

My breathing becomes jagged as I see my brother's face, hear his stupid laugh, imagine his eyes lighting up as he teased me growing up about what I got for Christmas.

I nearly drop my phone.

Dear God, let him be okay. Let them all be okay. Let this be some stupid meeting about healthcare or 401K's.

"What did they say?" I ask, my voice crackling with the tears I'm trying desperately to hold back. "Did they tell you anything?"

"No. They just said I needed to come to the headquarters as soon as possible."

Tears roll down my cheeks as she cries into the phone. "Are you alone?" I ask.

"Yes. I'm driving myself. I'm on Five Mile Road now, almost there."

"I think you're just ahead of me," I say, spotting a blue car a mile or so up the road.

"Why are you out here?" she asks, sniffling. "Did they call you too?"

I nod, then realize she can't see me. "Yes."

"Oh, Elin," she says, sobbing once again. "What can it be?"

"Linds, stop. We'll be there in just a minute. Maybe it's nothing," I offer, although I don't believe it. Not the way this has gone down.

I feel like I'm going to be sick.

"I'm here. I'll see you inside," she says and disconnects the call.

I look at Mr. Walters and he offers me a sad smile, so I look away. Pity isn't wanted. There's no reason for it. Everything is going to be okay.

ELIN

WE PULL TO the front door and I spy Lindsay's car in the emergency lane, but I don't see her anywhere.

"Do you want me to come in with you?" Mr. Walters asks.

"No, I'll be fine. Thanks for the ride," I say, jumping out of the car before it's to a complete stop and heading for the glass doors with Blackwater Coal printed in black across the front.

The warm air smacks me in the face, making my perceived suffocation even more real. I look frantically at the faces in front of me.

Men, women, some in suits, some in mining vests. Some wearing glasses, others hardhats. The one thing in common: the look of devastation and fear on their faces.

"I'm Elin Whitt," I sputter, slamming my purse on the counter. "Someone called."

For a brief moment, no one moves. I look from face to face, willing one of them to step forward and give me answers.

"Follow me, Mrs. Whitt," a large, burly man says. He starts down a long hall, turning to me as he walks. "I'm Vernon Trent, Chief Officer of Safety with Blackwater."

"What's going on?" I ask, peering through windows into offices as we come to the end of the hallway. I don't see Lindsay. "I need to find my sister-in-law. She got a call too."

A hiccup catches the rest of my words. Vernon stops at the doorway to a closed room. "She's in here. Please, follow me."

"This better be some stupid meeting about insurance . . ."

The door opens and I spy Lindsay pacing along the far wall. She turns as I enter, her mascara-streaked face racing towards me. I catch her in a hug, our arms winding around one another. I can't cry. I won't. Everything is going to be okay.

"It's fine," I say as promisingly as I can. "Shhh. Everything will be fine." Brushing her hair away from her face, I pull back to see her face. "Have they told you anything?"

"Not yet."

"Ladies." Vernon's voice fills the room, a commanding, yet kind tone that has us turning on our heels. He's standing at the front of the room, flanked by a woman in a navy blue skirt and jacket, pearls, and her hair curled like a '50's housewife. A man stands on his other side in a crumpled looking black suit and tie. None of them look pleased to be standing in front of us.

My stomach drops to the floor and I squeeze Lindsay as tightly as I can.

Vernon looks at his associates before clearing his throat. "We have some bad news. Please take a seat."

Thirty-Three

TY

M
Y EYES OPEN. I cough immediately, gasping for air, as my sight takes in an awkward, unfamiliar scene. The lamp on my helmet illuminates the floor of the mine and the dust that's permeating the air above it.

What the fuck?

My face is pressed into the wet, slimy ground and when I lift it, a sucking sound shatters the silence of the darkness around me.

Shivering, I try to get my bearings.

"Pettis! Stop!" My voice rings out through the mine, over the piercing equipment and past Cord and Jiggs, the two men that stand between me and him. "Stop!"

He looks at me over his shoulder. "Calm the fuck down, Whitt."

"No!" I shout, laying down my hammer and starting towards him. If he keeps at that angle, the ceiling will give and land right on Cord.

Pettis' laugh drifts over the sound of the machines and I realize that's exactly what he's trying to do.

"Stop, Shane!" I scream.

He turns to go back to the mining machine but realizes what I meant. He pulls back but it's just a moment too late.

The entire cavity we're in starts to shake—the walls, the floor, the ceiling overhead—knocking me off my feet.

"Run!" I scream, my voice drowned out by the sound of chunks of

black carbon toppling out of the seam and crashing in. "Get out!"

The noise of the equipment stops. The shouts of my crew melting away. The lights go out as my vision goes black as the walls literally close in on me.

I try to move my legs. I look behind me, where my body should be, but my head won't turn fully and the light won't make it through the dust anyway. I can't see them.

"Fuck," I mutter, my head not sure what in the hell is happening. There is no pain, or I can't feel it if there is. Struggling to make it to my elbows, my legs pressed to the ground, Cord's voice sounds from somewhere through the silt.

"Anyone hear me?" His voice is ragged and his words break as he begins to cough, undoubtedly expelling the debris floating in the air.

"Over here, Cord," I say, moving the air out of my face with my hand. Particles dance in the light, swaying to a song I don't hear.

I can't remember where everyone was when the walls gave way. *Where was Jiggs?*

Combing through my memory bank, I have him placed to my far left. By the shaft leading out.

Please, let him have gotten out of here.

I rack my brain for our location underground, thinking back to the map in my packet before we descended a few hours ago. We weren't incredibly deep, which would've given some of the guys a fighting chance to get out if they got a jump on it.

The odds are decent Jiggs made it.

What are the odds we'll get out?

Panic begins to set in, constricting around my chest. They aren't good, pretty fucking slim, but I have to stay calm. See who else is in here. Figure out how to stay alive.

Kicking my feet, I feel the weight moving until they're free. They're tight and sore and feel like dead weight, but they'll move. Yet with each swing, there's more pain.

"I can't move," Cord groans.

I roll over, wincing as my back and legs scream in pain. Blocking it out, I look around as I stand.

The dust is beginning to settle, the pungent smell of coal ripping away at my nostrils. The only sound is Cord struggling somewhere in front of me and water trickling to my right.

My headlamp shines in a circle as I turn, illuminating the destruction at my feet.

The wall to the right, the one we were mining into, has collapsed. I shine my light in front of it, to the last place I saw Pettis as he mined into an area that hadn't been bolted and secured. There's nothing but a heap of rubble about ten yards in from where he stood.

Gagging, I bend over at the waist and dry heave into the abyss.

"Shit." Cord barks from the other side of the little cavity formed by the cave-in and I stand, shining my light towards him.

"You over there?" I ask, my boots slopping through the mud as I stumble over lumps of coal and broken ceiling timbers.

"Yeah."

I see movement along the far wall, a few yards from me, and finally spot his face. It's as black as the coal on top of him, just the whites of his eyes poking out from the heap.

I clear his body from the debris and help him to his feet. His eyes are wide, a trickle of blood mixed with the soot running down his cheek.

"We're fucked, aren't we?" he asks.

A stillness settles over us. He feels it too because he looks away.

Instead of answering him, I take a deep breath. "Anyone hear me?" I call out.

Silence.

"Can anyone hear me?" I say again, moving my light to the front of the room.

The slope leading out of the hole is completely blocked, sealing us off from the rest of the world.

As I start to feel the weight of what that means, I see movement beneath a pile of broken black rock.

"Shit," I say, moving that way. Cord is behind me, his hand on my shoulder, as I guide us both.

We knock the rubble away, Cord focusing on the guy's legs as I work on the torso. Once the face is clear, I wipe frantically at the face to identify him.

The chest starts to move more quickly, and the man begins to cough and wheeze. Whoever he is, he's alive.

His eyes open and when they lock on me, a weak version of my favorite smile in the word flashes at me.

ELIN

LINDSAY GRABS MY arm as we sit on a '70's-patterned sofa. Her nails dig into my skin and it hurts, but I kind of like it. It keeps me present. Takes away from the numbness beginning to hit my nerves.

"Ladies," Vernon says, "this is Greta VanBraun with Blackwater and Reed Fascinelli with the Mining Safety Board. I regret to inform you that there's been an accident underground today."

"No," Lindsay sobs, her eyes wide with panic. I reach for her, pulling her to me, tears streaming down my face.

"Who's hurt?" I ask, my throat burning from the emotion.

A hint of a look of surprise glints across Vernon's face. It's just enough that it hits me straight in the gut, and I know there's more to it than that.

My arm sags off Lindsay's shoulder as I stand, even though my legs shake under me. "Someone is just hurt, right?"

"Mrs. Whitt, will you please sit down?"

The look on Greta's face chills me to the bone. I fall into my seat. "Where's Ty?" I ask, my voice so clear it even surprises me. "Where's my husband?"

"Mrs. Whitt, please—"

I cut Greta off. "Please spare me all the pretty language and answer my question. Where are my husband and brother? Where is Cord McCurry? If they're at a hospital, we need to get to them."

They don't speak, but they don't need to. The look on their faces says it all.

The volume of my wail screams through the room. Lindsay pulls me into her, her tears hot against my cheek. My ears are assaulted by her sobs aimed straight against my eardrums. But none of it matters.

Not anymore.

TY

"CAN YOU MOVE?" I ask Jiggs.

He groans and begins, with precision, to move his limbs. "Yeah," he coughs. "I think so."

Cord and I help him to his feet. He staggers a bit until he gets oriented.

"What the fuck happened?" Jiggs asks, taking off his helmet and feeling his head, wincing.

"Pettis was mining over there. I remember telling him to stop and he looked over his shoulder and everything started moving," I reflect. "That's all I remember."

"Who else is down here? Who else . . . you know, made it?" Jiggs says the words with a break to his voice, like the situation, the reality, is starting to smack him in the coal-black face.

"Us." The words ring around the space, sending a chill through all of us.

I put it out there plain as day because it's the truth and the sooner we accept it, the better. It's the first thing we learn in training. To stay cognizant of your situation.

This is our situation.

"Fuck," he hisses, looking around the darkened cavern. "How in the fuck are we getting out of here?"

I glance at Cord, who's looking at me. He knows what I know—that there's a blind man's shot in the dark that we'll ever get out of here. The odds aren't good. They're shit, actually. They'll try, I know they will, but I also know the numbers and factors and that we are fucked.

Before Jiggs can see my face, I turn away from him. Tears dot my eyes, the saltiness burning my cheeks in what must be cuts and scratches.

I haven't even checked to see if I'm bleeding. *What does it really matter now, anyway?*

Squeezing my eyes closed in an attempt to stop the tears, I see Elin. She's lying in our bed, her shy smile printed on her pretty lips. My hands clench at my sides, my tears just running harder now, because I would give anything to climb in that bed with her, soot and all, and hold her until I stop breathing.

"I'm sorry," I tell her in my brain, wiping my eyes with the back of my dirty hands. I can taste the acridness of the coal, feel the acid on my skin. Feel the sting in my eyes from the putrid dust.

Clearing my throat and spitting out a mixture of saliva and soot, the bitterness burning my mouth, I turn to my friends. They're looking at me.

Down here, I'm the man in charge. I have the training, the hours upon hours of sitting in a classroom and being lectured on this very thing. I know what to do, but looking around, feeling the realness of the moment, I know one thing: all that training is bullshit.

My lungs tighten in my chest as panic begins to take root.

"How we getting out of here, Ty?" Jiggs asks again. "What's the plan?"

I look at his face, barely a speck of skin showing through the blackness smearing his features. His eyes are wide, pleading with me for an answer.

Jiggs swallows, moving his weight from one side to the other, and I know he's about to lose it. That's going to use up what oxygen we have down here and make this worse for all of us.

"I'd say we're sealed. We aren't getting out up the ramp." I nod behind Jiggs to the wall of rubble that used to be our road out.

Racking my brain for protocol, I put together a plan. "They'll drill an air shaft as soon as they think the ground is stable."

"How much oxygen do we have?" Cord asks.

"Enough," I say with more certainty than I feel. "We can't panic, can't go using it up by being stupid. The best thing we can do right now is to stay calm."

"Stay calm," Jiggs mutters, blowing out a breath. "Yeah fucking right. We're trapped below the fucking surface and you want me to stay calm?"

It's in his voice—that ripple that comes right before someone loses their shit. I can't blame him, but I can't let it happen either.

"Hey," I say, my tone not one I usually use for my brother-in-law. "You want to make it out of here to see your wife and baby?"

The words drench him like a bucket of cold water. I ignore Cord's look, the one that asks if I really believe that's possible, and keep my gaze settled on Jiggs.

"Because you losing your cool down here isn't going to help anything," I say.

"My wife is up there!" Jiggs shouts, the words all too loud in the tight space. "I need to get out of here!"

I grab him by the shoulders and shove him backwards. "Guess what? My wife is up there too," I remind him, standing so close our noses nearly touch. "Your fucking sister? Remember her? So stay fucking calm, man."

His breath is hot on my face, his nostrils flaring as he waits for the next words out of my mouth.

Cord places a hand on each of our shoulders. "Settle down, boys," he says. The calm in his tone eases the tension between Jiggs and I, and we both blow out a breath. "We're gonna get out of here. Let's just ease up and get comfy because it could be a long minute."

Thirty-Five

ELIN

"LADIES, PLEASE LISTEN to me," Vernon says, squatting down in front of us.

I look at his face through Lindsay's hair. At first I only see his mouth move through the tears, fear gripping me in its strongest hold, blocking out his words. But when I make out "Ty," I pull away from Lindsay.

". . . aren't sure what caused it yet. Most of the crew escaped, but we haven't located Ty, Jiggs, Cord McCurry, "Grunt" Salis, and Shane Pettis."

"What do you mean you haven't located them?" Lindsay wails.

"We don't know where they are."

"Could they have gotten out?" I ask, not bothering to attempt to halt the trail of tears flowing down my face.

Vernon stands and joins his associates in a tight line. "It's possible. But, ladies, I think you should prepare for the fact that they may be trapped below."

"No . . ." Lindsay cries, wrapping her arms around my neck.

I sit, my posture rigid. I can't wail, can't sob, can't ask questions. My body starts to shake, my body temperature plummeting, and I know one thing: I'm in shock.

TY

THE WATER DRIPS down the walls, pinging into puddles. The sound chirps through the little room created by the cave-in.

It could be relaxing, in the right situation. It reminds me of the little fountain Elin had one time in the living room until Cord drank too much and knocked it over, breaking it into a million pieces.

"Okay, let's get a plan," I say, pulling myself together. "Does anyone have their radios?"

"The battery died on mine a few hours ago, before all this shit," Cord says. "I have it, but it's no good."

Jiggs looks around. "I have no idea where mine is."

"Mine was lying in water," I say, tossing the remnants of my shattered radio in a pile of coal across the room. "Battery is toast."

I survey the room. "Do we have any food in here?"

"How long you think we'll be stuck down here?" Jiggs asks.

"I don't know, honestly," I admit. "But probably longer than we care to admit." Again, I ignore a pointed look from Cord. "So, food. Lights. What do we have?"

Cord stumbles into the back corner and rummages around. A few minutes later, he steps into the light of my headlamp. "We have one lunchbox."

"That's mine," I say. My lips press together as I fight myself from snatching it from his grasp. I know there's a little note from Elin inside, as well as my lunch—the last thing she might ever do for me. My fists clench at my sides as I rip my eyes away from the metal bucket.

"Let's hope Elin packed you some good shit," Cord says.

Hearing her name out loud rips through my soul. I wonder where she is and if she knows. I hope someone is with her, comforting her, telling her it'll all be okay somehow. *That someone is lying to her.*

"We probably need to save our lamps," Cord points out. "It's gonna be dark as hell down here if we don't."

"This *is* hell," Jiggs snorts.

"No, you're right," I say. "Let's get a safe place to sit and save our lights. We'll flip one on at a time every now and then."

We begin clearing out a space on the floor for the three of us. We take pieces of rubble and build up a little pad over the mud and water that seems to never stop trickling in. We work silently, none of us making eye contact, like if we don't look at the others, maybe this won't be real.

We sit in a circle of sorts, Cord to my right, Jiggs to my left, my lunch box tucked in beside me.

"If we get real creative," Cord says, "we could convince ourselves that we're around a campfire. Especially the way these headlamps flicker and light up this little spot."

"We've had some good ones," Jiggs remembers. "Remember the one we had at Old Man Denham's farm back in our freshman year? We nearly let every single head of cattle out of that field."

I chuckle at the memory. "Not our best decision, boys."

"Nah, but it makes for a good story," Jiggs laughs. "Shit, that was the night I talked Lindsay into going out with me."

"I remember that," I say. "We were at The Fountain. She said she'd go for a ride with you if you beat me in a game of pool."

"And you let me." Jiggs laughs, but there's no denying the layer of sadness that creeps into the tone. "Thanks for that, Ty."

Shaking my head, I look at the small patch of black between us. "Ty?"

I raise my head slowly until I'm looking at Jiggs. His eyes are filled with a look that can only be described as pure fear, a look I've never seen on him before. A look that rips me to the core.

"Yeah?" I reply.

"We're gonna get out of here, right?"

"Sure, we are," I say, forcing a smile to make my uncertainty a little less obvious. "We'll be hearing the drill soon. We just need to be patient."

The air stills as we all decide whether we believe me or not. The drill will come. I do believe that. But will it come in time? And will it do any good? Those are two different questions.

"Hey," Cord says, rustling us out of our thoughts. "We need to save these lamps."

Our lungs all fill with air as we realize what this means. Total. Darkness.

One at a time, our lights go off. First Cord's. Then Jiggs'.

"Here we go," I whisper, raising my hand to my helmet and flicking my lamp off too.

The pitch black settles over us on the cold, wet floor of hell.

ELIN

THE PAPER CUP twirls in my fingers.

Around.

Around.

Around.

The water inside sloshes against the sides, threatening to spill out. It won't be cold if it does and touches my fingers. It's sat in there too long for that.

We've been in this room for six, maybe seven hours now. In some ways, it feels much shorter than that and in others, so much longer.

I should be getting home from work right about now.

Holding my stomach and closing my eyes, I remember my plan to tell Ty that we are having a baby.

I should be doing that now. Not . . . this.

The water ripples across the cup and I fight to focus on it. Sleep prickles at my consciousness, thanks to the shot by Doctor Walker. Of course, I had to tell him I was pregnant and when I realized that another person would know before Ty, I had a complete meltdown.

I look up as a knock sounds gently on the door. Vernon's head pokes around the corner.

"Can I get you ladies anything? Anything at all?" he asks.

"My husband and brother and friend."

His face falls. "We're trying, Mrs. Whitt."

"Try harder."

"We're discerning their location now. I'll update you as soon as I know more."

"You have to find them," I implore. "You don't understand . . ."

A part of me feels bad. It's not his fault, not specifically. Ty chose to go to work even though he knew the risks. But Vernon chose to be the face of Blackwater, so surely he expected some venom from me. If not, he should've reconsidered his decision.

"The Pettis family is in the room next to you and the Salis family too. If you would like to see them, it's the door on your left."

I nod, but have no interest in seeing them at this point. I don't even know them, not really, except Sharp, whom I loathe.

"And we haven't located any family for Cord McCurry. Do you ladies have any idea where to find them?"

My heart lurches in my chest and I look at Lindsay. "We are his family."

"I mean blood family."

"You don't understand, Vernon. We are his family."

He nods, not understanding, but getting my point.

"There is a Reverend Mitchell here to see you," he states. "Would you like to see him?"

"Yes. Please," Lindsay speaks up.

"We're holding all visitors unless you give us their names specifically. Is there anyone you'd want to see besides your attorney and doctor?"

Lindsay gives them the names of her parents. My heart breaks at the fact I don't have my parents here.

"Um, Ty's mom is on a cruise. I've called the cruise line and they're trying to reach her, so if she calls, please put her through. But I'm doubting she's reachable."

He looks concerned for a brief moment before smoothing out his features. Eric Parker told us when he visited earlier that Blackwater would try to segregate us from outsiders until this is resolved. He suggested we stay here for proximity purposes, but to fight for access for whomever we wanted to see. So far, we haven't wanted to see anyone.

"The media is asking if you have a statement . . ."

"They should contact Eric Parker if they have questions," I report.

"Very well. I'll send the reverend back."

I watch the door for the Reverend Mitchell's silver head to pop around the door.

"Did you choose pink and silver because it'll match the Reverend's hair?" Ty laughs, stretching his legs out on the tailgate of the truck.

Moon Mountain is lit up with a million fireflies twinkling around us. I press my cheek against his chest and cuddle against him.

"No, I picked it because it's pretty," I say, listening to his heart beat.

"You know what else is pretty?"

"What's that?"

"You."

"You think I'm pretty?"

TY

"YOU THINK I'M pretty?"

I watch the prettiest girl I've ever seen blush at the idea. How could she not know? How could she not have a clue that she's all I think about as she sits in front of me in math? How does she not understand she's all I've thought about when I'm alone since she showed up to our school ten days ago?

"I hope you'll think about being my girlfriend."

Her blush deepens as I try not to do something stupid and ruin my chances before I get this locked down. I'm afraid to say too much, smile too big, touch her too much just in case I'll burn any points I've managed to get with the gorgeous new girl in class.

"Really?" Her voice is soft, just like the faint scent of strawberries in her hair. "You want to go out with me?"

"Who wouldn't want to go out with the prettiest girl they've ever seen?"

A light flickers to my right. It's weak, an almost brown hue instead of the yellow light that usually comes out of the headlamps. Cord's face sags, bags evident under his eyes. "Everyone good?"

We all nod because anything more would be a lie.

The light flips off again and the darkness takes over.

"I fucking hate the dark," Cord laughs. "I always leave the light on in the bathroom down the hallway at night because I hate waking up to pitch black."

"My dad always said you're safer in the dark because the odds are even between you and whatever is after you," Jiggs relays. "I don't think this counts."

"This fucking sucks," Cord says, blowing a breath. "I need a fucking shower and I don't know if it's more to get clean or warm up."

Everything is damp. Even the little platform we built now has water just below the tops of the rocks. The chill is settling in our bones, making our bodies ache.

"Better get used to this not sleeping stuff," I say. "Lindsay is having a baby, you know."

"Yeah . . ." Jiggs voice trails off and I know he's considering our situation. But I need his spirits up. We need to stay as positive as we can for as long as we can.

Until we can't.

I can't go there. I feel like I should, to prepare, but how do you prep for . . . *that?*

"You're naming it after me, right?" I ask instead to distract me as much as anyone.

He snorts, the sound making me grin. I can imagine him shaking his head, rolling his eyes—but I have to imagine it because, although he's a foot away from me, I can't see him.

"Lindsay thinks it's a girl," Jiggs says.

"So, Cordelia, right?" Cord asks.

"No, assholes. I'm not naming my kid after you two," Jiggs

laughs. "After we get out of here, I might not want to ever see you again."

"I feel you there," I sigh, making them both chuckle.

"And as cold as I am," Jiggs says, "I might go along with her plan to move to Florida."

His voice softly carries through the cavern as he begins to cry. "Fuck it, you guys. I just want out of here. I'll move wherever the fuck she wants. I just want her."

The silence we've come to know intimately takes over once again as his crying tapers off. Our breathing rattles through the room, the drips of the water piercing the stillness. It's like a scary movie, and we're waiting on the predator to jump out.

"You know," Jiggs gulps, "if we don't get out of here . . ."

His voice breaks again and I reach for him but can't find him in the dark. My chest tightens as I scoot my ass along the jagged rocks until I'm beside him.

"Listen to me," I say, "we're gonna get out of here."

"Maybe," he says, his voice raw, "maybe not. But, you know, at least Lindsay will have—"

"Look," Cord interrupts, his voice booming over Jiggs'. "Shut up about this 'maybe not' bullshit. Okay? They'll come for us. You know they will."

"Yeah . . ." Jiggs says, sniffling. "This isn't fair, man. This wasn't supposed to happen."

"Elin says we all have a purpose in life," Cord says, his voice even.

"What?" I ask, irritation heavy in my tone. "To come to the pits of hell and die? I object."

"Maybe—" Cord is cut off by a faint sound that isn't our voices, isn't our breathing, and isn't water.

It's the sound of a drill.

Thirty-Seven

ELIN

"**H**AVE YOU EATEN anything?" Dr. Walker looks at me, then Lindsay, and back to me again.

I shake my head no.

"You both need to eat. For you and the babies."

Looking away to the paint-chipped walls of the conference room, tears blur my vision. My heart is broken. My soul ripped to pieces. My mind unwilling, unable, to consider my life in any way other than with a happy ending with my husband.

My brain spins out of control. If I don't keep it focused on a memory, a plan, an idea, it starts wondering where he is, if he's hurt, in pain, cold.

If he's dead.

Bile creeps up my throat, singeing the already burnt tissue from multiple trips to the bathroom before now. There's nothing left in my stomach. There can't be. Just the by-products of the agony I'm in.

I miss his smile, the way his laugh washes over me and makes me feel like everything is going to be okay. I need that. I need that now.

"Please be okay," I whisper. "We need you. You promised me you'd come home. You promised me you wouldn't lie."

"Can I get you ladies some fruit?" Dr. Walker asks.

WRITTEN IN THE $\mathcal{S}_{cars}$ 239

"I can't eat anything," Lindsay says behind me. Her voice is devoid of emotion. Like me, she's completely spent in every way.

She stands, grabbing the armrest of the chair and steadying herself. "I just keep thinking I fought with him for the last few weeks about moving. I just pushed and pushed and . . ." She bends at the waist, her head in her hands. "He left for work mad at me."

I spring to my feet and hug her, tears flowing down my cheeks. "He's never mad at you. He loves you so much."

"They should have some news for you soon." Dr. Walker chooses his next words carefully. "I know you're scared right now, ladies, and that's understandable. But can I be honest with you?"

My head turns slowly until I'm facing him. I'm unable to smile, to nod, to tell him he can say whatever he wants because I'm numb.

"Your husband and brother are both strong men. I've known Ty since he was a boy and would come into my office and ask for the requisite sucker and sticker before his appointment, not after. And Jiggs . . ." He chuckles and looks away for a moment. "I've known your brother since he came to me his freshman year for a physical for football. He made a not-so-gentle comment about me asking him to look away and cough."

The corner of my lip twitches. "I can only imagine."

"I'm sure you can," he says. "You know, in my area of expertise, we believe in the science of things. In cold, hard facts. But I've always believed, even in med school, that there was more to it than that. That people can feel other people's thoughts and wishes. And after all that schooling and thirty years of practice, I still do."

He kneels in front of me, glancing over my shoulder at Lindsay for a split second. "I know you're scared. You have every right to be. But you need to be strong. For you," he says, before tapping my belly, "for the baby. For your brother and husband and Cord . . . and for Lindsay."

"But I'm not strong right now," I whimper.

"You are stronger than you realize, sweetheart. I want you to dig deep and think about what I've said. Send your boys below some good vibes, let them know the world is praying for them and pulling for them."

My brows pull together. "The world?"

"It's all over the media, Elin. It's breaking news on the major stations. They have this place locked down tight."

"My God . . ." My head buries in my hands. "Will this make it harder for Blackwater to focus?"

"I think they're actually getting some help from experts they wouldn't have access to normally," Dr. Walker says. "I think this is a good thing." His face scrunches and he takes a deep breath. "But I think you need to prepare yourself in case this doesn't end up the way we want it."

"No . . ."

"Elin," he says, his hand landing on my knee, "I'm not saying it will, but I don't want you unprepared if bad news is delivered."

"You think there's a way to prepare for that?" My head buries in my hands before something pops in my mind. "Can you do me a favor?"

"Sure," Dr. Walker says.

"Can you make sure someone is taking care of Yogi? It's Cord's dog and he'll be pissed if we forget about his girl."

I begin to cry again when a sound catches my attention. A knock raps on the door and it pushes open. I'm glad for the distraction, realizing it might save me from punching the doctor in the face.

Vernon is followed by Greta, Reed, and another man in a blue pinstriped suit that introduces himself to Lindsay and I as she sits beside me.

"Any news?" I ask as Dr. Walker turns to leave. I grab his hand, needing his support. He moves behind me—one hand on my shoulder and the other on Lindsay's.

"Yes, actually."

My heart lodges in my throat, my hand squeezed tightly by Lindsay as Reed busies himself pinning a map of some sort to the wall in front of us.

"This is a bird's eye view of the mine," Vernon says, motioning to the drawing. "The area in that circle is where the miners should be."

"How far down is that?" I ask. I'm not sure why it matters, but it does.

"About three hundred to four hundred feet below the surface," Vernon answers stiffly. "The ramp they used for ingress and egress is sealed. We've tried to remove the debris and reach them through that channel, but it's too tight and we can't guarantee more internal collapse wouldn't happen if we disturbed the wrong area."

"So what do we do?" Lindsay asks.

Reed clears his throat. "Right now, we're digging an air hole into this spot." He uses a yard stick to point to a location inside the circled area. "This is where we believe your husbands to be."

My heart skips a beat as I stare intently at the little black dot on this dingy, white piece of paper.

"We've begun to drill, just a few minutes ago, a tube that will hopefully lead us to the men," Reed says.

"That's fantastic!" Lindsay says, sinking back in the sofa. "Oh, God, please let it find them. Please let it find them," she chants.

"I do want to point out," Vernon says, side-eyeing Lindsay, "that this does not come without risks."

"What risks?" I ask, glaring at him.

"Somehow, the crew mined into what we call an 'old works.' That's a mine that was dug before maps were taken of where the work was done. We didn't know it existed. But it does and it was there and once they bored into the side of it, that's what caused the collapse."

I fling forward in my seat. "So can we get to them from there? Can we find the opening to that mine and go in that way?"

"No," he says, killing the butterflies that frolicked hopefully in my stomach. "We have no idea where that mine opened and closed. Remember, we didn't know it existed until now. And usually these things are filled with water, which poses a threat."

"What kind of a threat?" I ask, feeling Dr. Walker's hand squeeze my shoulders.

"If the miners have managed to find an open space and it fills with water . . . there would be nowhere for them to go."

My hand shakes as I reach for Dr. Walker. He collapses his palms around mine.

"We can't do anything about that right now," Reed says. "But what we can do is try to reach them from the top. Like Vernon said, water is a big threat right now, and unfortunately, Indiana has a water table that sits right above where we need to be. We're going to have to cut through that to get to them."

"Wait," I say, sitting up. "But won't that drain down into where they are?"

"It could," Reed says warily. "But we're hoping the pocket we hit will be dry or low. There's really no way to tell until we get there."

"My God . . ." Lindsay moans, bringing her hands in front of her in prayer. "Please help us."

My gaze fixes on Greta. "Are you married?"

"Yes, ma'am."

"Then, wife to wife, bring my husband home."

Thirty-Eight

TY

WATER DROPLETS HIT me in the face, causing soot from my blackened face to run into my eyes. I wipe them as best as I can and listen as the drilling gets closer.

We stand in a line, our eyes towards the ceiling, illuminated by Jiggs' headlamp, waiting for any indication where the drill may break through. Waiting, too, for any indication that the ceiling may crack and we're buried into the dirt like fossils. The walls of this tomb seem to squeeze together with every minute that passes, the air tasting more putrid, the noise of the drill more deafening.

A hand lands on my shoulder and I look at Cord. He smiles, his teeth spattered with bits of black coal dust. His grin is easy, and if we weren't here, something casual like, "Hey, want to shoot some hoops?" or "Want to take Yogi to the lake with me?" would pass his lips.

But we are here. In this hellhole. One I'm beginning to think, with every creak of the ceiling, may be our final resting place. The "death" of "til death do us part."

Shivering, I blow out a final rush of air. "Do you think it'll hold?" I ask, nodding towards the roof that once was held upright by timbers. Those timbers have fallen, jags of rock and debris hang mercilessly from above like stalactites in a cave.

The drilling stops.

"I figure it's going to bust through over there," Cord says, nodding past Jiggs.

"Yeah," Jiggs agrees, his teeth chattering. "The water is dripping like crazy over there too. I'm guessing they're going through some sort of water table and it's pressurizing down here."

Cord and I exchange a look, knowing the possibilities. And that if the worst case scenario happens and this cavern starts to fill—there's nowhere to go.

The buzzing starts again, more powerfully this time, as we make our way to what used to be the ramp out. The walls shake, pieces of rock and ore falling away and crashing through the room.

My heart races, my blood soaring through my head, making me dizzy. I've never been so helpless. All I can do is watch the room shake ferociously, watch the water trickle in more quickly, listen to the sound of the drills scream. My fate is in someone else's hands.

"Hold on," Cord says over the chaos. The cavern shakes violently as the three of us crouch in a corner. I can hear Jiggs' prayers, the same one Elin whispers when she's nervous, one their mother taught them when they were little.

My heart lodges in my throat as I flip on my headlamp and aim it at the sound of the drill.

In one hard bolt of energy, the end of the metal tool pierces the ceiling where we had been camped.

We jump back as chunks of the ceiling give way and a steady stream of water flows down the wall. Before I can process this, I hear voices.

Springing to our feet, we amble to the trickle of light from above. Chills break out over my dingy skin as we shout up, angling our bodies under the light.

"This is Fred Jaspar," we hear from the top. "How many of you are down there?"

"This is Tyler Whitt," I shout. "With me are Jiggs Watson and Cord McCurry."

"So there are three of you?"

"Yes."

I look at Jiggs, his eyes glowing. He pats me on the shoulder in relief.

"Tyler, do you have the location of Grunt Salis or Shane Pettis?"

"No, sir," I yell up, the light starting to blind my eyes. "I think Pettis was killed in the cave-in, but we don't know about Grunt."

"How are you holding up? Are any of you injured?"

"No," I yell up, shielding my eyes with my hand. "How are our families?"

"Your families have been notified. They're safe and waiting on an update."

"Can we talk to them?" Jiggs shouts over me.

"Right now, we want to focus on getting you out of there," Fred replies. "We will let your families know we are in contact."

I turn my back on my friends and look into the darkness. My nose itches, my throat blocked by a lump the size of a chunk of coal.

"Can you . . ." I say, sniffling, turning back around. "Can you tell them we love them? Tell Elin I love her, okay?"

My voice breaks and Cord's right arm falls around my shoulder. I can't do it anymore; I can't be the strength for the group. Whether that makes me weak or not, it doesn't matter. I just need to hear her voice. I need to tell her I love her. Not through an intermediary, not through someone that's never met me.

"There's no way we can talk to them?" Jiggs asks, either reading my mind or feeling the same way.

"I'm sorry, that's against protocol right now," Fred says.

"You know what?" Cord barks back. "Fuck your protocol. Your fucking protocol got us stuck down here, so the least you can do is let these guys talk to their wives."

"We're going to need you to stay calm," Fred says, his voice so calm, so nonchalant we could be talking about the weather. "Let's get a plan together and get you out of there and then you can talk to them face-to-face, all right?"

"I . . ." I say, but Cord shakes his head at me.

"What's the plan?" Jiggs asks. "How you getting us out of here?"

"We're going to try to bore a shaft big enough to get you up, but we need to get our ducks in a row first."

I watch as the water continues to flow down the side of the wall. "You know we might have a water problem down here, right?"

"We're aware." Fred's voice is tight and I read exactly what he's saying.

"Shit," I mumble.

"We'll send some food and water down. Some extra lights. I need you guys to hang tight and don't disturb anything, okay? Someone will be up here every minute if you guys have any questions. Just holler up."

"All right," Jiggs says. "Hurry the fuck up, though, will ya?"

"We're doing everything we can."

I imagine Elin's face. "Fred?"

"Yeah?"

"Do more than you can. We need out of here."

ELIN

THE KNOCK IS quick and I turn on my heel from my pacing spot in the back of the room. My hand goes to my throat, probably because I stop breathing every time someone knocks.

"We have news," Vernon says as he enters. He, too, looks like he's aged years over the past twenty hours. Bags are piled under his eyes, his clothing now wrinkled and stained with what looks like spilled coffee.

Lindsay walks across the room and holds my hand. Our entwined knuckles shake as we search his features for some indication of good or bad.

"We've made contact with your husbands. They're alive," he says.

"Thank God," I say, my entire body shaking with the force of my emotions. I bend, my knees starting to go limp. "Are they okay? Are they hurt? Did you hear about Cord?"

"Cord is with them. It's just the three of them in a hole that was formed in the cave-in."

"Thank you, thank you," Lindsay repeats, releasing my hand and clasping hers in front of her face.

"We've sent food and water down and they are aware of our plans to get them out."

"Can we talk to them?" I ask, my heart pounding in my chest. "Please?"

"I'm afraid not," Vernon says, wincing.

"Why not?" Lindsay asks. "We're their wives. Jiggs is her brother too! That's bullshit!"

"I know you feel that way," Vernon apologizes. "This is standard protocol. We have to focus on the operation at hand and you aren't permitted out there. I'm sorry."

Lindsay and I turn to each other, burying our faces in the other's shoulder, our sobs racking our frames.

"They did ask us to tell you they love you."

I just cry harder. This should be a relief, that they're alive and well, but it's not. It means they're aware they're stuck a few hundred feet below the surface. It means they've probably witnessed their friends die. It means a miner's biggest fear has been realized by my husband, brother, and friend.

"Vernon?" I ask, wiping my eyes. "What are the chances we will get them out?"

"I can't say."

"Yes, you can," I say, narrowing my eyes. "What is the percentage that all three of them will get out of there?"

"We're doing the best we can."

"That's not good enough."

"Mrs. Whitt," he says, his voice full of anguish, "that's all I have. We are doing everything in our power to bring them home."

He walks to the door and opens it, but pauses before leaving. "If you ladies need anything else, I'm right out here."

Thirty-Nine

TY

CORD TOSSES A pebble. It hits a puddle of water and splashes. Years of fishing and skipping rocks tells me that the water is deeper over there than a simple wet patch.

Jiggs' light goes off on his helmet as he leans against the slick mine wall. He mumbles in his sleep, something about a transmission. Cord and I grin, but don't laugh. Any other time, we'd heckle him relentlessly, but not today. Not now. We just let him enjoy the simple annoyances of a transmission.

The glow from the light illuminates the trash from the food and the emptied bottles. I lift a leg, my body cold, wet, and aching. My clothes are completely soaked through, even though the mining bibs are supposed to be waterproof. I guess they aren't made to sit in this shit for hours on end.

Or days?

"How long you figure we've been down here?" I ask Cord, keeping my voice down so as not to wake Jiggs.

He tosses another pebble. "Fuck if I know." Another pebble launches. "Hopefully not much longer."

Another pebble goes sailing.

"I've been thinking . . ." I force a swallow. Once this is decided upon, it will be a sealed deal. And as Foreman, it's my decision. I remember how many decisions I've had to make and how many

I hated making and laugh. I'd give anything to trade those stupid choices with this one.

"If the bore works," I say, "we need to agree on who goes out in what order."

Cord's eyes darken. "I go last."

"No," I gulp, the words stinging my throat. "I have to go last. I'm the boss."

"Fuck that," Cord says, the remaining debris in his hand rocketing across the room. "You two have wives, families. I'll go last."

"I can't do that, Cord."

"Sure you can."

Blowing out a breath, I steady myself. "I will agree Jiggs goes first. Lindsay is pregnant. That gives him seniority, in my opinion."

Cord nods, his mouth opening for a split second. He shakes his head and growls through the room.

"What?" I ask.

"Nothing." He removes his helmet and sits it beside him. "Okay. Jiggs first. I agree with that. Then you."

He looks pointedly at me, a fire to his gaze that I don't see often.

"I'm the Foreman," I point out. "I took an oath to get my men in and out every shift."

"I really don't give a shit," he chuckles angrily.

"Damn it, Cord. If something happened to you, do you think I'd be able to live with myself knowing I left you behind?"

"That works both ways, Mr. Foreman. I'm not about to go up and tell Elin, 'He'll be right here.'"

Staggering to my feet, I wince as my left leg screams in agony. "It's Jiggs. You. Then me. Got it?" I bark.

He watches me closely, his lips forming a thin line. Finally, he shrugs and stands, grabbing his helmet off the ground. "Whatever, Whitt. I'm gonna go take a leak."

His boots splash in the water as he makes his way into the darkness. I watch him until I can't see him anymore, then I turn to Jiggs. He's smiling in his sleep, his face streaked black, making him look like a cartoon character.

My knees buckle as the situation slams into me. I catch myself on the wall.

"Dear God," I whisper, feeling my lashes touch the grit on my face. "Please get us out of here."

ELIN

"I LOVE YOU."

Even though I didn't say the words out loud, I can hear them ricochet through my mind.

Ty's face is all I see, his wide grin highlighted vividly in my mind. I see his thick lashes, the little freckle on the right side of his nose. The way his dark hair contrasts with his fair skin.

It's comforting, the only relief I can find in this madness. I feel connected to him this way, to imagine him in front of me and talking to him.

"We've been through some crap lately, huh?" I say, although not out loud. My words, again, are for he and I only.

I block out Lindsay talking quietly on her cell phone across the room. I ignore the faint sounds of the office that shares a wall of this conference area we've settled into over the last day. I concentrate on Ty.

Tears wet my lashes as I let that thought wash over me. "You're a survivor," I tell him. "You've made it through hell before. And I need you now more than ever."

My hand goes to my belly and I fight the tears. "I have a surprise for you, Ty."

I catch a sob before it escapes and I draw Lindsay's attention. Right now, stressed to the max, the lights dim, my life on pause, I need this moment with my husband—real or not.

"You have so much to do here yet. I need you to fix the back door. I need you to make sure the furnace is still on. I need you to hold me," I say, even my not-real voice breaking.

My body quakes with the tears that beg to spill, my back lifting off the brown fabric of the chair.

"Get my brother and get Cord and get out of there," I beg. "Do you hear me?" I scream inside my head. "You can't leave me here! Not again."

A man's voice makes me jump, nearly catapulting out of my chair. My lids fly open, only to see Vernon standing at the front of the room.

Lindsay gives me a strange look and I realize I must not have heard him knock.

"I just received an update from the mining board. We will begin boring into the hole within the hour," he relays.

I glance at the clock. It's nearly noon, Ty's day off. "That's fantastic!" I exclaim.

"It's great news," he says cautiously. "Just remember, this is not a guarantee." He holds his hands out as Lindsay and I balk. "I don't want to scare you, but I want you to be aware of the risks."

"Which are?" Lindsay asks.

"We have flown in an expert in this kind of thing. He has designed plans to extract miners numerous times before, so we have reason to be optimistic. But you have to remember, we are battling Mother Nature. There are no guarantees."

The room suddenly feels too small. The air too stale. The lights too fake.

I begin to pace, walking back and forth across the laminated floor. "I need to get out of here," I say, stopping and looking at Vernon. "Can we get closer to the mine?"

"I can get you into a different room here, certainly. But we aren't authorized to get any closer to the mine. And I strongly suggest not going outside, unless you want to give a statement to the press. They're camped out, waiting for news, just like we are."

My head tilts towards the ceiling and I feel the weight of the world on my shoulders.

"I'll work on getting a fan brought in. Maybe circulating the air will help?" he asks.

I watch him like he's crazy. No, a fan won't help. No, circulating the air won't help.

Having my husband and going home will help.

He seems to sense my thoughts and backs towards the door. "We will do our best to update you before any news hits the media. They are outside filming. If you'd like to watch, I can bring in a television . . ."

Lindsay looks at me and I stare blankly at him. He leaves.

Forty

TY

JIGGS SITS ON top of a lump of coal, his head buried in his hands. Water laps at the tops of his boots, just like it does mine. It leaks inside my boots, the bitter cold stinging my toes. Our teeth are chattering as we struggle to stay out of hypothermia. It's been this way for a couple of hours now.

My spirits are falling, as much as I try to keep them up for all of us. I'm tired, cold, achy. And I have this overwhelming fear that's taken root in my gut as my energy wanes that this isn't going to end well. Every hour we're down here increases the chances we won't make it out. That's why they suggested we write these letters. They know the odds.

Shivering, my heart as broken as the walls of this cavern, I look into the darkness. So many things I didn't do, so many things I put off, so many things I took for granted because who would've thought this would've happened to me.

I look at my friends.

To us?

Cord takes the pen from me and rips a sheet of paper from the notepad the top sent down. I can see the paper wet as his damp fingers touch it.

A heaviness sits on us, silencing us all. Once they start boring, which they informed us will happen shortly, our contact with the outside world will cease. All attention will be put on the bore and the reservoir of water sitting on our heads, the same water that's slowly filling the room.

"I'm done," Cord says after a while. He folds the paper into quarters. He puts it in the baggie and when Jiggs and I don't make an effort to drop ours into it, he crushes the opening with his hand and sighs.

"Just . . . give me a minute," I eke out, watching the paper tremble in my hands.

If shit goes wrong, these will be my last words to my wife. To the love of my life. To the woman I would do anything for and love beyond measure. I wish I had more time to write this, more time to be able to find the words to tell her all the things I want her to know, to give her some sort of guidebook on how to do the things she doesn't know how.

I look away into the darkness and blow out a breath, even the darkness a blur through my tears.

I love her. So damn much. And if I don't make it out of here, I'm okay with that on my part. I mean, I hate I won't get to experience life with her, but what will I know once I take my last breath? Nothing.

I hate it for her. For the pain she'll go through, for having to recalibrate her life. I feel like I've let her down, and I just wish I could talk to her, face to face, one final time, and beg her to forgive me and tell her how much she means to me and hold her in my arms and . . .

The tears come fast and hard.

Sucking in a quick breath, I look at the words on the note in my hand. They're incomplete. A ramble of topics and words and emotions and things to make her laugh, but it's the best I can do.

My words mirror the man I am: a failed attempt at making things right.

"We're ready to start!" a voice booms from above.

I look at Jiggs as his head lifts to mine. His eyes are bloodshot, his hair caked with soot. "Here we go," I say, reaching for his letter.

He kisses it before putting it in my hand. I drop them into Cord's bag.

He stands and places them in my lunch box. Tying a rope around the handle, he tugs on it and we watch it rise to the surface as water speeds down to the floor.

ELIN

A PLATE OF nibbled fruit and sandwiches sit on the table in between us. Paper cups of water sit, virtually untouched, next to it.

Lindsay's face is swollen, her lips cracked and red. Her skin is blotchy, her hair a tangled mess. It's such a contrast to her usual made-up appearance that it breaks my heart.

"How are you?" I whisper, my throat parched.

"About the same as you." Her voice is husky, matching mine. "You know you look like a mess, right?"

A hint of a smile plays on her lips and, instantly, a bit of pressure releases from my shoulders.

"You haven't looked in the mirror recently, huh?" I tease.

"Aren't we a sight?" She leans back in her chair. "How long do you think it will take?"

"I have no idea."

We sit in silence again, each of us coming to terms with the next piece of the puzzle. How the next few hours will determine the rest of our lives.

"They're going to be fine," Lindsay says out of nowhere. "I know that sounds crazy and optimistic, but I believe it."

I half-smile, unable to give her more.

"I fell asleep earlier—today? Yesterday?—and I had a dream. I was giving birth to this baby, a girl, if you're wondering, and Jiggs was with me, holding my hand. I felt so calm, so happy. It has to be a glimpse of the future because I could never feel like that if he wasn't here. I just couldn't." She looks at me earnestly. "They're going to be okay, Elin."

"They have to be," I say, wishing I had felt as sure about it as Lindsay. "I can't . . ." I gulp, "I can't imagine going through life without either one of them."

"I know and that's why they'll come back to us. They have a guardian angel watching over them. I feel it."

I pick at a sandwich and avoid her stare. Even though I've tried to convince myself this will end well, I don't feel that way. Maybe because I've heard Ty talking about mining disasters. Maybe because I feel like he's been spared once already. Maybe because I understand the dangers more than she does. Whatever the reason, I just can't find that peace about it.

"I was thinking," she says, her voice lifting me out of my daze. "We should have a double baby shower."

"I can't think about that right now."

"Sure you can," she says, resting her elbows on the table. "You have to feed the result in your mind that you want. If we are imagining this party together, our boys there, that gives the universe the energy we want it to have."

Laughing, I roll my eyes. "I don't know how much of that universe energy stuff I believe."

"Well, I do," she says simply. "And I'm going to be over here choosing the theme and the finger foods, so if you want a say in it, I'd speak up."

"You're nuts," I say, feeling an ease seep in my bones.

"I am," she laughs. "So should we wait until we know what we're having or should we just go green and yellow and—"

A knock hits the door, cutting her off. The positive air evaporates from the room as Vernon walks in.

"The boring has started," he says, walking over to the table. He forces a swallow before producing two baggies. "Your husbands sent these up for you."

My stomach hits the floor as I stare, unmoving, at my name written in Ty's handwriting on the dirty piece of paper in front of me.

Forty-One

TY

T HE BORING EQUIPMENT screams over our heads, shaking everything around us. Mixed with the water gushing in like a river has been unleashed, it's like being in a giant washing machine.

The water is now up to my waist. A sea of cold, black water that's thick like soup from the debris and mud and muck, rippling in a nonstop motion from the commotion above.

I barely hear the sound anymore. It was loud, so loud, at first. But that was untold minutes ago. Hours, maybe. Now it's just a new normal as we wait to see if the shaft hits bottom.

My heart strikes against my ribs, my lungs battering them too as I struggle to stay calm. To stay alive.

Ducking chunks of rock from the ceiling as all four walls of the room judder and quake from the assault of the boring machine, I'm pulled into one direction: survival.

"Ty!"

I read Cord's lips more than I hear his voice as he yanks on my arm, pulling me off my feet. One hand lands on his chest in an attempt to catch myself, my chest submerging in the muddy water. A boulder the size of a small car smashes into the water right where I was standing.

A chill rips through me, more from the fear of what could've happened than from the ice-cold water.

Jiggs grabs my other arm and helps me to my feet. His teeth clamor together, his cheek cut but the blood clotted together by black gunk.

I'm exhausted. The fatigue I feel is reflected on my friend's faces.

"Just a little longer," I shout, looking as optimistic as possible. They nod, reading my lips, but my words do nothing to help their spirits.

Cord's headlamp flickers towards the sound of another boulder smashing into the water. As it scans the cavern, it pauses on the north wall and the steady flow of water pouring down the walls.

"Stay calm!" I try to shout over the shrill screams of the boring machine.

"Fuckkkkkkkk!" Jiggs shouts, eyes wide, as we dodge falling rocks from both above and on either side of us.

"Shit!" Cord screams, his face contorting in a mix of agony and fear as a rock strikes his left shoulder. He sags at the impact, his knees buckling, threatening to drop him into the water pooling around us.

Jiggs and I grab an arm and pull him up, Cord wincing in pain, as we huddle together in a corner and try to stay alive.

"Stay calm," I repeat, my face inches from theirs.

"They have to be close!" Jiggs shouts, looking over my shoulder at the spot where the ceiling is bowing and flexing. "Surely to God they're close!"

"Ah!" we shout in unison as the noise becomes too loud to take and the boring machine drops through the ceiling.

We shout in celebration, tears flowing down our jet black faces, as we hug one another in an attempt to celebrate as well as keep each other from collapsing into the water.

The machine is silenced as it begins its ascent back to the top.

"You boys okay down there?" a voice shouts from above.

"Yeah!" I shout back. "Cord got a little banged up, but we're here!"

"How's the water situation?"

I shine my headlamp around the room. The water is now rushing into the room full-speed. "Coming in quick!"

"We'll have the box to you in just a few minutes. We're gonna have to work fast! You'll get in and pull the rope and we'll haul it up. Got it?"

"Yes!"

I look at my friends' faces. A combination of relief and fear is etched through every line.

Looking at Cord, I give him a final shot to reneg on the agreement we made earlier, that Jiggs is the priority. He nods.

"Jiggs," I say, looking him in the face. "You're going up first."

ELIN

I NEVER KNEW one piece of paper could weigh so much.

Holding it in my hand, palm open, I look across the way at Lindsay. Her eyes are wide as she looks at Jiggs' note in her hand. Turning her back to me, she walks to the front of the room and slips out the door.

I brush my fingers over my name, scrawled in Ty's penmanship and stained with water and dirt. It reminds me of the inside of his truck—everything had its place, but none of it could escape the mine dirt. Just like this letter.

With my heart strumming at an ear-splitting level, I carefully unfold the paper.

The edges are torn and stained and a big drop of something has hit the middle, making the words there hard to read. I start at the top.

"Dear Elin,

If you're reading this, I'm guessing I didn't make it out."

"No," I whisper, blinking back tears. Jaw set in defiance, I redo the folds of the paper and enclose the letter in my hand. "You *will* make it out," I say out loud. "I won't read this if that's what it means."

Anger flashes through me, a zip of energy that I embrace.

"Get your ass back here," I demand, not even caring if someone hears me and thinks I'm crazy. "Stop this 'guessing you didn't make it out' bullshit and come home."

I pace a circle, feeling the electricity soar in my veins. I take a deep breath.

"Ty, if you hear me," I say out loud, "I need you back here. I have something to tell you, and this time, you better fucking come home."

Swiping the water cup off the table, I take a long drink. The water is lukewarm, but it feels good sliding down my throat. I down it all.

Setting it back on the table, I continue my plea. "Jiggs, if you hear me, I'm not about to host Thanksgiving at my house from now on. So figure out your shit and come back here. You've got a wife to take care of and a baby to raise. And don't tell Ty, but a niece or nephew too."

I blink back a tear and sniffle. "Cord . . ." my voice breaks as I think of my sweet friend. "You never, ever fail me. Somehow, you always figure out what I need or what I need to hear and you deliver. Every. Time. Right now, I need you to deliver your sweet self, along with my handsome husband and ridiculous brother. Do you hear me?" I ask, my bottom lip trembling. "That's an order."

I fall into a chair at the table and listen to my cries resonate through the room.

"Ladies," Vernon says, rushing into the room without knocking, Lindsay on his heels.

I stand immediately, springing to my feet, my heart stalling in my chest. "What?"

"One of the men is on the way up."

I suck in a breath, my eyes floating to Lindsay. Exhaling, it comes out in shaky, tear-filled breaths. "Which one?" I ask.

"I don't know. I just got word that one is in the slot." He looks between us. "We have a television out here if you want to watch. I can clear the room out."

"Yes," I say, nodding emphatically. "Please."

He goes before us and we can hear his voice booming through the other room, followed by shoes hitting the floor. I grab Lindsay's hand and we race across the hall into Room E11.

It's empty. A large flat screen television is lit up on the far wall, one of the national television stations on live. It's muted, but we get the idea. The words scrolling along the bottom make it clear what's happening: Miner #1 is coming to the top.

"I wonder who it is," Lindsay says to no one in particular. Her voice is a mere rasp. "God, I feel guilty because I'm praying it's Jiggs. But I know how much you need it to be Ty and . . . Cord . . ."

"There's a good chance it is Jiggs or Cord," I say. I fight back the poison in my stomach. "I can't imagine Ty coming up before them."

My spirits sink, just a bit, at the realization. I feel guilty about that too, but I can't help it. He's my husband.

Forty-Two

TY

THE MAKE-SHIFT ELEVATOR lands, sitting on top of the water. A part of me, a huge part of me, wants to slide inside, pull the rope, and get the fuck out of here.

But I can't.

I'd never forgive myself if they didn't make it out and I did. And how could I look at my wife and know I killed her brother?

"Jiggs, get in there," I say, grabbing his shoulder and pressing him towards the box.

Water roars into the chamber like an open sieve. It inches up quickly, now chest-high.

"I can't leave you guys down here," he cries, tears streaming down his face.

"Yeah, you can," I say. "You have a kid coming and I need someone to watch my wife and no one will do that like you. Now get your ass in there."

"Promise me you'll be up," he says, climbing inside. "Promise me."

"We promise," Cord says. "Now hurry the fuck up."

Jiggs reaches over head and yanks the cord. The machines groan as he is lifted up and out of sight.

"One down," I mutter to myself. Turning to Cord, I blow out a breath. "You're next."

We wait for the box to lower, but it doesn't come. I peer up and can see the glow of the lights at the ground level, but no movement from the box.

"We're having a problem with the gears!" someone shouts down the air shaft. "We're trying."

"This water is chest high!" I shout. "Hurry the hell up!"

I look at Cord.

He looks at me.

ELIN

"COME ON, COME on, come on," I repeat as we watch the man being escorted onto a stretcher. "Who is it?" I shout.

We can't see close enough to tell, just a figure of a man that could be any of the three. My heart is in my throat, Lindsay's hand nearly breaking mine, as we watch with bated breath.

My hand is on my stomach and I whisper, "Daddy promised to come home, little one. He'll come home. Hang in there."

"It was Jiggs," Vernon says from behind us.

We whirl around as Lindsay screams, her hand going to her mouth. "Oh my God!" She looks at me and pulls me into a hug.

I'm stunned, frozen in space. I hear her talking and watch her ask me something, to which I nod. She leaves the room with Vernon and I'm standing alone, watching a television screen where nothing is happening.

I flick the buttons on the side until the sound comes on.

"They're still working on the gears, Gerald. The problem stems from the lowering harness. We're being told it's urgent they retrieve the other two miners as quickly as possible because water is filling the cavern below. Everyone listening, pray for these men."

Gasping, I back up until I'm against the wall. My legs sway beneath me as the television blurs from the tears.

Forty-Three

TY

THE CART BEGINS to lower in our direction and I heave a sigh of relief. Then reality strikes.

The water is at my throat, sloshing around against my mouth. It's cold and thick and bitter.

I angle my chin towards the ceiling and look at Cord. "Your turn, buddy."

He shakes his head.

"Cord, get the fuck in there!"

"Only one of us is gonna make it, Ty."

"Don't say that," I shout. "Get the hell in that cart and get up there before neither of us makes it!"

I grab his arm, the shoulder that got banged up, and he winces. Easing up, he takes advantage and I find myself spinning in the water.

My head jerks to his, my eyes wide. His teeth clenched, a look of pure determination on his face.

"No, Cord," I say, my voice cracking as I realize what he's doing. I fight back with everything I have left in me, but he overpowers me.

"Get in there, Ty."

"No!" I shout as his hands find my shoulders and he shoves me into the cage. We continue to struggle, the water inching up. The walls of the shaft begin to crumble, water splashing in our faces.

He reaches inside and pulls the cord. Immediately, the cart starts to move upwards. "What are you doing?" I scream, tears pouring from my eyes. "Cord! Damn you!"

"Take care of Yogi for me," he shouts over the sound of the dirt giving away.

I see his eyes in the sea of darkness as I ascend. I collapse into a heap on the floor of the makeshift elevator, trying desperately to hear his voice.

"Thanks for everything you've ever done for me, Ty," he shouts as he slips out of sight. "I love you, man!"

"Cord!" I shout, slumping against the back wall, sobbing.

ELIN

"MRS. WHITT," VERNON'S voice says beside me. "One more is on the way."

I'm afraid to look, but there's no way I won't. Taking a few tentative steps toward the television, I hold my breath.

The man makes it out of the cart, on his hands and knees, before a blanket is thrown over him and he's helped to his feet.

"Who is it?" I ask, wheeling around. My heart threatens to explode in my chest. "Who was it!?"

Vernon pokes his head out of the door and pulls back inside. "It was Ty."

I fall to my knees, weeping into my hands.

Forty-Four

TY

"**G**ET CORD!" I scream, my words broken with grief.

I know there's no chance. The water was too high and the channel was disintegrating as we rose. The cart will never be able to reach him. I know that, but I can't believe it. I can't give up.

"Get Cord," I shout again, my vision blurry as halogen lights shine brightly on me. "Hurry!"

"We're going back down after him," a man says to me, but I don't see his face.

"You have to get him!" I throw my helmet to the side and tug at my hair. "Get him. You have to fucking get him!"

"Why did you do this to me?" I scream as tears stream down my face as I sob into the night. "Why? Damn you, fucker!"

My head buries in my hands as my body racks with grief that my best friend just gave his life for me. "Damn you, Cord!"

No one approaches me for a few minutes, giving me time to get myself together. Whether I look together or not on the outside, I'll never be the same on the inside. A piece of me will be down that hole, a part of me as jagged as the walls of that room.

"Where's my wife?" I ask, finally taking a proffered towel and wiping at my burning eyes. The white linen is smeared with grease and debris. "Where's Elin?"

"We've sent someone for her. We need to take you to the emergency room, Sir."

"Not until I see her," I say, refusing to get into the ambulance. "I need to talk to someone. I need to know if they got Cord."

A man in a black business suit comes into the tent set up with a look of defeat on his face. "Mr. Whitt?"

"Did you get Cord? Tell me you got him. Please . . ."

"I'm sorry. We hit water."

"No!" I wail, covering my face with the towel. "No!"

ELIN

"HE'S IN THERE." Vernon points to a grey tent.

I start running, bumping into people, tripping over cables and wires, ignoring requests for me to slow down and questions about who I am. I run, my focus clear: to get to Ty.

Shoving the tarps open, I quickly scan the room. But I hear him before I see him.

My throat closes shut, my heart splintering, as I hear him sobbing from the other side near the ambulance.

Sprinting to the sound, I see him. He's sitting on a chair, covered from head to toe in black mud. He's leaned over, his face buried in a towel, his body shaking, nearly convulsing.

"Ty!" I scream and he looks up. I run to him and he stands, catching me as I nearly leap in his arms. "Oh, baby!" I cry, running my hands through his hair, burying my face in the crook of his neck.

I pull back and kiss his face, his lips, as he pulls me the tightest he's ever pulled me into him before. His entire body is covered in some kind of oily grease. It's caked in his hair, his ears, his eyes.

"Are you okay?" I ask, wiping the muck off his face. "Tell me you're okay. Talk to me, baby. I need to hear your voice."

"I'm fine," he says. "But Cord . . ."

My heart stops. "Cord?"

"He didn't make it."

"No!" I gasp, my legs threatening to go out from under me. Lurching forward, my heart splintering into a million pieces, I reach for my husband.

His big, beautiful eyes fill with tears and our cries mix together, a haunting, lonely sound, as we sink to the ground.

"Cord!" I sob. "No . . ."

Those friendly eyes, his charming smile, his cheeky grin—it all flashes before my eyes. His voice drifts over my ears, not so much words, but the timbre. The ease of his spirit, the kindness in everything he did washes over Ty and I as we sit, entwined, on the dirt floor.

Ty breaks down in my arms, his body shaking violently. "I told him . . . I told him not to . . ." His words are barely able to be understood through his wails. "God, Cord. Why?"

Pulling my husband as close to me as possible, I soothe him the best I can in the midst of my own suffering. Just as I feel myself start to go over the ledge, I feel him. I feel Cord. Like a rush of warmth from a mid-afternoon sun, I know his spirit is here.

Forty-Five

ELIN

HIS LASHES ARE splayed against his cheeks, his skin cut and nicked from the ordeal. He's clean now, lying in a hospital bed. I sit in the chair beside him and say a prayer of gratitude that it's just for observation and a little hypothermia. That he's going to be as good as new.

Jiggs is in the room next door, sleeping off his injuries too. Lindsay and I have switched rooms a couple of times over the past twenty-four hours, mostly because I didn't want Ty alone and I wanted to get a visual on my brother.

Jiggs has been awake some and we've talked. He's shared a little of what they went through, but I can tell it might be awhile, if ever, before he really wants to speak about it. The hospital said they'd send in grief counselors to help them talk it out, if they wanted.

Ty has slept almost constantly since we got here. The doctor said to let him rest, that it was the best way to heal. I've been able to sleep some, as long as I'm holding his hand. Even then, it's a fitful sleep because he mutters Cord's name and my tears fall again.

Like he feels me watching him now, he opens his eyes. It's a slow, sleepy process, but one that makes me smile.

"Hey," I say softly, bringing his knuckle to my mouth and kissing it. "How do you feel?"

"All right, I guess," he says. "Better now that I see your face."

"I've been here the whole time."

He grins and I watch as it takes effort for him to manage the expression. The cut down his left cheek ripples, making him wince.

Even though he's a little battered, a little bruised, I think his damage is internal. A broken heart. A scarred soul that may never be repaired. Like mine.

The loss of Cord still feels unreal. I expect his goofy smile, his warm voice to walk in the door at any minute and give me hell. I'd do anything to hear him call me a pit bull, to give Ty a hard time about playing pool, or Jiggs shit over the way he drives.

Nothing in our lives will ever be the same and I feel the loss of Cord McCurry constantly. We all do.

"How's Jiggs?" Ty asks, struggling to get comfortable. I help him adjust in his bed before he tugs on my arm. "Will you lie with me?"

I laugh. "I don't think the nurses would like that."

"I don't give a shit. I just spent . . . how long? . . . without you. I want you next to me."

"How can I resist that?"

Slipping off my shoes, I climb in bed next to him. I rest my head on his shoulder, like I do every time we lie together, and drape an arm over his torso, careful to avoid the wires and bandages.

"Jiggs is okay," I say finally, my words soft. "He has a few more dings than you and a broken rib, but he's fine. Raising some hell over there."

He laughs, his chest rising and falling, but I hear the hesitancy in it.

"How are you? Really?" I ask.

"I don't know. You know, I'm physically okay. I don't feel too bad. I just . . ." His voice trails and his body stills. "I don't know that I'll ever get Cord's face out of my mind. Or what he did for me. For us."

I squeeze him tight and blink back tears.

"He thought the world of you," Ty says, sniffling, his voice breaking. "When we were going through our shit, he would be my voice of reason. He would tell me to keep at it, to not give up. That son of a bitch . . ."

We cry together, our hearts mourning the loss of one of the best people to ever walk the earth. To a sweet boy, a sweet soul, that maybe didn't realize he knew how to love, but loved more than anyone I've ever met.

"I feel like we have to honor him," I say, wiping my eyes with the bedsheet. "He gave his life for us to be together. We have to figure out how to give back to the world in his name."

"We could never give back enough for what he just gave us," Ty says. "It's a hard gift to accept."

I rise up and look him in the face. "But it's one he gave knowing the consequences. For you to not just accept that takes away from what he did."

He shrugs, not agreeing, not disagreeing. Instead, he changes the subject. "I want to take a vacation. Just me and you."

"Where to?"

"The ocean. Cord always wanted to see the ocean and never made it. I want to do that. For him. Sound okay?"

"Sure," I say, my heart racing. "But I might not be that much fun."

"Why's that?"

"Well," I say, angling my body so I can see his face. "I can't eat seafood."

"Sure you can. I know you don't like shrimp, but I think you'll like lobster. And crab rolls."

The corner of my lip twitches. "And my round belly might not look good in a bikini either . . ."

"What are you talking about?" he says, brushing my comment off. "You're hot as fuck and I want to see youuuu . . ."

He stills. His eyes go wide, head cocking to the side. "What are you saying?"

"I'm saying," I say, bending over him so that my lips hover over his, "that I'm having your baby."

"Really?" His voice is full of hesitation, his eyes twinkling, yet guarded, like he thinks I'm kidding.

"No, I'm making it up," I giggle. "Yes, really! I'm pregnant, Ty."

He pulls me to him, nearly suffocating me. Giggling, I try to pull back. "I can't breathe!"

He lets my face loose, but then smothers it in kisses. His lips are still swollen from the accident, but that doesn't stop him from kissing me senseless.

I settle in beside him again, noting the smile etched on his face. It's inked on mine, as well.

"Mr. Whitt?"

We look to the doorway. A man is standing there with a large manila envelope in his hand.

"Are you Tyler and Elin Whitt? This is room 5431, isn't it?"

"Yes," Ty says. "What can we do for you?"

"I'm with Blackwater. My name is Hugh Umbrose. How are you tonight?"

"Better than I have been."

"Well, I'm actually here to see your wife." Hugh hands me the envelope. I sit up and take it. "This is a copy of Cord McCurray's papers. He listed you as his next of kin."

I drop the papers onto the sheets. "What?"

"You are listed as his next of kin. As far as Blackwater goes, you are in charge of his business."

I look at Ty and he just smiles.

"But we aren't . . . I mean, I'm not his family," I say, picking up the envelope again. "Not by blood."

"Sometimes family isn't made by blood, Mrs. Whitt. Sometimes it's a choice, and Mr. McCurry chose you."

TY

MY REFLECTION STARES back at me in the mirror. I don't look bad, just a little cut here and there. My hair needs trimmed and my limp is back pretty heavily, but there are no lasting effects of the accident.

Not physically, anyway.

I lay my tie around my neck and wait for Elin to come and do it. I'm not even going to fuck with it. Not only because I won't get it right anyway, but because I like her attention on me.

I need it.

I crave it.

She's the only thing that keeps me together.

Sleep has become my enemy. I wake up in cold sweats, sometimes from seeing Cord's face slip into the darkness, sometimes as I feel the earth shake beneath me and listen for the rocks to start falling. Jiggs has this problem too. They say it'll go away eventually. Maybe. Either way, I can deal with it because Cord gave me the chance.

I smile as I think back on his life. No one loved him like a parent, no one loved him like a husband. Yet, even with the absence of that kind of unwavering affection, he knew it.

I'm proof.

It's made me realize how selfish we are with our emotions.

How we blame other people for the decisions we make or the lack of opportunities we have and how stupid that is. Cord had an excuse to get out of anything; he had the hardest life of anyone I know. Yet he never used it as a crutch, and he didn't let it keep him from choosing love. Even if he didn't realize it.

"Hey," Elin says from behind me.

I turn to see her. Her eyes are puffy.

"What's wrong?" I ask, reaching out and cupping her cheek.

She sighs. "I felt like I should go through that envelope from the hospital," she says. "And I found this."

She holds up a piece of paper that stills me. It's white notebook paper with smears of black.

"Cord wrote this while you were underground. And it has my name on it," she whispers.

I fold her into my arms and rest my chin on her head as I remember us writing them. I had no idea he was writing to her, but I can't say I'm surprised. "Does it say anything important?"

She pulls away. "I'll read it to you:

"Well, this sucks."

She laughs at the little stick person in a state of obvious frustration that was clearly drawn for her amusement.

"I've had a lot of time to think down here. I've thought about a lot of things, but I keep coming back to what you said about everyone's life having a purpose. I'm sitting here in this hole the size of a small room with water freezing my toes off and your husband and brother making me crazy with their bickering and I'm wondering—how in the hell did I get here? Maybe my purpose in life is to be tormented by them assholes. Both of them."

Another stick person makes her giggle and she looks up at me, then clears her throat before continuing.

"In all of my life, you made the biggest difference." She looks at me, needing a second to gather herself before continuing. *"Even growing up, as kids, you showed me how to fight for people, how to stand up for what's right. You never knew it, but a lot of who I learned to be was by watching you and the empathy you had for people, even in times that were*

hard. You're going to be an amazing mother."

Her voice cracks and I grab her hand and squeeze it.

"I want you to know that I'm going to do everything I can to deliver your family back to you. And if I don't make it out of here, I don't want you to be upset. I mean, cry, because that feeds my ego a bit, but realize that maybe this was my purpose in life, like you said. And if that's the case, I'm okay with that. I really am. Remember that story I told you once about "insane decisions"? This one was premeditated. Remember that. Always.

Life's not for the faint of heart, that's for damn sure. But what doesn't kill you makes you stronger, and this, my friend, won't kill you. But I don't know how much stronger you can get.

"There's a winky face," she says, sniffling back tears.

"Thank you for taking an interest in the kid from foster care that pulled an attitude on you in the cafeteria line in junior high. I don't know why you did, but it proved to be the luckiest day of my life. It was the start of a family I never had.

"Thanks, Pit Bull. I've never really said this to anyone, but I love you guys.

"Cord."

She breaks into tears and I hug her tight. "I had no idea he thought of me like that," she sniffles. "No clue."

My tongue is tied, the idea of my friend being gone too fresh to discuss. Hearing his last words, the words I watched him write on that piece of paper read out loud, is haunting.

"We need to go," she says, reaching for my tie. "We can't be late for his funeral."

She works getting my jacket situated when I look at her. "He knew you were pregnant, didn't he?"

Her hand stills. "Yes."

"And I didn't know?"

She looks into my eyes, tears filling them. "It was Cord that told me I was pregnant." She goes back to work on the tie, clearing her throat. "He would've been a great husband and a great father someday."

I force a swallow and look away, blowing out a breath. "Did you read the letter I wrote you?"

She shakes her head. "No. I couldn't. I mean, I tried. But it started with 'I guess I didn't make it' and I couldn't read on." She finishes working my tie, pats my chest and steps back. "There you go, handsome."

I nod, thankful she didn't read the letter. Maybe we'll read it together at some point and maybe we'll let it sit in a drawer. I don't know. All I do know is that I'm grateful she didn't *have* to read it.

Forty-Seven

ELIN

SWORE I'D never set foot in here again. After the funeral service for my parents, I could barely drive by the little building on Main Street without breaking down. Yet, just a few years later, I stand in the very same place, giving another eulogy for someone I love.

The microphone hisses as I adjust it. I vaguely wonder if I can just shut it off, but that seems more of a hassle than it is worth.

Taking a deep breath, my lungs fill with the scents of a hundred flower arrangements surrounding the casket of my friend. Yesterday was calling hours. Ty, Jiggs, Lindsay and I stood at Cord's side and watched as mourners lined up down the aisle, out the door, and around the corner. They stood on the sidewalk in the pouring rain until it was their turn to enter to pay their respect to a man that deserved it.

I can't look over there. My feet are glued behind the podium, stuck in place by the gazes of people filling the seats facing me. The director brought in every chair they had in storage and it still isn't enough. Through the windows, I can see shadows of people standing on the sidewalk outside, listening to the service through speakers. It's almost too much to take in.

My hands tremble as I lay a piece of paper on the wooden stand in front of me. I constructed words as beautifully as I could late last night, wanting to say the perfect things as a goodbye to my friend. I can't see any of it.

Head bowed, lip quivering, I choke back the sob that shakes my chest. Lindsay rushes to my side, a handkerchief clenched in her hand. Her arm stretches across my shoulders and I turn to her.

We cry. Even when I'm sure there aren't tears to be spilled, they come out in waves. Before I can start to pull myself together, Ty and Jiggs are pulling us into one giant embrace.

We stand, the four of us, our fifth wheel missing, and feel the loss of him more than ever before. Arms entwined, heads touching, tears mixing—we grieve the loss of a person that is simply irreplaceable.

I glance up, wiping the tears from my face. A small gasp escapes my lips. Half the people facing me are standing, the other half on their way to their feet. Chins tucked, hands folded in front of them—it sends chills through me.

Jiggs slips his wife under his arm and guides her back to her seat. Ty presses a soft kiss to my forehead and asks me with his eyes if I'm okay. "I'm fine," I whisper. He seems unsure as he rubs his fingers down the cuts just starting to heal on his cheeks.

Finally, he takes his seat in the front row and I'm left watching the townspeople take theirs as well.

"I want to thank you all for coming today," I say, my voice heavy with emotion. "I know none of us want to be here. I'd rather be home, listening to Ty and Jiggs and Cord argue over who is the better mechanic."

A few chuckles roll through the room. My eyes find Ty's and he smiles, urging me on.

"Cord left me in charge of his affairs. When the paperwork was handed to me, I wasn't sure how to take it. Me?" I point to myself. "Why me? Then I saw how messy his house was and I realized it was some form of payback."

Lindsay's grin relaxes me and I take a deep breath. "Cord was a complicated guy in some ways and, in others, he was so simple. On one hand, he frustrated me like no one else on the planet. He wouldn't do what I told him and he called me Pit Bull," I say, rolling my eyes, "even though I hated it."

The words end as I choke back the tears. "That's a lie," I sniffle. "I didn't hate it. What I will hate is not hearing it again."

I glance at the casket. My breathing ragged, my shoulders vibrating with the emotion that threatens to spill out across the parlor. He looks so peaceful, like he might sit up and give us his easy smile at any minute. It's devastating.

"They say people don't remember words. They remember how you make them feel. I disagree. I will remember so many things that came out of Cord's mouth." A smile tickles my lips as I taste the salty tears streaming down them. "I'll miss him bossing me around and giving me advice, even when I don't want it. I'll miss the way his laugh sounds in the middle of Thoroughbreds on a Saturday night. I'll miss the way he'd get me to do what he wanted without me realizing it."

I try to find Becca in the sea of faces. I know she's there. I saw her earlier, but the tears make everything smear together. "This is so unfair," I say, squeezing the words out between sobs. My gaze meets Ty's and I have to grab ahold of the podium for support when I see the anguish on his face. His hands are clasped together on his lap, his gaze fixed on the casket at the front of the room.

"I wish I could talk to him just once more. To tell him . . ." I take a second to catch my breath. "To tell him thank you for sending Ty and Jiggs back to me. To tell him he was right about so many things. To tell him how much we all love him."

My tissue is completely soaked, the white material breaking apart in my hand. I press my palms against my eyes. I know I look like a complete disaster, but it's nothing compared to how I feel.

"What happened in the mine was a tragedy. I'd give anything to go back to that day and keep them all home. But I can't.

"Even though he didn't admit it and maybe he didn't even realize it, but Cord McCurry loved more purely than anyone. His love didn't come with strings. There were no contingencies with his friendship. If he liked you, that was it. I think we can all learn something from that."

I stand tall, clear my throat, and feel a sudden burst of clarity. "Cord's life was cut unfairly short and I refuse for it to be in vain. His death will not be something we cry about today and go to work tomorrow and forget. I won't allow that."

"Cord gave his life for my husband and brother. His bravery, his selflessness is unparalleled. I challenge each of you to live your life the same way."

Adjusting the microphone again, I find Becca. She's watching me with rapt attention, her eyes swollen from crying.

"One of Cord's most annoying traits was that he was always right. It didn't matter if it was about Jiggs' truck or my marriage, he had an uncanny way of knowing what the right answer was." I glance at my brother. "Sorry, Jiggs."

The crowd chuckles again.

"His little snippets of guidance taught me many things, but the most important were about relationships. That sometimes you have to take a step back and breathe. That you can't make *insane decisions* when your head is a mess. That even when you can't walk in someone else's shoes, you do have to try them on."

Glancing at the casket again, I smile. "It's not just the words we speak in a moment, but the weight of words over the course of time that matters. The words you choose every day add up. You are the words you speak, whether that's constructive or destructive. Cord was a light. His legacy, the heft of the words and actions he left behind, are proof."

"We need to live like Cord," I implore. "We need to treat the people in our lives, whether it's our spouse, parents, or friends, with care. Give them the benefit of the doubt. Lend an ear. Be sensitive to the trials they might be going through that we can't see."

"We can let our friend live through us in the way we treat one another in the good times and in the bad. Relationships can get messy. My own marriage was in shambles not too long ago." I look at Ty as his face tightens. "It was Cord that reminded me to fight for what I wanted, even when I was scared. To live and love bravely. It takes courage to love. But to have someone to love and to love you back is worth every bump in the road."

I smile at my husband and watch his features soften. "Life isn't easy. Love isn't for the faint of heart. You have to just put your fears aside and go for it. I learned that from Cord, the man that thought he couldn't love," I laugh. "Cord never quit on the people he loved, even when things got hard. Even when he was deep in the Earth. Even when he knew the end."

Leaving the podium, I walk across the burgundy carpet and peer into the casket. My hand rests on his as I give Cord one final smile. "We love you. So much."

I look back to the crowd. "You are all here to pay your respects to one amazing man. Don't let it stop when you walk out the door. Love fully, even when it gets hard. Give forgiveness, even when you aren't sure the other guy deserves it. And in every friendship you're in, don't forget to actually be friends."

I gaze across the sea of faces until my gaze lands on Tyler Whitt. He smiles the same smile he gave me the morning he asked me for a piece of gum so many years ago.

As I start to take my seat and a hymn begins to play, a peace settles over my soul. Ty takes one of my hands and Jiggs takes the other. I squeeze them both, the warmth in their palms comforting me.

Forty-Eight

ELIN

Six months later...

"**A**RE YOU SURE I'm not too heavy?" I start to lean off Ty's lap, but he pulls me down again against his Arrows' shirt.

"Will you stop it? You aren't too heavy."

"I'm huge," I say, rubbing my swollen belly. "This baby is going to be ten pounds. I know it."

"You'll be the prettiest ten-pound-baby-carrier I've ever seen," he teases, rubbing my nose with his.

I settle against him as we sit in a loveseat in the nursery. The sun streams through the windows, the tree outside casting shadows on the golden walls.

Baseball decorations adorn the walls and crib, and sure enough, a signed picture of Lincoln Landry on the closet door.

It's the perfect room for little Cord, even if it is a little cheesy. But Ty's gusto to decorate and his enthusiasm for his vision—how could I say no?

We rock gently back and forth, feeling the late afternoon sun on our skin.

"Did you get your homework done?" I ask him.

"Yes, Mother," he mocks, kissing me on the shoulder. "I'll be glad when *my* homework is done and I'm giving it out instead."

"Wait until you have to grade it," I point out. "Not so fun."

"Remember how fun grading papers is with me?" His eyebrows waggle and I laugh. "Besides, you're not going to do that for me? It'll be geography papers, and I hate to say, much more interesting than your cut and paste sheets."

"Maybe you can take them over and get Jiggs to help you. That nine-to-five job of his at the power plant isn't enough to keep him occupied. Lindsay is ready to murder him," I laugh. "She was saying yesterday that it's a good thing they didn't move to Florida. Without you to entertain Jiggs, she'd be out of her mind."

Ty rolls his eyes. "You'd think he'd have that truck working by now with all the time he has on his hands. Maybe Delia can help him when she gets older."

"Speaking of Delia," I say, grinning, "I told Jiggs we'd watch her tomorrow night so they can have a date night. Jiggs had me make reservations for them and order flowers and everything."

"It doesn't count if you do it for him."

"Yes, it does!" I laugh. "I just hope you want to cater to me like he does Lindsay after I have Cord."

"Don't I already?" he says, kissing my cheek.

"You do. Just remember me when your little sports buddy arrives in the world," I laugh, hearing the back door squeak. We wait as heavy footsteps walk through the house and the nursery door opens.

Dustin's head pops around the corner. Yogi bursts in at the opportunity and plops down at our feet. I reach down and scratch her behind the ears.

"Hey, can I go play some ball with Jason?" Dustin asks.

"Yes. Dinner is at six-thirty, so make sure you're back by then," I say, smiling at my new foster son. He returns the gesture, a softness in his eyes that's just begun to settle in.

The Case Manager from Child Protective Services said Dustin had lived in five different homes since being turned over to them. That helped explain his attitude and behavior issues. Once we passed the foster care courses and pulled some strings, he moved in and things have changed.

His grades are markedly better. His disciplinary record at school much cleaner. And the lightness in his step much easier.

Dustin told me he'd never had a room of his own and never went shopping for his own shoes. The day he picked out his own bed and basketball shoes was one of the happiest days of my life, just because of the joy on his face.

It's the little things. I knew that before the accident, but I know it more now. It's not about money, it's not about cramming in a week's worth of work in one day. It's not about getting from point A to point B and it's surely not about getting irritated over the little things in life. As a matter of fact, that's what it's all about.

Life is about stopping to chat with Ruby at the counter at The Fountain while she makes my Bump. It's about planning the Thanksgiving menu with your sister-in-law and arguing about who is hosting it this year, burning dinner because your husband won't keep his hands off you. It's about setting up Becca with every man I meet so she finds her happily-ever-after even though I don't have time and arguing with your foster son about his curfew and making a scarecrow every fall.

Some of those things might hurt. Life does pack a punch. But it's the scars that make us who we are, that tell the story of the life we lived.

"What are you making for dinner?" Dustin asks.

"Baked chicken and pasta. Maybe an angel food cake."

I look over my shoulder to see Ty beaming at me. He takes my hand in his and strokes my knuckles with the pad of his thumb.

"Awesome!" Dustin grins and closes the door behind him. His footsteps beat down the hall again and he leaves, the door squeaking.

"Are you ever going to fix that door?" I ask.

"Nope."

I look at him and make a face. "And why not?"

His cheeks flush just a bit, a shade most people wouldn't notice, but I do.

"What's that all about?" I ask, chuckling.

"Want the truth?"

"Absolutely."

He shifts my weight on his knee and looks me in the face. "When I was trapped, I kept thinking about how I needed to be here to fix the door and the furnace and all the things you don't know how to do. So now I don't want to fix them because it reminds me of my job here, if that makes sense?'

I kiss his full lips. "It does. But you have lots of jobs here. Can you fix the back door?"

His lips press against mine again, his hands starting at my cheeks and skimming my neck, shoulders, until they land on the tops of my rounded breasts.

"I can think of another job I'd like to take care of around here, if you're feeling like it."

I look at his handsome face. "I'm always feeling like it."

"Then let's go."

ABOUT THE AUTHOR

USA TODAY AND Amazon Top 10 Bestselling author Adriana Locke lives and breathes books. After years of slightly obsessive relationships with the flawed bad boys created by other authors, Adriana has created her own.

She resides in the Midwest with her husband, sons, and two dogs. She spends a large amount of time playing with her kids, drinking coffee, and cooking. You can find her outside if the weather's nice and there's always a piece of candy in her pocket.

CONTACT ADRIANA

ADRIANA CAN BE found on all social media platforms. Look for her on the ones you frequent most!

Her **website** is the place to go for up-to-date information, deleted scenes, and more. Check it out at *www.adrianalocke.com*.

If you use Facebook or Goodreads, there's good news! Adriana has reader groups in both places. Join Books by Adriana Locke (Facebook) and All Locked Up (Goodreads) and chat with the author daily about all things bookish.

ACKNOWLEDGEMENTS

THIS WAS A story that took so many formations, it's amazing to see where it ended up. There are so many people to thank for helping it get here:

Before anything, I'd like to acknowledge the Creator of the Universe. Thank you for blessing me with another opportunity to do what I love. Not only that, thank you for blessing me with so many generous, kind people to help make it happen.

I may write the words, but Mr. Locke gives me the faith, love, support, and space to make it happen. Thank you, My Love, for doing all the things I ask (and all of those that I don't). You work harder than anyone I know and, while I'm not sure why I was given you, I'm not giving you back.

My Littles can't read my books (yet—maybe never). That doesn't stop them from supporting me in their own ways. It makes it so much easier to spend hours writing when you roll out of the office to see their little faces asking, 'Did you finish? How's it going? You need a drink?' They're my life, plain and simple. I couldn't ask for more patient and supportive children.

Even at my age, I'm still a mommy's girl. There are nights she makes dinner and drops it off before the Littles are home from school because she knows I'm slammed. She lends a hand picking people up from practices and never misses a baseball game. Did I mention she does this while undergoing chemo? Yeah. She's a rock star and I couldn't do this without her.

To my extended family in all directions—thank you all for your incredible support. Every little thing, from passing out ink pens to watching the Littles to spreading the word about my release dates matter. And I couldn't appreciate it more.

Jenn C is my right hand, my note taker, my sanity. Without her, I'm a blubbering, chaotic, disorganized mess. And lonely. Thank you for pushing me, making me laugh, sending me pictures, and giving me hell. Stop traveling. I hate being without you. I love ya.

Kari and I met so randomly a few years ago. Even as our friendship grew, I had no idea it would turn into *this*. She's my other half, the person that knows me and what I like and what I mean even when I don't. So much of everything I do goes back to her in one way or the other. Thank you for being you, Kari—the most talented person I know. And my PIC. Forever.

Susan read this book, despite her life going at a million and six miles per hour. I don't know how she gets through a day and that's without throwing my books into the mix. Thank you for taking time for me. You make me smile each and every day.

Carleen read this a hundred times. Each time, her notes were so smart, so thorough, that I stared at the screen . . . and then got to work. There aren't enough words to explain my gratitude for your time, eyes, and love.

Ashley R read this story (multiple times) with so much passion, so much determination to get it 'just right' that I was floored. Thank you for your honesty. Thank you for your willingness to talk to me on the phone and hammer out the little things. Thank you for being you and sharing your talent with me.

Jen F jumped on board the beta train, having never worked with me before. Sometimes that can be an awkward exchange, but not this time. I appreciate your words of wisdom and the rawness in which you shared your point of view. You made such a difference to this manuscript.

Candace, Erica, and Joy didn't hesitate to lend their eye to the final product. Without your attention, ladies, this book would be riddled with mistakes. (And that one chapter wouldn't have been included, Candace!) Thank you for setting aside your lives and lending me some of your time. You are the best!

Thank you to Ashley P, Mary Lee, Robin, and Michele for reading this in its earliest, messiest stage. You were all forward with your comments, delightfully insightful, and generous with your time. I appreciate you all.

Mandi is my Pres (if you've read Wherever It Leads, then you get it). If not for her, I'm generally moody and indecisive. ;) You know all the things I mean to say, my friend. That's the beauty of our friendship—I don't even have to say them. #Easy

Suzie and I outlined this book while she sat in the parking lot of Nordstrom Rack. I'll never forget that night. Her enthusiasm for this story, her demand that it be written and be written next made this happen. Thank you for being my supporter, voice of reason and, most of all, my friend.

A long time ago, I was talking to Gail on the phone and telling her what it was like where I live. Immediately, the writer in her jumped up and shouted, 'Write that story!' I laughed at her, but she insisted. Even though I didn't write it then, I have now and I thought of her and her excitement over this prospect throughout the process. I hope it works out half as well as you'd hoped, Gail.

Once again, my team came through in a big way! Thank you to Lauren Perry with Perrywinkle Photography for the gorgeous picture of Ghent Scott. Hugs to my friend Kari March with Kari March Designs for taking my vision of the cover and making it happen (with your magical tweaks, of course!). Kisses to Lisa with Adept Edits for your patient work on this manuscript. God bless you. There aren't enough thank you's for Christine at Perfectly Publishable. Not only is her work the best in the business, but our friendship is one of my most treasured. Kylie and her team at Give Me Books was a delight to work with for my fourth time (I think!) and I was honored that Erin at Southern Belle Book Blog would take me on for this project as well. I also would like to give a shout-out to Jenn Watson with Social Butterfly PR for being one of the sweetest people in the business. Thank you all for making this happen!

Without Books by Adriana Locke, I probably would still be

tinkering with the first chapter. You ladies (and gentlemen!) push me, encourage me, and send me so much inspiration that it's impossible not to write. You're my happy place. Thank you for your incredible support in everything I do.

And thank you to Sam Hunt. Without your music, I would still have writer's block.

Locke, Adriana, author.
Written in the scars

JAN - - 2019

CPSIA information can be obtained
at www.ICGtesting.com
Printed in the USA
LVHW04s1320170918
590405LV00006B/1221/P

9 781539 458753